MW01634551

# Summer and Sagebrush

Also by Helena Linn:
*Winter in the Bunkhouse*

# Summer and Sagebrush

by Helena Linn

*Seven Cross Lazy L Productions*

Summer and Sagebrush
by Helena Linn

Published by

Seven Cross Lazy L Productions
P.O. Box 308, Big Piney, Wyoming 83113
307-276-3506
helenal@tribcsp.com     www.7crossproductions.com

©2011 by Helena Linn



Publisher's Cataloging-In-Publication Data
(Prepared by The Donohue Group, Inc.)

Linn, Helena.
    Summer and sagebrush / by Helena Linn.

    p. ; cm.

    Sequel to: Winter in the bunkhouse.
    ISBN: 978-0-9817649-1-7

    1. Ranchers--Fiction.  2. Ranch life--Wyoming--Fiction.
3. Families--Wyoming--Fiction.  4. Wyoming--Fiction.  5. Domestic
fiction.  I. Title.

PS3612.I559 S96 2011
813.6                                                    2010914166

Book and cover design by Sommers Studio
www.sommstudio.com
Cover art by Donny Marincic
www.marincic.com

Edited by Gail M. Kearns
To Press and Beyond
www.topressandbeyond.com

Book production coordinated by To Press and Beyond
Printed in the United States of America

I am grateful to God and my beloved parents,
Philip and Elva Marincic, for life, love, and the great
gift of growing up on a cattle ranch in Wyoming.
I dedicate this book to them and to the love of
my life, Bob Linn, and to our wonderful family of
children, grandchildren, and great-grandchildren.

# Chapter One

**Jake and Kate** stepped through the archway of St. Ann's church with barely enough time to shield their faces from the rice being thrown at them from every direction. When they'd been pelted with the last few handfuls, they were met with hugs from Kate's new nephews and niece—Jessie, Danny, and Abby.

Moments later, Jake's mother Maureen, Kate's friends Cameron and Jean, faithful ranchhand Charlie Grady, and Jake's twin brother Jesse and his wife Mary Anne, were congratulating the newlyweds. Kate and Jake had been of the same mind: they wanted only those closest to them to be present for the Mass and wedding vows on that warm Indian summer day of October 20, 1958, in Saratoga, Wyoming.

After receiving everyone's wishes for their happiness, Jesse took Jake by the elbow. "Mary Anne said everything is ready in the parish hall."

A simple but beautiful cake, along with punch, coffee, candy, and nuts were all tastefully arranged on a side table covered with fine lace. Kate commented on how elegant the table looked, and Mary Anne confided that Mother McClary had given the lace tablecloth to Jesse and her when they got married.

The wedding party stood quietly while Father Hardy asked the blessing before they sat down at tables arranged in a triangle. By the time Jake stood to thank everyone for coming, they had enjoyed a wonderful prime rib dinner prepared by Mary Anne and Jesse. Kate added her thanks to her new brother- and sister-in-law for the meal and providing music for the Mass. "Mary Anne, I am happy to have such a talented sister," Kate said.

"And we're glad to have you as a part of our family," Mary Anne replied. Everyone applauded, and in the age-old tradition clinked their glasses. Jake kissed his bride. After they opened their gifts and asked Charlie to take them with him as he returned to the ranch, Kate and Jake said goodbye to their family and friends.

"Mom, we'll be back to fetch you in the morning. I know you're anxious to get back to Dad in Arizona and I'm anxious for him to meet Kate."

"Don't worry, son, I'll be ready." She winked at Kate. "If you're a little late, I'll understand."

Just outside the parish hall door, Kate cried, "Oh dear, look at my car." She was dismayed at the sight of her Buick covered with shaving cream, and cans tied at the rear.

Jake rushed her through the driveway to the back of the hall and opened the door to his pickup. "I figured those kids would do just that. Come on."

They pulled away and Kate glanced backwards to see their wedding guests laughing and the kids looking disappointed that they'd taken off in a different vehicle.

"Now, tell me where we're going," Kate demanded lightheartedly. "You've kept it a secret long enough." Her voice raised a tone or two when she asked, "And in the pickup?"

"You'll see," was all he said.

Kate recognized that they were on the road to the family ranch, several miles southwest of Saratoga, where they had been staying the last few days. But she had no idea where they were going when Jake turned off onto a narrow graveled road that followed a fence line.

"What are we doing way out here?" she asked. Jake patted her thigh and concentrated on driving over a two-track trail that appeared to be heading into the mountains. Minutes later a log cabin and some corrals came into view.

"Do you mean we're going here on our honeymoon?" she asked in disbelief.

"Well, no. Only for tonight."

She could tell that Jake intended just that when he took their small bags and a jug of water out of the pickup and told her to come on. "You'll like it," he said confidently.

She wasn't so sure but there was nothing left to do except follow him in through a homemade door into the rustic but clean log cabin.

"It's our cow camp for the summer while the cattle are up here. That little wood stove came out of a sheep wagon."

Kate looked around. A Dutch oven sat on the floor under the cast iron skillet hanging near the stove. She pulled her jacket tighter against the chill of the room and was glad to see that the wood box was full. She opened the door of the homemade cupboard, which held a few dishes and a small metal pan that stored some silverware.

"How come the silverware isn't in a drawer?" Kate asked.

"Because the mice can't get into that cupboard."

Jake set about building a fire.

Kate started laughing and shook her head. "I might have known that your idea of a honeymoon was not a trip to Bermuda."

---

Kate awoke the next morning to see Jake smiling at her. *How is it possible to be so happy,* she wondered.

"Good morning, wife," he said, interrupting her reverie. "Daylight's burnin'. If we're going to get a good start to Arizona, we'd better get a move on."

Kate yawned and pulled her shoulders tight, then stretched full length. She was up, had her feet in slippers, and her robe on before Jake even moved a big toe. "I thought *we* needed to get a move on."

"Sure, I was just enjoying the view." He threw the blanket back and put his feet on the floor, then reached for a shirt.

"I don't suppose you have a shower in this little honeymoon cottage of yours?" she asked, knowing it wasn't likely.

"Nope, just the next best thing to it." He caught her hand and led her out the door.

When she realized he was heading for the creek a few yards away, she shrieked, "No, uh-uh, no way."

Protesting but unable to stop Jake from disrobing her and taking off his shirt, he pulled her into the icy water.

Before she knew it, she was up to her shoulders and shivering. "I'm . . . I'm freezing," she said between gasps.

"I'll be happy to un-freeze you." He started out of the creek just before she cupped a handful of water and tossed it at him.

When they were back on the bank, Kate managed to get her robe and slippers on, but the robe was too wet to give any warmth, and her teeth were still chattering.

Jake took her hand to lead her back to the cabin. "Wasn't that refreshing?"

Kate made a face at him. "I think I just married a crazy man."

He kissed her affectionately. "You're right. I am crazy. I'm crazy about you."

"I'm glad of that," she said, pausing. "Just don't get any more crazy ideas, okay?"

———•———

Kate could see that Jake hadn't brought anything along for breakfast so she wasn't surprised when he said he was going out to start the pickup and they'd head for town as soon as she was ready. About a mile down the road Jake said, "I like your friends Cameron and Jean Wyatt. I could tell they were pleased that you asked them to come, and Jean seemed especially glad that you asked her to be your matron of honor."

"Cameron was my dad's best friend. I would have asked Margo if she still lived in Jackson but she's so far away. In fact, I asked Mary Anne but she thought I should let my old friend Jean have that honor. Mary Anne said she was happy to take care of all the arrangements." Jake slowed for a curve and Kate added thoughtfully, "Mary Anne is special, always looking out for everyone else and quietly takes care of what needs to be done. I'm really going to like having her for a sister-in-law."

"I guess you can tell that my family has already grown to love you, and they all told me I'm a lucky man."

"Then I won't tell them about the skinny dippin' this morning. They'd think you've lost your mind." She laughed, "And they'd think I'd lost mine to let you dunk me in the creek in October. That water is near freezing."

"To tell the truth, it's cold in the summer too."

They rode in a comfortable silence for several minutes. "By the way, I told Cameron we would come to Denver as soon as we could to get my new name and yours on the investment papers," Kate said.

"There's no need to put my name on them. That's your money and you need to keep it that way," Jake replied firmly.

"I won't do that. Anything I have is yours too." Hoping he wasn't as adamant as he sounded, she jokingly added, "Of course I want what you have to be mine too."

"What I have *is* yours. But it's my job to take care of you, not the other way around." A quick glance let her see his lips set in a tight line and his fingers drumming on the steering wheel.

*Uh, oh,* she thought, wondering why he would feel so strongly about sharing the money she had. "Well, we'll talk about it later," she said, which didn't seem to help his mood any.

Finally, he said, "I thought we would have a nice breakfast at the Saratoga Inn before we pick up Mom and head for Arizona. She's anxious to get back to Dad. He was really upset that he couldn't make the trip." Jake looked her way briefly. "I guess this trip to Arizona isn't much of a honeymoon but . . ."

Kate leaned over and squeezed his arm. "I think this is a perfect way to start our marriage. I want to know both of your parents and we aren't exactly kids who need to get to know one another. We already know what it's like to live together."

Sounding a bit embarrassed she added, "Well, not really, there's . . . well, you know . . ."

He laughed at her coyness. "Oh, yes, my sexy little wife, I know."

"Oh, Jake, you're embarrassing me," she said snuggling against his arm.

After a bit, Jake said, "We shouldn't be gone from the ranch too long." He took hold of her hand but she couldn't help thinking about his reaction to her suggestion about the money.

———•———

While Jake studied the menu, Kate decided on one egg, bacon, and toast and then looked around, admiring the western décor. She was caught off guard when the attractive couple who had just come into the restaurant headed for their table. *Someone who knows Jake,* she surmised right before the woman spoke.

Jake looked up, and with a quick glance at Kate he stood to acknowledge the couple.

"Well, fancy meeting you here," the woman said disdainfully. Jake extended his hand to her but she ignored it and moved close to him. "Darling, you must kiss the bride," and with that she planted a kiss on his lips. "Grant and I were married two days ago and we're here to pick up some of my things before we leave for the Caribbean."

"Congratulations," Jake said, with little enthusiasm. He shook hands with Grant. "I'd like you to meet my wife, Kate. Kate, this is Laurie Wagner . . . uh, Laurie . . .?"

"Hayward," Grant put in and reached across the table to shake Kate's hand.

The waitress came with the coffee Jake had ordered and said she would be back to take their order.

Laurie looked directly at Kate. "Surely you don't live on that ranch out in the middle of nowhere."

Kate was quick to respond. "Oh, yes, I love our home and it's in such a beautiful valley."

Laurie turned to Grant. "I've been there. It's so primitive—no electricity or running water. I really must thank Jake for jilting me at the altar," she said pointedly to all of them. "If we had gone through with that wedding, I would never have met this wonderful man. He's a partner in a huge law firm in Denver and his home is in a wooded area. It's all so luxurious and grand."

Grant looked uncomfortable. "We need to let these people have their breakfast, dear." He took her arm. "Nice to have met you," he said, nudging Laurie away.

Jake wished them a safe trip and sat down at the table. When they were out of earshot, he blew out a breath and said in a low voice, "Whew!"

"You didn't tell them that we were married yesterday. How come?" Kate asked.

Jake grinned. "Well, that would have put a damper on her announcement." The waitress was coming their way when Jake leaned over and whispered, "I could have told her I married a wealthy widow—she would have wondered how wealthy."

Kate thought that over for a few seconds then turned her attention to the waitress when Jake asked, "Have you decided?"

The waitress left with their order then Kate turned to Jake.

"Laurie seems happy with her new husband, doesn't she?"

Jake shrugged. "I suspect he will have his hands full trying to keep her happy." He grinned and added, "Right now, all I care about is making you happy."

She smiled at him. "You're good at making me happy."

All the same, she couldn't help being aware that the woman he had once cared about was sitting in the same room.

# Chapter Two

**A week later** they were on their way back to the ranch in the foothills of the Wind River Mountains of Wyoming. Kate looked over at the boulder strewn hills and sage covered flats with their dusting of snow. She and Jake had spent four glorious days in Arizona with his parents.

"What a contrast," Kate said. Jake glanced her way and she added, "From Arizona, I mean. The weather was warm and comfortable there but I guess we'd better get used to winter again."

Jake kept his eyes on the road ahead. "Actually, this is mild compared to some fall weather around here, but there's plenty of time for winter." He topped a rise on the road that soon dropped down on the other side. "Recognize that ditch?" he asked.

"As a matter of fact, I do. My life has never been the same since I landed in that snow bank almost a year ago."

"Mine either," he said contentedly.

A while later, Jake turned off the county road and slowed the car to cross the cattle guard between two tall posts that supported a log with the McClary Ranch sign. He continued down the lane toward the ranch buildings. "It's good to be home."

"There's the Bunkhouse," Kate said and a wide smile spread across her face lit by the setting sun.

"You said you loved that house but if you don't, it's too late now," Jake said.

"I meant every word. It's a beautiful house. I like everything about the ranch. Of course, I'm not too fond of that separator but I like the cream and butter, so I guess I'll just have to put up with it."

Jake shrugged his shoulders to indicate a response.

"Unless you want to take over washing all those discs," she added.

"Not a chance. That's woman's work."

In the months Kate and Jake had been snowed in on the ranch, neither of them had been comfortable enough to tease, but now their lightheartedness came natural to them. After recognizing their love for each other, old tensions melted away like icicles with the warmth of a coming spring. The trip home from Arizona had given them time to talk over their dreams for their life together. Having lost her four-month-old Jeremy brought back sad moments during a discussion about having children, but because Jake shared her hope of having their own children, she let herself imagine what their future might hold.

Jake stopped the car at the front gate where it would be easiest to unload. He set three suitcases on the porch, opened the front door, and waited for Kate to catch up with him. As she reached the top step of the porch Jake took the bags she was carrying and set them down alongside the suitcases. He scooped her up in his arms and stepped over the threshold. "I've waited for a long time to do this." Holding her close, he whispered, "Welcome to the Bunkhouse, Mrs. McClary."

Back on her feet, Kate drew in a deep breath and clasped her hands in front of her. She noticed Jake was suddenly lost in his own thoughts. "Whatever are you thinking, Mr. McClary?"

"I'm thinking that now this house is your house too."

"I love you and *your* house."

"This is *our* house and I do like it, but it's you I love."

They went out to bring in the rest of the things from the car— some groceries but especially the gift from Jake's folks.

When Jake opened the back door of the car, Kate said quickly, "Be careful with these two boxes of china your family gave us." There was a wistful note in her voice when she added, "I've never had a full set of china before and this is such a lovely pattern."

Jake set the boxes on the floor in a corner of the living room. He caught Kate's hand and led her toward the kitchen. They heard Charlie coming in the back door. "I'll put our things in the bedroom later. Let's see what no good Charlie's been up to while we've been rolling in the hay."

"I heard that," Charlie said, stomping his feet on the kitchen rug as he opened his arms to give Kate a big hug. "Nothing much has changed here. I've got supper ready . . . you know, the usual."

Kate looked down to find Buster staring up at her with pleading eyes. She knelt, took the dog's face in her hands, and put her cheek alongside his. "I missed you too," she said softly.

Jake and Kate finished getting everything on the table while Charlie dished up the stew. During the meal, he wanted to know everything about their trip and how Jake's parents were doing.

"Jake's dad can't get around too well but he has a sharp mind. Mom is the sweetest thing and I fell in love with both of them," Kate offered.

"Dad was disappointed that he couldn't come up for the wedding but it helped that we were able to take Mom home and let him meet Kate. He said I'm one lucky cowboy and to take good care of that girl."

Charlie winked at Kate. "I bet he told you to make sure he behaves himself too."

"You've got that right, Charlie," Kate laughed and shot Jake an amused look.

"Katie, I was so honored to walk you down the aisle. It was the perfect wedding."

"I wouldn't have had it any other way."

Then Charlie filled them in with how things had gone at the ranch.

"I put a new hinge on that gate in the second stall and mended Mac's harness. That bull you bought at the sale this fall keeps going through the fence. Had to put him back in the pasture twice. I fixed that fence so he won't get out again."

Jake got up and bounded down the two steps into the living room to pick up a box from the sofa. He handed it to Charlie. "We appreciate your hard work and taking good care of things here."

"Wow!" Charlie exclaimed when he lifted brand new spurs out of the box. "I've been thinking about new spurs ever since I lost a rowel on my old ones. These are pretty fancy . . . thanks a bunch." He put them back into the box and stood up to help clear the table.

"Just leave everything, Charlie. I'll do the dishes," Kate said.

"Well, okay, I'll milk the cow and slop the pigs. They've been living 'high on the hog' the last ten days with no one to use much milk or cream." He laughed at his own pun and headed for the mudroom door.

Jake filled the fireplace box with logs, and then separated the milk while Charlie took the eggs he'd gathered from the hen house into the cooler. Jake went out to bring in an armload of kindling for the kitchen stove. He came through the kitchen door just as Charlie said, "I sure am glad to have you two back home."

"We're glad to be home, aren't we, Kate?"

"We certainly are. It's been a hectic few weeks." She checked the sourdough crock. "Pancakes for breakfast in the morning?"

"You bet," Jake said. "Well, Charlie, looks like things are back to normal around here, huh?"

"Just the way we like it," he answered. "And, Jake, you *are* one lucky cowboy."

Charlie went off to bed and Jake put a log in the fireplace. "Well, I see Jerry's glad you came home." He lifted the big cat off Kate's lap and pulled her out of the recliner in front of the fireplace. "Let's move these recliners out of the way and bring the couch over here. What do you think?"

Kate stepped to the other end of the couch and helped move it in front of the fireplace. Jake put a recliner at an angle on each end of the couch forming a kind of semi-circle. He sat down on the couch and beckoned Kate to join him. Snuggled close, they quietly watched the flames lick around the log.

Finally Jake spoke up. "Look, we need to set some rules around here."

Kate was startled until she saw Jake's mouth working to suppress a grin.

"First of all, I think you ought to bring in the wood and carry out the ashes. And you're not to climb on that rickety old ladder that you fell off of last year unless I'm right here."

Kate stared back at Jake, nodding in agreement.

"You need to learn to milk the cow," he continued, "in case Charlie and I have other things to do. And I think it would be good if you iron the sheets, just in the summertime. No need to iron the flannel ones."

Kate looked into Jake's twinkling eyes. "Of course, and what will you be doing while I'm slaving away for you?"

"As you know, I'm tired when I come in, so I need time to relax."

By this time, Kate was hardly able to keep a straight face. She held her hands together and bowed, "Of course, Master McClary."

"Cut that out, you little minx." Jake pulled her into his arms and kissed her. They continued to watch the fire and talked about all that had happened during the preceding months.

"They were good at the hospital to let me quit without even a week's notice," Kate said.

"And it was darn fortunate that your landlord bought all the furniture you had in the apartment, so you really left Jackson the way you went—with one car full of your belongings, as I recall."

"Yep, and I'm glad I was able to be here in time to go with you to bring the cattle down from the mountains. But then, I hate seeing those calves weaned from their mamas."

Jake gave her a steady look. "I know, but you've got to understand . . . by that time those cows are pregnant with the next calf, so the young ones need to fend for themselves. I never like seeing the yearlings go to market either, but that's how we make our living."

"Grandpa always said he hated to let any of his stock go. Sometimes I thought he knew every cow even though they didn't have a name. I know every horse he had was special to him."

"Your grandpa was a good rancher and a real gentleman. Everyone around here had a lot of respect for him and your grandmother."

"Thanks for saying that." She raised her eyebrows and said firmly, "But you need to know that I have no intention of learning to milk a cow."

Jake countered with his own raised eyebrows. "Oh?"

"Grandpa told me never to learn to milk because then everyone would expect me to do the milking. The truth is I don't want to do it anyway."

Jake started to laugh but Kate poked him in the ribs and said, "Listen here . . . you can strike that rule about ironing. I'll carry in wood and take out ashes if necessary. I already told you I won't milk the cow. So much for your rules, but I have one for you."

"Oh?"

"Yes, I absolutely refuse to let you work with that mean horse of yours anymore. He could have caused more than a broken arm, you know."

From Jake's noncommittal expression, it didn't look like he was taking Kate seriously. She gave him a disgusted look.

"I mean it. That horse is dangerous, and Charlie told me you were determined to tame him. You work with horses all the time so you must know that horse could really hurt you. And here we are miles from a doctor. I simply can't be worried about something that doesn't need to be." She sat back into the cushions and folded her arms defiantly.

"I'm glad you care so much, but I'll tell you the truth."

"What's that?"

"The truth is I sold Red and another horse to a rodeo contractor last summer."

Kate jabbed him in the ribs again. "And you let me go on like that?"

"It was funny to see you so worked up," he said as he pulled her close again. "I knew Red was never going to be gentle enough to ride. I caught him a couple of times but never did get a bridle or saddle on him. So I broke a couple of good horses last summer and I think you're really going to like Misty. She's kind of a gray color with a dark gray mane and tail."

"I like Candy."

"Candy's getting old. You need a horse with more spirit, like your own."

"Maybe you're right, but if Misty is anymore spirited than I am, she might be hard to handle."

"I'm glad you said that and not me." Jake laughed. "I suppose we'd better get you a saddle and your own bridle. You rode Mom's saddle when we went to bring the cattle off the forest, and of course she doesn't mind, but you ought to have your own."

"You're good to me, Jake."

"Well, when I wasn't good to you, you tried to leave, and I can't let you do that ever again. Also, I want you to be happy with me . . . and with the kind of life we live here."

"I am, and I already know I like the kind of life you live here."

A thoughtful look came over Jake. "I always got the idea that being a nurse was important to you."

"Yes, that was one of the best decisions I ever made."

"Are you feeling bad about having given it up?"

"I liked being a nurse, but being your wife is far more important to me."

Jake tightened his hold on Kate's shoulder as she burrowed deeper into his chest.

"Besides, I would never be happy living in a city again after living here."

Jake drew in a long breath. "When I told Mom that Orland's granddaughter was at the ranch last winter she wondered how you would take being snowed in for so long. She said she thought you loved being on the ranch with your grandparents in the summer, but going through a winter out here is a different story."

"Yes, she told me she was glad that I had been through a winter here so I'd realize what I was getting into."

"Kate, are you disappointed that I didn't take you on a real honeymoon?"

"Our honeymoon has been perfect so far . . . well, we could have left out that dip in the creek."

"Are you still harping on that?" Jake asked, amused.

"Seriously, spending time with your parents was special. Besides, you can always take me on a cruise someday."

"A cruise?"

"Oh, I forgot," she said, teasing him, "ranchers don't go on vacations."

"Well . . . maybe some do. Like I said, my life has never been the same since you showed up, so who knows what might happen next."

The fire was dying down. It had been a long day and Kate was ready for bed. A little while later Jake joined her. "Guess what. It's snowing." They didn't need to remind each other that they were about to spend another winter in the Bunkhouse.

"That means tomorrow you should make a list of everything we need for the winter and we'll go for supplies before winter sets in."

"Yes . . ." she started with an impish grin on her face.

"And don't you dare call me master!" Jake pretended to be stern.

Kate let Jake cradle her in his arms and they soon drifted off to a peaceful sleep.

# Chapter Three

**Kate** opened the top of the Dutch door and watched the men heading for the corrals. She cupped a mug of coffee in her hands and thought how it felt déjà-vu-like as she watched Jake and Charlie catch the horses and lead them through the barn door. When they brought the harnessed team out to hitch to the sled, she turned her attention to washing the breakfast dishes and the separator. When the kitchen was cleaned to her liking she set about making a list of supplies for the winter.

The snow hadn't amounted to much yet. The cattle were in the meadows at the Orland place so Jake and Charlie could start feeding at the farthest fields from the house and move closer as the winter progressed.

Listing the groceries, laundry supplies, and paper goods they would need for several months, she remembered how Jake and Charlie had liked her cottage cheese and pear salad topped with a spoonful of mayonnaise and a cherry. Jake and Charlie had been surprised that she even knew how to make cottage cheese. She added maraschino cherries to her list. She wrote down lettuce, fresh tomatoes, celery, and several bags of carrots, and then included six heads of cabbage and a few loaves of bread that would keep until they could use it all. Spices and condiments would also be needed. Jake had said to put potatoes, onions, apples, oranges, and grapefruit on a separate list because they would be stored in the cellar. They would buy canned vegetables and fruit by the case so those were on another list. When she had written down everything she could think of, Kate looked over her lists and worried Jake might get upset about what it was going to cost. She needn't have been concerned; he hardly looked at them when he and Charlie came in that afternoon.

Even though it had only snowed about eight inches, the weather had turned cold after several weeks of sunshine and moderate temperatures. Charlie kept saying he was sure they were going to pay for it later.

The next morning they set out in the pickup for the forty-mile ride to Pinedale. Kate got herself comfortably situated between the two men. "This is cozy," she said.

"She learns fast," Jake said to Charlie. "Did you notice how she hurried to get in the middle so she wouldn't have to open a gate if we came to one?"

Kate joined in their chuckles but insisted she had never thought of that. "Now that you've pointed it out I'll be sure to get in the middle in the future," she announced.

Charlie mentioned they usually got a haircut when they went to town, but he didn't need one this time because he'd had his hair trimmed just before the wedding.

"I don't need one either," Jake said. "Anyway, we have our own barber now, remember?"

"Is that so?" Kate asked. "I'll have to think about it when you two get to looking shaggy again."

Jake glanced at Charlie and feigned hurt. "I guess we were pretty shaggy lookin' last spring when she took pity on us, huh?"

"You just want me to chop it off so you tightwads don't have to pay for your haircuts," she quipped.

At the grocery store, Kate handed Jake the bulk lists she had made. He looked them over. "Maybe you'd better do this and I'll go see if I can get a loan at the bank," he said jokingly. She wrinkled her nose at him and he pulled a shopping cart out for her. "Let's meet at check-out when we're through."

Jake gave the case goods and bulk lists to a stocker who went to find the items they wanted, then he took care of selecting bacon, ham, some chicken, and a couple of small turkeys. He left the cart near the checkout counter where Kate had already parked two carts with soap, paper products, and personal items. When he found her, she was choosing fresh fruits and vegetables and looking a bit stressed at the amount of provisions piling up in her cart.

"Whooee, maybe I shouldn't turn you loose in a grocery store," Jake said with a frown.

"Should I put some back?" she asked anxiously, distressed at his remark.

"I'm kidding. Buy whatever you need, even what you just want." He emphasized his words with a loving smile.

The stock clerk had their bulk purchases ready to go. As the checker added up items, Jake and the clerk carried things to the pickup. Kate relaxed and marveled at the stockpile of goods they'd bought and couldn't imagine running out of anything by spring.

Jake paid for their purchases and they went to pick up Charlie at the Cowboy Shop where he'd been buying Levi's and winter gloves.

Jake chose The Stockman's for supper. As the waitress led them to a table, he wasn't surprised to see the Petersons eating their evening meal. Kate recognized Jackie Peterson as one of the women who had come to help her with the branding dinner the previous spring. They stopped to say hello and the couple greeted the three of them warmly.

"Well, congratulations you two," Jackie said right away. "We're sure happy for you." She smiled in Jake's direction and added, "You got yourself a pretty wife and a great cook."

Jake hardly had time to reply when Sam Peterson wisecracked, "I s'pect you've warned her that she's going to be snowed in all winter with you two galoots."

"Oh, yes, I've been warned," said Kate amiably. Privately she wondered if any of the neighbors suspected she had already spent a winter with the two galoots.

Jake took Kate's elbow, indicating they should move on to their table where the waitress was placing menus.

When the Petersons were finished with their meal, they stopped by and asked Jake about his folks. Before departing, Jackie spoke up, "Be sure you get down to our place before the snow gets too deep. We have electricity now," she said with obvious excitement. "I hardly know how to act when I can flip a switch and have light! You're the last ranch up the valley so I hope you get your electricity next summer. It's such a convenience," she gushed.

The waitress arrived with the chicken-fried steak they'd ordered and Kate was glad she had asked for a half order, especially when Charlie suggested they ought to have ice cream for dessert. "Might be a while, you know," he told Kate.

All of the supplies were in the storeroom the next morning, but Kate decided that she would finish cleaning the kitchen before she put the groceries on the shelves. She did the breakfast dishes and washed the separator then started on the kitchen. She did what she could before time to fix dinner but there wasn't time to clean all the cupboards. She left the rest for the next day.

Thanksgiving was only two weeks away and more than anything Kate wanted the house to be immaculately clean. In spite of Jake's warning, she went to the garage to get the rickety old ladder. To her surprise she found a new metal stepladder. She brought it into the house and proceeded to climb it to reach the cobwebs and clean the windows.

Later, when Jake came in and finished washing up he found the ladder leaning against the wall in the living room. "I see you found the ladder," he began, "didn't I tell you to wait until I was here?"

"If I'd waited for you nothing would have gotten done."

He shook his finger at her. "Now you broke that rule so you'll have to be punished."

Kate folded her hands and made a small bow.

"Don't you dare say it," Jake warned.

"But Master McClary . . ."

Jake cut her off and pressed his lips firmly on hers. "You're the limit. How can I get you in line when you look at me like that?"

They were locked in each other's arms when Charlie came through the door, stomping his feet. "Suppose you two lovebirds can break it up long enough to feed a hungry man?"

"Guess we'll have to," Jake said, winking at Charlie.

Dinner was ready as soon as Charlie came back from washing up. When Jake reached for another helping of potatoes that had been fried and then simmered in cream, he commented, "I'm surprised you had time to fix us this good dinner when you spent the morning washing windows. I didn't know fried potatoes needed cream to make them taste this good."

Charlie took the bowl from Jake. "I never had these before you came, Katie. You make a tasty meatloaf too." He helped himself to more meat and passed the platter to Jake.

Kate was feeling the muscle strain of climbing up and down the ladder, but didn't say anything. She turned the conversation to what Jackie Peterson had said at the restaurant the night before. "What did Mrs. Peterson mean when she said they got electricity and she hoped we would get it next?"

"Well, we have an electric company trying to get electricity out into the country," Jake replied. "They've worked at it for several years and they've been bringing it to this part of the county lately."

"So our ranch is next in line?"

"I suppose so but no one has contacted me about it. They'll probably want an easement to come the shortest distance, which is through the meadows, but I won't let them do that."

"It would be hard to maintain and Jake doesn't want tracks across the fields," Charlie concurred. "Can't say as I blame him."

"Same with a telephone line," Jake added.

"I understand, but it would be nice to be able to stay in touch with your folks by phone, Jake," Kate said quietly. "Do you have to pay for all this? I would like to help . . ."

"Absolutely not!" Jake's emphatic response startled Kate even though she wasn't exactly surprised. Moderating his tone, he said, "If we have to pay for poles and lines from the county road to our house it will be a ranch expense. Don't worry about it. We'll manage."

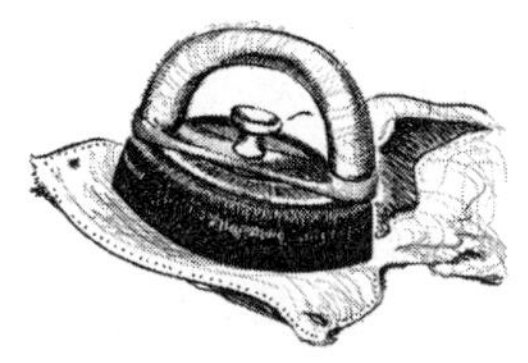

# Chapter Four

**Trying** to iron clothes and linens with sad irons was something Kate thought she might never master. Either the iron was too hot, too cool, the handle slipped, or she burned her fingers. Now, as she unhooked the handle from one iron and managed to fit the handle onto another, she found that the iron was almost too hot for the tablecloth she was trying to iron.

Last winter she had scorched a blouse and left a black mark on one of Jake's shirts. Yet another time the handle came loose and before she could connect it to the iron and move the iron to the stove, there was a hole in a pillowcase exactly the size of the iron.

She hadn't heard Jake come into the kitchen when she muttered, "I hate these irons!"

"How come?" he asked, making her jump and drop the iron directly on the tablecloth.

She managed to pick it up before it burned the material, and then practically slammed the iron back onto the stovetop. "Never mind," she responded curtly.

"Ooh-kay," he murmured. "I'm going out to bring in some wood." He came back into the kitchen with an armload of kindling that he dropped into the wood box behind the stove.

"I'm sorry," Kate said. "I just can't seem to keep these irons at the right temperature. Having an electric iron would make life a lot easier."

Jake listened but kept quiet.

"Guess I'm not a very good pioneer."

"Well, it seems to me that you cope real well. You might be a city girl but you're a rancher at heart," he said, trying to ease the tension. There hadn't been much of that since they'd arrived at the Bunkhouse.

"Right. Just don't expect a nicely ironed shirt. I'm sure you noticed that I didn't do a lot of ironing last winter."

"Well, so much for ironed sheets," he said wryly as he winked at her.

Kate hung her newly ironed apron on a peg and pulled the irons to the coolest spot on the stove about the same time Jake came back into the kitchen from stacking logs near the fireplace. He folded the ironing board and took it to what they sometimes called the milk room and sometimes called the laundry room. Mostly they called it the mudroom. It was that too.

Later, while the men were doing chores and Kate was getting supper ready, she realized that it wasn't only the sad irons that bothered her so much. It was also Jake's ongoing stubbornness to let her pay for anything, much less the idea of her offering to pay for electricity to be brought to the ranch. It would imply that he wasn't capable of taking care of her and the ranch. But she sure would like to have an electric iron.

———•———

Several inches of snow fell early in December. With the plow Jake had attached to the front of their pickup, he was able to plow the road following each snowstorm, and the road was still passable. After breakfast one morning, Jake announced that he would be in by noon and they should go into Pinedale. He had several things to take care of and Kate needed to be ready to go with him.

"But I've started mixing the bread. It might not be done," Kate protested.

"Charlie can bake it. You said you wanted to get some more lettuce and tomatoes before we get snowed in. And there was something else . . . what was it?"

"Yams."

"Well, here's your chance. I'm pretty sure we won't get out again this winter."

Dinner was ready when the men got in. The bread was in the loaf pans and Charlie said he would bake it. Jake insisted they didn't have time to eat. Charlie told them to get going and he'd take care of things at home.

Jake's first stop in Pinedale was at the bank. Kate wanted to wait for him in the truck but he insisted she go in with him. "You need to sign a card so you can write checks on our accounts," he told her.

Kate hesitated. This was news to her.

Jake hopped out and went around to open her door. "You're a partner in the ranch, you know. You'll have to write checks so come on."

When they'd completed all their errands, they stopped at The Stockman's for an early supper. Kate hadn't had time to think through what she wanted to say to Jake until they were on their way home.

"I've been thinking," Kate began.

Jake cast a questioning glance her way.

"I suppose we can't really do much about it until spring when we can get away for a few days, but we need to go to Denver so we can meet with Cameron." Before Jake could say anything, she added, "I need to change my name on my investments and add your name to them too."

"Uh, uh," Jake said emphatically. "I've already told you, that's your money."

"You said I'm a partner in the ranch. If that's so then I intend to be a full partner and I want to put some of that money into the ranch operation. We can keep some of it invested."

Jake wracked his brain for a response, but he wasn't quick enough to counter Kate's well-thought-out solution.

"You see, my father left me insurance money, plus a business and property to dispose of. Then Grandma left me the money she and Grandpa had saved from their ranch and what they got from selling it to your family. They hadn't used much so it all came to me." She swallowed hard before continuing. "Then there was insurance and property that I sold after David died. Trust me; it all added up to a substantial amount of money that I would have never used up, even if I hadn't worked." Kate put her hand on Jake's thigh. "So, are we partners or not?" Her tone left no room for argument.

Jake was silent for several moments. Finally he said, "We're partners . . . all the way."

She pressed her cheek to his shoulder. "Good!"

—•—

A couple of days later, they awoke to another foot of snow and it was still snowing. Being snowed in for the next several months wasn't the daunting prospect it had been the winter before. In fact, Kate looked forward to the peace and quiet.

On the first day of heavy snow, she was watching from the Dutch door when the men drove the sled through the gate into the ranch yard after feeding the cattle. When she saw Jake jump off the sled and line up poles so Charlie could drive the sled across them, she remembered asking them last year why they did that. Jake had explained that the poles kept the sled runners from freezing down. He had said, "If that happens the horses might not even be able to pull the sled free and something could be broken in the process."

Jake and Charlie shook snow from their caps and coats before they came in to the mudroom. Both of them commented about the tantalizing smell of fresh bread in the kitchen and then went to wash up. Jake helped Kate get dinner on the table. She poured coffee, took the pot back to the stove, and then sat at her place. Kate said the blessing and passed the plate of roast beef to Jake while Charlie took a hot roll and passed the basket over to her.

"Guess we're snowed in, huh?" she asked casually.

Charlie grinned. "Think you can stand another winter penned up with a couple of ol' coots?"

"I couldn't be happier. By the way, are you guys two ol' coots or two galoots?"

"Charlie, I wish you wouldn't call us names like that," Jake said. "She could hold that against us fine gentlemen." They all laughed happily.

It was a few days later when Kate fully realized they were back in the routine of the previous winter, except for one big difference. This winter Jake kissed her before he went out to feed and usually when he came back in. And because nothing had changed with life on the ranch, but virtually everything was different since they'd married, Kate attempted to have enough done in the house so she could go out with Jake on occasion.

It never ceased to amaze her when all the cows were looking in the same direction, and more often than not it was because there were coyotes off in the distance.

Charlie made it a point to hand the reins to Kate after he drove out of the stackyard so she could drive the teams while he and Jake pitched hay off the sled. One day she told Charlie, "You know, they would head for the feed trail all by themselves if you told them to."

"I know, Katie. But you'd better hang on to the reins anyway."

On days when the skies were clear and the sun shone brightly, she liked to go out across the fields on the cross-country skis that Jake had given her for Christmas last year. Charlie cautioned her to watch for the moose he'd seen down by the willows.

"Oh, I stay out in the open. I haven't forgotten being face to face with that mama moose."

One morning while filling their coffee cups, Kate mentioned the four coyotes she'd come across while skiing near a grove of aspens.

"We saw 'em too," Jake remarked. "Charlie said he saw one pawing through the snow like he'd found something to eat. They must have some pretty lean days."

"Makes you wonder how all the wild animals survive with all this snow," Charlie opined.

"Some don't, you know," Jake said. "Remember how many deer carcasses we found last spring? Sometimes they just don't have enough to eat. I can understand when an animal dies naturally and I've always appreciated that people have had to kill an animal to eat. What really hurts is to see a deer that tried to jump a wire fence and got hung up. I hate knowing one died like that."

Jake and Charlie talked a lot about the natural world and the environment, especially when sitting at the table enjoying an extra cup of coffee after a good meal. Kate learned a great deal by listening to them talk about what needed to be done on the ranch and how the cows were doing; they would predict how cold it was apt to be or when a storm was on the way. She often thought, *They're so easy-going about everything. I like that.*

At night Kate's prayers thanked God for the peace and tranquility of her new life. It was comforting to know that she and Jake and Charlie agreed on *most* things, especially now that Jake was coming around to her way of thinking about their financial arrangement.

One night after supper Jake said that he had a chore for Kate to do the next day and wouldn't tell her what it was. She only hoped it was something she *wanted* to do.

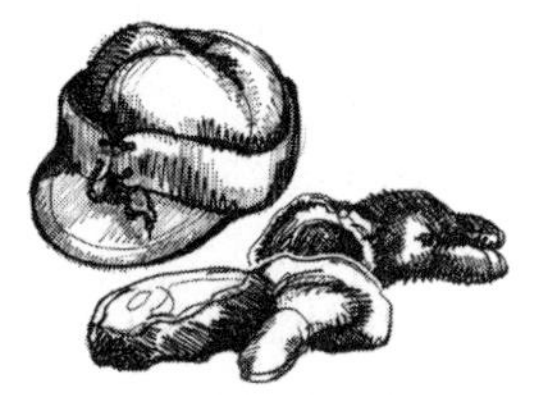

# Chapter Five

**Sleep** didn't come easy to Kate that evening. She woke up several times during the night speculating about what Jake wanted her to do tomorrow. Jake's steady breathing and the warmth of his body was comforting. She knew he wasn't lying awake thinking about the next day. When Jake got up to put logs in the fireplace, she asked what time it was.

"Four o'clock. I think the clock chiming woke me but it's also getting cold in this room."

"I know." He came back to bed but it was a while before his body radiated warmth again.

In spite of her lack of sleep, Kate had breakfast in the warming oven when Jake and Charlie came in from doing the chores. "Would you fill the boiler before we eat, so the water will be hot?" she asked Jake.

"Sure enough."

"And then pour it into the washing machine before you go out to feed. I need to do laundry."

"I wanted you to go out with us to feed today."

"Is this what you were talking about last night?"

Jake nodded. "Yes, that's part of it."

"Not a chance. I've got too much to do around here."

"Well, I guess there's plenty of time," Jake said on his way out to fill the boiler.

---

The next morning Kate was ready to go with them. They'd fed out two loads of hay when Jake came to the front of the sled where Kate had been driving the team. "Okay, now head for the gate over there," he said, pointing toward some pine trees.

It was tough for the teams to make a trail so Jake took the reins. "Now I see what you're up to," Kate said.

"Yeah, you have to pick out the tree this year. I'm surprised you didn't notice the axe tied on back there."

It didn't take long before Kate spotted a perfectly formed pine tree. It wasn't as tall as the one they'd had the year before but it was just as beautiful. Jake chopped down the tree while Kate and Charlie admired the skill with which he did it.

"Well, Katie, it looks like you got the best lookin' pine tree in the whole valley," Charlie said as he helped Jake lift the tree onto the sled.

By the time Kate had dinner on the table, Jake had the tree fitted in the stand. They got out the decorations but decided it was too late to start the trimming. Charlie begged off decorating the next day too, saying he needed a nap. When Jake and Kate finished putting the final touches on the tree, Jake placed a log on the fire and they sat down to enjoy the fragrant pine aroma in the room.

After a while Jake got up to do the chores and Kate followed him to the mudroom. "I'll gather the eggs . . . you have enough to do."

"You can milk the cow if you want," he said mischievously.

"I don't want to—and I'm sure Mrs. Cowley doesn't want me to either," Kate replied while putting on her down jacket. "There's a limit to this partnership business. I'll make you a deal, I won't milk the cow . . . I can't anyway. And you won't iron the sheets . . . you can't anyway."

"Well now, Mrs. McClary, who do you think did my ironing before you arrived at the Bunkhouse?"

"Probably no one since your mother did it for you."

Jake picked up the milk bucket and held the door for her. Their easy banter had put them in a jolly mood, and Kate didn't seem to mind that their big thermometer on the fence registered thirty-two degrees below zero.

Supper that evening was vegetable soup left over from the day before. When everything was back in place and the fires stoked, Charlie, Jake, and Kate sat in the living room to watch the reflection of the fire on the shimmering icicles and glistening ornaments. By nine o'clock, it was their usual bedtime.

The next afternoon Jake managed to plow the ranch yard between the house and the barn, but he hadn't made any attempt to plow the lane after the last snowstorm.

"From now on, we'll have to ski out to the mailbox," he reported when he came into the kitchen after parking the snowplow in the shed.

"Oh, dear," Kate said.

"What's that mean?"

"I ordered some Christmas presents for you and Charlie from the catalog and they haven't come yet. It might be a bigger box than we can carry that far."

"We'll take the toboggan to get the mail next Tuesday," Jake said, relieving Kate of her worry.

But the package wasn't there on Tuesday, and that put Kate into a tailspin. Charlie told her not to fret and wanted to bet five dollars with her that it would get there in time for Christmas.

"I'm not betting . . . because I want you to be right," she said cheerfully. She already had gifts for both Jake and Charlie so there would be things under the tree but she wanted their shirts, wool socks, and new playing cards to give them more packages to open. She had also ordered fruitcake and a tin of mixed nuts along with some wrapping paper.

Kate had had a lot of time on her hands living in Jackson the previous summer so she had crocheted afghans for Charlie and Jake. At the time, she wasn't sure how she would get them to the men but now they were in beautifully wrapped boxes in the closet.

———•———

Jake and Kate enjoyed playing the piano and guitar, frequently at Charlie's request, and oftentimes they played the phonograph and danced. They had all learned the lyrics of *Put Your Little Foot* and Charlie taught them how to dance to it, which they did together. Charlie and Kate usually started, and at the right moment Charlie twirled Kate around to meet Jake and then he would do the same and send her back to Charlie.

"I'm glad you looked through the records and found the music for this dance," Kate told Charlie after a half hour of lively steps and fancy whirls. "It's one of the ones I like the most."

Jake confessed to his favorite part of the lyrics: "While the moon's shining bright and the music's just right and you're holding me tight, we will dance through the night . . ." to which Charlie accused him of being a hopeless romantic.

Ignoring the remark, Jake pointed to Buster who had been watching Kate's every move. "He's supposed to be a cow dog, but I guess he thinks you still need protecting. You've downright spoiled him, treating him like a kid."

Even though they all laughed, Jake's words hit a nerve in Kate. Remembering how hard it was for her to get pregnant in her first marriage, she was worried about her chances of getting pregnant again. Jake hoped they would have three or four children. He was so lighthearted when he'd said, "We need boys to help out on the ranch and you ought to have some help in the house."

⸺•⸺

Kate went with Jake to the mailbox the following week and her package had arrived.

"Good thing I didn't bet with Charlie. I would have lost," Kate said.

Her order wasn't the only one to arrive; there was a big package from Montgomery Ward addressed to Jake as well. She barely had time to get everything wrapped and under the tree before Christmas Eve. Thankfully the men were late getting in that day. They'd brought in hay for the corral in expectation of an easier day on Christmas morning.

Kate prepared supper and then got dressed in the same ivory silk shirtwaist top and her black woolen ankle-length skirt that she had worn last Christmas Eve. She fastened the same little straps of her shoes over the tops of her feet. She'd even put up her hair with a silver clip at the crown. She was at the stove, reaching for the plates she had put in the warming oven, when Jake came through the kitchen door. Just like the year before, he gave her a lingering look and a wolf whistle, which this time sent her into his arms. He pushed her away. "Let me clean up. You'll get that snazzy outfit all dirty." She planted a kiss on his cheek, already fuzzy with a growing beard.

Next, Charlie came in and gave her an admiring smile, telling her how glad he was to see her wearing the squash blossom necklace he had given her last Christmas. He headed to his room to do his own clean up.

The men had turned the calf in with the milk cow so they didn't have to milk. Since Kate didn't have to wash the milk bucket and both men helped with the dishes, they were finished early. Even so it was dark by the time they were ready to open their gifts. Kate got a hug from each of the men when they opened the packages with her handmade afghans. They each had a box of chocolates for Kate, who had been eyeing several nicely wrapped boxes with her name on the tags. Charlie handed Kate his gift to her.

"Oh, thank you Charlie, this bracelet is special. And it matches the turquoise necklace." She slipped it on her wrist and then opened a big box from Jake to uncover a coral colored blouse with a muted blue and gray patterned wool vest. "Perfect. I love them," Kate said, holding up the shirt and vest.

After that, they watched Charlie open a big box with two shirts and a warm jacket they had found for him. "How did you know my shirt size, Katie?"

"I wash your shirts, remember," Kate said warmly.

"Oh, sure you do. These are too good looking to wear to work though. I guess I can dress up once in a while and go to the Bunkhouse dance."

"A dance is a good idea. Just don't go thinking you can waltz my wife around too often," Jake teased.

Kate handed Jake a pretty package. "This one's for you." She watched for his reaction as he tore off the paper and lifted the top off the box.

"Wow, isn't this high class, Charlie," Jake said, admiring the leather jacket Kate had bought for him. He leaned over and kissed Kate, who breathed a sigh of relief.

"Your mother helped me pick it out when we were in Arizona."

Jake lowered his voice and said, "I guess Kate doesn't want people to see me in that old corduroy anymore. Now, I'll look like a rich rancher."

Charlie chortled. "Yeah, it's a real cover-up. You're still going to look like a cowboy—bowlegs, run-down boots, and a ten-gallon hat—with a fancy leather jacket." Kate was enjoying their good natured chitchat.

Jake said they should open the gifts from his parents now and handed Charlie a package included for him. Several paperback western novels delighted Charlie. "This is great. I was running out of things to read. Thought I might have to read a cookbook."

"You always know how to crack a joke and make us laugh," Kate said, looking at the books.

Jake and Kate got plaid western shirts that matched. They were nearly overwhelmed at the big box of candy, nuts, books, and all that Jesse and Mary Anne had sent. Among the gifts were pictures of Jessie, Danny, and Abby. Kate studied them, remembering how gracious the kids had been to her and how they liked to tease their Uncle Jake. She handed the pictures to Jake and pointed out that the kids' ages were written on the backs of them.

"Gosh, look at Jessie. He just turned twelve and already looks like a teenager," Jake remarked. "With that big smile and his curly hair, all those Saratoga girls will be hoping for a prom date with him." He looked carefully at the next picture. "I think Danny looks a lot like his dad. He's more serious and probably more studious than Jessie, but they get along pretty well. Both like to play baseball and they're good cowboys. Danny must be ten . . . yep, that's what it says," he confirmed when he turned the picture over.

"That young lady is cute as a button," Kate said when they got to Abby's photo. "She's eight now, it says here. Her hair is curly but not as dark as the boys. And she has beautiful light blue eyes. What a delightful family Jesse and Mary Anne have," she added wistfully.

Jake took Kate's hand, letting her know he understood. It was never far from their minds that they wanted to start a family of their own.

"Those kids never had school pictures before. They were home-schooled when they lived here," Jake said, handing the pictures to Charlie.

Charlie looked over each picture and then left the room without a word. Jake and Kate eyed each other wondering what was up. Charlie came back moments later, carrying his Bible. "Martha and I always read the Christmas story on Christmas Eve. Do you mind?"

"Please do," Kate and Jake chimed together.

Charlie sat in one of the recliners and opened to St. Luke's gospel. Kate settled on the couch before the fireplace with Jake holding her close. For several minutes after he finished they sat quietly, thinking about the events of that night so long ago. Then Charlie stood up, leaned over, and planted a kiss on Kate's forehead. "Thank you both for a wonderful Christmas." On his way to bed he passed the window to the east. "You ought to see this full moon—a mighty pretty sight."

Jake got up, put a log on the fire, and walked over to the window. "Kate, come here quick." He grabbed the big blanket from the small sofa, opened the door, and led Kate out onto the porch, wrapping them both in the blanket.

"Oh, look," Kate murmured in awe. "It's just like the night we saw those frost diamonds!"

Jake held her tight and whispered, "That was the night I realized I was in love with you."

Kate swallowed hard. "And you never told me."

"I wanted to. Don't you remember I asked if you'd ever marry again?"

"I know, but . . ."

"It had only been a few months since you lost your husband and baby and you were sure you would never marry again. I didn't think you'd even be able to love someone else—especially me after the way I'd treated you on your sixteenth birthday."

Enthralled with the sight of the moon just above the horizon, making the snow glisten and sparkle, they were caught up in the scene until Kate shivered and Jake loosened the blanket so they could get back where it was warm.

The next day after the men had done what work they had to do and were enjoying Kate's turkey dinner and pumpkin pie, they all agreed it had been a special Christmas. Jake suggested they play cards after cleaning up the table.

"Do you know how to play pinochle?" Charlie asked.

Neither Kate nor Jake knew the game but they were eager to learn. Charlie brought out pinochle cards from his room and shuffled the deck. "Martha and I played a lot of pinochle. I wanted to teach Jake way back then but he was too busy chasing the girls and didn't have time to play cards with old folks."

"Don't believe him, Kate. I don't think he ever asked me—and I didn't chase girls." He leaned toward Kate and said slyly, "They chased me."

"I'm sure," she replied dryly.

Charlie laughed at the two of them.

Charlie wrote out what each combination added up to. For several hands Jake and Kate had to consult the list to see if they might have a family in a trump suit or at least be able to count three hundred for a double pinochle of two queens of spades and two jacks of diamonds. Both of them soon learned what counted and how to take tricks. Unfortunately, Jake too often depended on the dummy hand to have exactly what he needed and he would overbid. But it wasn't long before he fully understood the game and held his own. Charlie was good at the game, but Jake and Kate were sharp card players and kept him on his toes.

From that Christmas night on they added pinochle to the list of games they liked to play. Poker was still Charlie's favorite, and Jake preferred cribbage, mainly because he'd won most of the games recently. Kate challenged them to play Scrabble occasionally, knowing she was better at that than they were.

As winter progressed, more snow fell and the temperatures dropped to bitter cold days and nights. Most evenings they were too tired to dance or play cards. Sometimes Kate played the piano while the men listened. Occasionally Jake brought out his guitar and they played and sang together.

Kate doubted she would ever get cabin fever.

# Chapter Six

**Late January** of 1959 was colder than the previous year. Frostbite was a big concern of Kate's, not for herself as much as for Charlie and Jake. They trudged in daily from their chores with frost on their beards and eyebrows. Even with felt liners in their boots and leather mittens lined with sheepskin, she was sure their hands and feet could freeze. But they never complained.

On one especially cold day she spoke up. "I worry about you two freezing out there."

"Our sheepskin-lined coats over our denim jackets keep us warm enough," Jake answered without much concern. "We even have to take off the coats and wear the jackets while we're pitching hay. They're lined with flannel so we do okay."

"And those scotch caps with the ear flaps keep our ears from freezing," Charlie said.

"Nevertheless, I can't help worrying about you two out there in this bitter cold."

One sunny morning Kate put off washing the dishes and separator so she could watch Jake and Charlie hitch the teams to the hay sled. She threw on a heavy sweater and opened the top of the Dutch door. With her hands cradled around a mug of hot coffee, she watched a rein arch over the backs of the horses. Charlie caught it and climbed onto the sled holding all the lines. Jake came from behind the horses and stopped to adjust something that seemed to be caught. He looked toward the house, and for a moment she felt his eyes on her. Then he blew her a kiss. She was touched by his gesture and hastily sent back a kiss before he turned away. Shivering, she shut the door and then stood with her back to the fireplace until she was warm.

*First things first,* Kate thought, as she collected what she needed to stir up bread dough. When it was covered with a tea towel to let it rise, she washed the breakfast dishes and the separator, swept the floors of the kitchen and mudroom, and then poked kindling in the kitchen stove. She browned a pot roast and left it to cook slowly. By then the fireplace needed more wood. When she'd taken care of that, she sat down and pulled a robe around her. She often sat and picked up some needlework or read a while. Today her thoughts were bittersweet. She was keenly aware of how her life had changed since David and Jeremy died. She didn't like comparing Jake with David, but the simple fact was that she was happier now than she had been in her first marriage. Sadness seemed to overcome Kate every time she took in this realization.

In spite of trying not to, she saw such differences in David and Jake that she couldn't deny them. David loved her, but he lived and breathed medicine. He worked hard and provided well for her, but by the time he got home in the evenings he was either tired or had his nose in a medical journal. He always made time to spend with Jeremy after supper and then retired while she sat up to nurse the baby and get him settled for bed. Naturally, she was the one to get up during the night to attend to the feedings and changing.

Her thoughts turned to Jake and the little things he did to make her feel special, like the kiss he blew from the corral and his easy teasing. As soon as he came in from doing chores, he would take her in his arms and give her warm kisses before he went to wash for a meal. Sometimes she had to pick off bits of hay, or splinters from the wood he'd carried in, that stuck to her hair or clothes but she didn't mind in light of how good he made her feel. It hadn't been that way with David, and there she was comparing them again.

In her frustration, she got up to check on the roast and stopped to pet Jerry. Surprisingly, he had stayed on the small sofa near the steps instead of jumping into her lap. There was plenty of time before Jake and Charlie would be in from feeding. They had to open a new haystack that morning and lead the cows to a new feedground, which would delay them, so Kate went into the den to find a book to read. The cabinets under the bookshelves were topped with a narrow shelf. There were several magazines on the shelf near Jake's desk. They were new and Kate doubted he'd read any of them. As she leafed through the pile, they held little interest for her until she came upon a horse magazine and another from Alaska. A letter dropped out from between the two of them and fell to the floor. It hadn't been opened and the postmark was from the summer before, but Kate could tell it was from Laurie, Jake's ex-fiancée and the woman they'd met in the restaurant with her new husband.

Kate placed the letter on the mantle and sat down to read a magazine, but curiosity kept her from enjoying it. She was glad when it came time to get the potatoes, carrots, and onions cooking with the roast.

After a late dinner, Jake and Charlie took a nap before it was time to milk and do the chores. Afterwards neither wanted anything more to eat and Jake hit the hay early.

Jake turned to her when she crawled in beside him.

"Oooh, you're cold," he said when she snuggled against him.

"I know. It feels good to get into bed where it's warm."

He chuckled. "Sweetheart, you have the darndest way of making your point. I thought you wanted to be in bed with me, and all you really want is for me to get you warm."

—•—

The next evening Jake was sitting on the couch when Kate came in from washing the milk bucket and strainer. He motioned for her to sit next to him. They watched the flames shoot up from the log on the fireplace and he told her about the coyotes they'd seen that day. "We haven't heard them howling much lately. But we haven't been outside at night and we can't always hear 'em in here."

Kate pulled a robe over both of them. "They don't come close to the house, do they? I've never seen any around here."

"They would if they thought they could get into the chicken house. Before Jesse built the one we have, he said they lost most of the hens one night. 'Course, it could have been some other varmint, like a skunk."

"I haven't seen a skunk since I moved here."

"They come around once in a while but . . . their powerful odor . . . and porcupine quills are things we can live without. It's tough to pull quills out of a dog's jaw but I've had to a couple of times." He was a bit surprised that his comment didn't get a response but Kate hardly seemed to have heard.

Kate stood up, took the letter from the mantle, and handed it to Jake. "This was in with some magazines in your den. You must not have seen it, it hasn't been opened."

Jake looked it over. "I didn't need to read it. I'm sure it says the same thing the others said."

"This came in July."

Jake gave her a wide-eyed look. "I think I hear a bit of jealousy. Are you wondering if I was thinking of Laurie at that time?"

"I'm not jealous," she protested. "But I admit I'm wondering why you were still writing to her when . . ."

"I wasn't writing to her. She wrote to me . . . always saying she made a mistake and wanted us to get together again." He opened the envelope and took out the sheet of paper. "Here, read it."

"I don't want to read your letter."

"Well, I'll read it to you then." Not surprisingly, Laurie had written just as Jake had said. There was an angry note at the end demanding why he didn't have the decency to answer her letters. After he finished, Jake tossed the letter onto the table.

Then Kate made a confession. "Remember last winter when you had a broken arm and I went to the mailbox with you?"

"Sure, I remember everything from the time I laid eyes on you in the ditch."

She lifted her eyebrows as if to say, "really?"

"There were two letters from Laurie then. Of course, it wasn't any of my business, but I did have to wonder if you two were mending your fences."

"We weren't mending fences." He winked at her and added, "I do that with Charlie."

"Be serious, will you? The morning we had breakfast in Saratoga after our wedding and she brought her new husband over to our table, I think now that she was telling you off in a polite way."

"Probably was, although I didn't think it was so polite . . . pointed but not polite. I think it was February or March when I wrote to her and told her we were not suited to each other and I wished her the best. If she was going with what's his name . . ."

"Grant," Kate offered.

"Yeah, Grant . . . or planning to marry him, she didn't tell me. If the truth were told, I threw away a couple of letters after I let her know it was over." He gestured toward the letter on the table. "Since I didn't answer them or this one, I guess she realized I meant what I said."

Kate was thoughtful for a few minutes. "So you didn't tell her about me before we saw her and her husband in Saratoga?"

"Sweetheart, by the time you'd been here a couple of months, I certainly was not thinking about Laurie. The day you left the ranch, I was afraid you were gone for good and I have never felt as lost as I did then. I wanted to hightail it to Jackson and ask you to marry me but I was afraid you would turn me down."

Kate thought over what Jake was saying, but didn't offer a reply.

"I had some hope the day I spent with you on the anniversary of David and Jeremy's death. You seemed glad I was there. But then there was haying and a lot to do with everyone here."

"I was thankful to have you there," Kate said. "You made the day bearable and I had been missing you. After that, I started wondering how I could come back gracefully and ask you to marry me."

"Well, for heaven's sake, why didn't you? You could have saved Charlie all the trouble he went to trying to get us together."

They laughed about that and enjoyed the fire a while until Jake yawned and got up to put logs on the fire. "Time to go to bed," he said, offering her a hand up.

He picked up the letter and tossed it into the fireplace.

# Chapter Seven

**Wet clothes,** sheets, and towels hung on every available rack in the mudroom as well as on a clothesline Jake had rigged up in there. Kate had swept and mopped all the floors, set the table, and had dinner ready. She liked knowing that the house was clean and in good shape for the weekend—it gave her a sense of accomplishment—even though weekends were pretty much like every other day on the ranch. Besides, Jake, Charlie, and she tried to do as little work as possible on Sundays. Although there was some necessary work to be done, they considered it a day of rest.

Thinking she had some time before the men came in, Kate sat down to read and had almost fallen asleep when the kitchen door opened and startled her. She jumped up so quickly that she knocked over a glass of water from the table next to the couch. She muttered, "Rats," as she headed for the kitchen for a rag to wipe up spilled water and the broom to sweep up broken glass.

"I saw you get up from the couch. You must have been sleeping while we were out there in the cold slaving away for you," Jake said jovially.

"Oh sure, I was sleeping! Take a look around and you'll see *I* was slaving away for *you* all morning," Kate replied, scowling at him. "Surely you know that man's work is from sunup to sundown, but a woman's work is never done."

As she stomped toward the living room, she heard Charlie say, "Sounds like Martha. I guess all women say that."

"We'd better tread lightly, she's a little grumpy," Jake replied. "Maybe she's gettin' cabin fever."

"Cabin fever . . . never!" Kate yelled back.

"Most women would, cooped up here with two galoots for several months," Charlie said sympathetically.

Kate came back into the kitchen. Jake looked at her with concern. "Seriously, don't you get a little bored and tired of the day-to-day work and chores? Especially without a woman to talk to?"

"I'm where I want to be with the man I cherish, in a lovely home in a beautiful valley. I couldn't ask for anything more than that."

"Not quite true," he said softly.

She snuggled against his chest. "No, not quite." His hold tightened. "We can't be impatient," she added. "God will send us children . . . we've prayed for it."

"I know," he whispered.

———•———

The bitter cold and occasional wind in April made calving season miserable for Jake and Charlie. They took turns checking the heifers. Generally Charlie took the first night shift and Jake relieved him about midnight. Sometimes Kate went with Jake, but mostly he wanted her to stay in the house to keep warm so she wouldn't catch a cold. None of them had had any cold or flu symptoms for the past two winters, but by the middle of April, Kate began coughing and her chest hurt with congestion, and they were all reminded of the risks of someone getting sick and no way to get to a doctor. The men worried about her and Kate was just as worried but tried to keep from them that she had symptoms of pneumonia.

When Jake and Charlie brought the chilled newborn calves into the house, Kate didn't even offer to take care of them.

The men insisted she stay in bed most of two weeks and often found her on the couch in front of the fireplace when they got in from feeding.

"It's warmer here," she told Jake one afternoon when he brought her a cup of soup. Charlie appeared with a mug of hot tea and some crackers, which he placed by the soup on the little table next to the couch.

They both sat down to make sure she took some nourishment. She sat up and reached for the mug of tea. "You two can't get sick.

I've about used up all the tea and honey. We don't have much Vick's left either." She smiled weakly. "You don't need to worry anymore. I'm feeling much better today."

"We're glad of that," Jake said. "You still look peaked and weak so don't get up too soon. We don't want you to have a relapse."

"Did you eat?" Kate asked with her usual concern.

"Sure, we had some of that soup. We might be eating that for a while—Charlie made a big pot of soup yesterday."

"It's very good, Charlie," Kate told him when she had taken a spoonful.

A few days later early in May, Kate was able to join Jake and Charlie for breakfast. Jake said, "It's a relief to see that you're recovering. You've had us damned worried."

Charlie added his concern too. "I kept thinking we needed to get you to a doctor but it didn't seem like a good idea to pull you on a sled out to the road then send you off with the mailman to town. We're just glad that you're a good nurse."

"Thanks, I'm feeling better. Kinda weak though."

"Don't worry about anything. We'll do what needs to be done until you're back on your feet," Jake said. "Then you'll have to get things back in shape . . . slave," he added, in his usual kidding way.

They were all in a good mood and Kate asked Jake if they were through calving.

"Most of the heifers have calved now."

"You said you've lost two so far," Kate said. "I still shudder at the thought of that mama cow that lost her baby last year."

"Seeing a calf die makes me forget that the money is lost too."

"Of course, I should try not to be so overly sentimental about it all. I just can't help it."

Jake sent her a wink. "My dear, you are just naturally sentimental."

Finally, nearly all the cows had calved and there were signs of spring. Kate watched every day for new blades of grass or buds on the willows and lilac bushes. Snowdrifts had begun to shrink into slushy piles, and water dripped off the roof during the middle of the day.

Feeling good again, Kate often sang *Oh, What a Beautiful Morning* while she worked away in the kitchen after breakfast.

Jake snuck up on her one particular day while she was mashing potatoes in a pot on the stove. "It's good to hear that beautiful singing voice. What's the occasion?"

"It's spring. The snow is melting and I saw something green coming up in the flowerbed this morning. Isn't that great?"

"It is, but that means spring work is beginning. The note from Sam Peterson yesterday said they're setting the times for brandings and wondered when we wanted to brand." He pumped a glass of water. "I think I can get through to the county road so I'll drive over to Peterson's this afternoon and get that settled." He finished his drink and set the glass on the counter. "I guess you know you'll be cooking for the branding crew before too long. We should be able to go to town. If you need anything for the dinner, we'll go to Pinedale soon."

"Okay, but I want to go to the other brandings so I can help the women with the meals."

"Good. The women all help with dinner just like the men help with branding." Jake grinned appreciatively. "You make a pretty good rancher's wife, you know that?"

"It's too late now if I don't."

"I think I'll keep you," he said, tweaking her cheek gently.

"Go get ready for dinner. I'm trying to make gravy and you're a big distraction."

The three of them helped with brandings at the Peterson's, the Dixon Ranch, and Holden's. Kate took her dinner rolls each time. Jackie Peterson and the other women agreed that none of them could make rolls as good as hers.

Before they left the last of the neighbors' brandings, everyone assured Kate and Jake they would be on hand to help with their branding the next week.  The women asked what they should bring to go with the beef stroganoff Kate was planning as her main dish. Jackie said she'd bring the pies. Janie Holden offered to make a green bean casserole and Eleanor Dixon had the fixings to make a salad.

They were headed for home when Kate piped up. "I must say, it felt strange to be with people again. Last year, not seeing anyone but you and Charlie for several months didn't seem to bother me."

"Does it bother you now?" Jake asked.

"Not really. I like wintertime, but I'm glad to get together with Jackie and the other women in the spring. They're all so good-natured and they enjoy each other's company. I don't think any of them get snowed in like we do, though."

Jake gave her a quick glance. "Oh, they do, but not for as long as we do because they live closer to the road." He motioned to the gate they were passing through. "Since the county only plows to the gate on top of this big hill some families leave a car out by the road if their place is snowed in." He slowed for a pothole. "Some of them have kids that ride a school bus to Boulder so the road is plowed for the bus to get to the last ones on the route."

Their own ranch road was a challenge. The snow had melted but there was still some mud, and the ruts that had formed made it slow going.

Charlie had been quiet the whole way. He spoke as they drove up to the Bunkhouse. "You must be tired, Katie. Don't fix anything for me. I'm full from that big dinner and as soon as the chores are done, I'm off to bed."

"I'll do the chores," Jake told the older man. "But if you don't mind, I wish you would start the fire in the fireplace before you go to bed."

Kate patted Charlie on the arm. "Take him up on it. I'm going to gather the eggs and I'll wash the milk bucket but that's it for tonight. It's been a long day for all of us." She smiled at Charlie, thinking what a kind and gentle man he was.

———•———

The day before branding, as they were cutting up meat for the stroganoff, Kate told Jake that she'd prefer doing the whole meal herself. Everyone expected to help and she didn't want to hurt any-one's feelings, but that's the way she felt.

"Right," he said, indifferently. "Are you going to brown this meat now or should I put the kettle in the cooler?"

"I'd better do it now. I need the morning to do the rolls. I've cooked the eggs but they will have to be deviled in the morning . . . those women make such big meals. I hope mine turns out okay."

"You don't need to worry. You can do it. Remember last year? They all thought you had a wonderful meal."

"Last year I didn't know what I was getting into. It was pure luck and a good memory of Grandma's cooking."

"Of course, Charlie and I knew you were a good cook but those ladies thought you were passing through and we'd conned you into cooking dinner for a branding crew. They thought we were lucky ducks."

---

The day of their branding, the stroganoff was simmering in the oven, the noodles were made and cut up ready to be cooked in boiling water, and Kate was preparing the rolls when the other ranch women began to arrive.

Kate wasn't surprised that Eleanor and Janie, in Levi's and boots, took off right away for the corrals where they usually gave the shots and kept the irons hot. Jackie Peterson counted the grownups and the teenagers who'd come to help wrestle calves.  She took plates and silverware to the table and had fourteen places set on the long table in no time. Together, Kate and Jackie dished up pickles, olives, butter, and jam and then sat down to have a cup of coffee before it was time to bake the rolls.

"We always enjoyed having Mary Anne and Jesse as neighbors but you and Jake are just like them," Jackie offered. "I guess we all wondered if you would like it here, being a city girl and all."

"I've always lived in a city, but I'm a country girl at heart." Kate replied. "I spent summers with my grandparents on the Orland Place just east of here when I was growing up." She sipped her coffee. "Of course, I didn't spend the winters out here. I was always disappointed that we never had Christmas with Grandma and Granddad."

"I remember Jake saying that you came through here hoping to see your grandparent's ranch again, and then got stuck with fixing the branding dinner last spring." She stopped before adding, "You and Jake must have hit it off right away. Love at first sight, I guess."

Kate thought, *apparently, the neighbors didn't suspect that I spent the winter alone with Jake and Charlie.* She'd worried a bit that they might speculate about what she was doing there with two men all winter long. Finally she said, "The McClarys moved here the year before my last summer at the ranch. I'd met them and they were all great about helping out when Granddad got hurt."

Kate went to put the rolls in the oven and Jackie poured another cup of coffee for each of them. Kate directed the conversation away from herself and asked Jackie about her family.

"You know Brett and Cassie. They've been at all the brandings. We have another daughter Betsy who is married and lives in Idaho. "I'm hoping we can get over to see them before too long, but summers around here are so busy." She sipped her coffee and added, "Maybe they'll get here for a few days. Her husband is a farmer so they keep busy too."

By the time they got up to finish getting dinner on the table, Jackie had filled her in on many of the details about the other families in the valley and whose kids had just gotten out of school for the summer. She confided that Eleanor and Janie fussed every year about having to cook dinner at their own places. "They would rather be out with the men . . . if you know what I mean," she added conspiratorially.

"I'm glad the corral dried up before the branding," Kate said as she spied the crew coming toward the house. "I've never seen so much mud and manure come into the house as we've had these past weeks."

"I know all about that," Jackie laughed.

After everyone left, Kate told Charlie, "It's good to see all those people but I sure do like how quiet and peaceful it is right now."

Later on in bed she related Jackie's comment to Jake about how they must have hit it off right away. "Love at first sight, she called it."

"I thought love at first sight had to do with strangers. Anyway, I hope you didn't tell her how it really was."

"I wouldn't dare, knowing how fast news travels in this valley. And it sure wasn't love at first sight."

Jake drew Kate close and wrapped his arms around her. "But it sure is wonderful the second time around . . . at least for me."

"Well, if you put it that way, I'd say I have to agree."

# Chapter Eight

**Kate rode out** on her horse Misty with Jake and Charlie a week later, trailing the cattle to the desert. She patted Misty's neck as she rode alongside Jake. "This horse is gentle and easy to ride. I'm glad you broke her for me."

"She was easy to break . . . never did buck. Can't say the same for this cayuse. That's why his name is Buck." Jake turned back for a cow that had stopped to eat a few blades of grass, then came back to join Kate. "He's a good horse, though, even turned out to be a good roping horse. I've worked him pretty hard."

"Jackie Peterson told me that you are the best roper around and the other ranchers like to have you do the roping for brandings." She grinned at him and added, "That made me very proud."

"Well, that's nice but I'm not the only one—the other guys can rope too." He looked at her saddle. "Are you comfortable? We can change the length of the stirrups if you want."

Kate shifted her weight from one stirrup to the other. "Seems just right to me. This is a beautiful saddle and the bridle looks good on Misty. You outfitted me with the best. I can't thank you enough." They rode on for several miles before Kate asked, "How far do they go out here?"

"We're about there. You'll see a gate around the other side of the hill just ahead of us. We'll turn 'em in there. They'll stay out here until the first part of July when we can take them to the summer pasture on the forest. The feed is good out here and I checked the reservoirs last week. They're in good shape too."

"I hope I get to go along when you move the cattle to the forest. Moving cattle is fun, isn't it Jake?"

"Well, not always fun, but it's one of the more pleasant chores on the ranch," he replied.

"I guess it wouldn't be much fun in a storm, and it could be a long day of riding but it's a nice outing for me."

They pushed the last of the cattle through the gate. "Just look at those cows . . . they sure go after that green grass growing between the sagebrush," Jake said.

Kate looked over the great expanse of sagebrush. They sat on their horses watching the cows graze and the calves run and play while they waited for Charlie to reach them. "Jake, I'd almost forgotten about the sagebrush. We've had snow for so long and with hay meadows all around the house, I haven't seen the sagebrush. I love that silvery green/gray color and it has a wonderful sage smell." She got off her horse and picked a fragrant stem to pull through a buttonhole so she could enjoy its tangy scent.

"I like sagebrush, too, but I guess I never was as awed by it as you are."

"We need to get some growing in the yard," she said dreamily.

Jake frowned. "What did you just say?"

"I think we ought to have some growing in the yard. It smells so fresh and good."

"Kate McClary, there are miles and miles of sagebrush all over this prairie, and you want it planted in the yard?" He took a deep breath and added, "Do you have any idea how hard it is to grub sagebrush to make a field that will grow hay . . ."

"Well no, I've never seen anyone do that. But I really do want to plant some sagebrush in the yard."

"And who did you have in mind to do that?"

Kate's eyes twinkled as she batted her eyes at him.

"Okay, I get the message." He stared at sagebrush all around them and then looked askance at Kate.

Charlie rode up, grinning. "Well, the cattle are happy, I'm happy. Are you two happy?"

Jake shook his head at Charlie. "I think I just agreed to plant some sagebrush in the yard at the Bunkhouse. Can you believe that?"

Charlie barely suppressed a laugh. "I guess if it would make Katie happy, you'd do that."

"Couldn't be happier, Charlie," Kate said, reaching over to Jake. They rode along hand-in-hand most of the way home.

———•———

One warm sunshiny morning Kate informed Jake that she intended to set out the bedding plants she bought the last time they were in town. "It's a perfect day for planting."

"I hope they don't freeze," was his retort to her plan.

"Oh, for heaven's sake, it's almost the middle of June. They won't freeze."

He just raised his eyebrows and shrugged his shoulders as he went out the door.

She had just finished planting the flowers where she wanted them to be when she heard a pickup coming. Kate took off her gloves and brushed at the dirt clinging to her knees. She had just recognized her neighbor when she heard Jackie Peterson call through the open window of the truck, "Hi, Kate."

Kate walked to the fence and said, "Jackie, glad to see you." She opened the gate and added, "Come in. I just finished here."

"Gosh, you're ambitious. I never get much done in my yard but yours is looking great."

Kate led Jackie up the front steps and stopped to take off her shoes. When Jackie started to do the same, Kate said, "Don't take off your shoes. Mine are dirty. I'll clean them up later." She shut the screen door and left the front door open to the sunshine. "How about a cup of coffee or tea?" she asked.

"Tea would be nice." Jackie looked around and told Kate how much she'd always loved the Bunkhouse.

Kate went to the cookie jar and put some of her homemade oatmeal and raisin cookies on a plate to serve with the tea.

"I came to ask you and Jake to come to our house for supper on Friday night," Jackie said. "We thought it would be fun to play cards." As an afterthought, she added, "You ought to bring Charlie, too. We usually play bridge, but we could play poker or whatever you like."

"Sounds like fun. Jake and Charlie are at the barn. I'll ask them as soon as they come in, but I'm sure it'll be fine."

Jackie didn't stay long, saying that she had to go into town before she went home. "We'll see you Friday night . . . is five-thirty okay with you?"

"Yes, thanks for asking us."

She waved goodbye and stood with her arms folded on the top rail of the fence. It occurred to her that their neighbors might think they were antisocial people. She made up her mind to dispel any such thoughts in their minds and do some inviting herself in the future.

When she told the men about the plan, Charlie opted out. "You two go on. I'm sure I'd be too tired to go out that late."

Kate suspected that he might be feeling like a fifth wheel but he sounded sure of himself. Jake mulled over the idea and then said, "If you want to go, it's fine with me."

By Friday Kate was looking forward to spending the evening with the Petersons. She was ready and would have left supper for Charlie but he assured her he'd make himself a roast beef sandwich and not to bother with anything else.

When Jake appeared wearing his new leather jacket and new Levi's, Charlie said it was a good thing he was duded up because he was taking a pretty lady out. Charlie winked at Kate. "Have a good time," he told them.

At breakfast the next morning, Kate said they had enjoyed the evening. "We'll have to have the Petersons over here sometime."

"We'll do that . . . after haying," Jake said without much enthusiasm. He seemed to have had a good time the night before but she knew him well enough by now to know that he was content to stay home unless they needed to go to town for supplies.

———•———

A few days later, Kate was out walking when she spotted Jake on his horse. He'd been riding the fences to find where a couple of cows and their calves had gotten out just before they took the cattle to the desert.

Jake trotted up to Kate, his cowboy hat shielding the sun from his face. "Fine morning for a walk," he said.

"When I get the time, I like to walk out to the road and wander around through the sagebrush." She held up an object for him to see. "Look at the arrowhead I found this morning," she said.

"Just remember to check for ticks when you get back to the house."

"I saw a horny toad this morning. Granddad used to take me out to look for horny toads and rabbits in the brush." She waved in the direction of a hill on the other side of the creek. "I walked over by that butte. There's some really tall sagebrush we could get for the yard."

"Oh, yes . . . let's do that. It'll be such fun," Jake said with a hint of sarcasm.

"Well, be that way."

"Quit looking at me like that. You're the limit, you know? What will you do if I say no to planting sagebrush in your yard?"

"I'll think of something," she said with a silly grin.

"I wish I hadn't asked," he replied. He held out a hand to give her a lift. "Here, put your foot in the stirrup and I'll help you up." They rode on home with her arms around his waist and both of them singing *Home on the Range*. As they rode up to the barn, Charlie was standing at the gate with his arms folded and a big smile on his face.

———•———

Each morning by the light of dawn, Jake and Charlie had their horses saddled and were ready to go out irrigating. Jake went over to the Orland Place, which was farther away, so Charlie was usually back at the Bunkhouse first. He would do the chores and then he and Jake would come in for breakfast about the same time.

"The mosquitoes are fierce today," Jake commented one morning. "I guess we ought to be glad the horseflies and deerflies haven't showed up yet."

Charlie looked up from his plate of pancakes and eggs. "Don't ever kill a mosquito, Katie," he said soberly.

She could hardly believe her ears. "Don't kill a mosquito? Why not?"

Charlie went on just as straight-faced as before. "If you kill one, all the others come to his funeral."

When it registered what he had said, Kate burst out laughing, and Jake, who'd known what was coming, joined her. She wiped the tears of laughter from her eyes. "How'd I ever end up here with you two galoots?"

"I guess you parked yourself in a snow bank where we could find you," Jake replied.

Charlie finished off the last morsel on his plate. "Yep, you're one lucky girl to be stuck with us galoots."

"Hey, both of you, stop ribbing me or I won't make us that angel food cake I was planning on doing this afternoon."

"Gosh, now we've done it," Jake said. He gave Kate an insincere penitent look.

"Wanna hear another joke?" Charlie asked. "I've got plenty."

"Save it," Kate replied. "I've got to think about exactly where the sagebrush should go. One thing's for sure, it's never boring here. I'm perfectly happy. That is, I will be when I have some sagebrush in the yard." She picked up two serving bowls and made her way to the kitchen.

She was almost out of earshot when Kate heard Charlie chuckle as he asked Jake, "Want me to help you with that sagebrush?"

# Chapter Nine

**Kate would have** preferred to be out with the men while they mended fences, moved cattle, and irrigated, but there was too much in the house to keep her busy. It was warm enough now to hang clothes and linens on the clothesline outside. More than anything, she loved the fresh smell of sheets just off the line this time of year. When needed, which was often, Jake or Charlie would fill the gas washing machine with hot water for her. Between the three of them, there seemed an endless flow of laundry to be done.

"When I went into town the other day I saw how much progress they've made with the telephone line," Jake said as he topped off the washing machine.

Kate's eyes lit up. "How long will it take them to get here?"

"I'm hoping maybe by September . . . before snow flies."

"Jake!"

His eyebrows went up. "Yes?"

"You promised we would make a trip to Denver and here it is nearly haying time. You've put me off long enough."

Kate followed him into the kitchen where he sat on a stool and ran his fingers along his chin.

"If you can't go with me, I'll go alone."

"I don't want you to go to Denver by yourself. So that's settled." He paused and said thoughtfully, "We'll have to shut the water off pretty soon so the meadows will be dry for haying. In fact, we're running short of water now." He added playfully, "So when do we leave?"

"You're impossible, you know that?"

He got up and stood in the open doorway. "Takes one to know one," he quipped.

She picked up a hand towel from the laundry pile and threw it at him. He caught it and tossed it back to her.

———

Kate made a trip to Rock Springs to do some necessary shopping. While she was there she called Cameron Wyatt. They had exchanged a few letters since he and Jean attended the wedding so he wasn't surprised that Kate wanted to get her surname changed and Jake's name added to her investments.

"It'll be good to see you two. We want you to stay with us, of course." Cameron said.

"Jake won't stay long. He and Charlie have been mending harnesses, fixing teeth on the rakes and sweeps, sharpening sickles, and all those chores getting ready for haying season, but we'll come whenever it's convenient for you and Jean."

"Can you get here by next Monday?"

"I'll check with Jake but we ought to make it by late Sunday."

"Great, we'll count on it." Cameron hesitated before hanging up. "Kate, I had a call a few days ago and intended to get a note off to you."

Kate suddenly felt uneasy about what he was going to say.

"Your mother called me wanting to know how to get in touch with you. I wouldn't give her any information without your okay. But I said I'd let you know."

"Surprise" hardly seemed adequate to explain how Kate took that news. "It is not okay with me," she replied. "I don't have anything to say to her or any desire to see her. I don't like having you in the middle of this, but will you tell her that if she calls again?"

"Yes, I will, although maybe not in so many words. Knowing how you feel, I certainly won't encourage her to try and locate you."

That evening Kate wasn't her usual self. She mentioned that she told Cameron they would be there Sunday night. She was unusually quiet and didn't join in the supper conversation with Jake and Charlie.

"I'm looking forward to going to Denver even though it'll be a short trip," Jake offered as Kate hung up the tea towel after washing the milk bucket.

"Me too."

"I think we should stop to see Jesse and Mary Anne on the way home."

"That's fine."

Jake looked intently at her. "Is there something on your mind, Kate? You're awfully quiet."

"I've been thinking about my talk with Cameron. My mother called him and asked how to get in touch with me. He didn't offer any details, but he wanted to know what I thought."

"And what do you think?"

"I don't want to see her or even talk to her."

Jake folded his arms and leaned against the counter. "I'm surprised. You're usually such a compassionate person. I don't understand why you wouldn't want to make peace with your own mother."

Kate became quiet again. She hadn't expected Jake to feel this way about it.

"Maybe she's missed you all these years. Or she has cancer or a bad heart. *Maybe* she regrets leaving you and wants to make it up to you."

"Maybe," Kate said without much conviction.

———•———

After morning Mass in Rock Springs the next Sunday, Jake and Kate were on their way to Denver. When they arrived, they enjoyed a meal with Cameron and Jean, talking over how things had changed in the past year.

"We're glad to see you so happy, Kate. After you lost David and Jeremy, we worried about you getting on with your life. Going to the ranch seems quite providential now," Jean said.

"I know your dad would be pleased," Cameron put in. "He told me several times how bad he felt that he couldn't raise you on the ranch, but he was grateful to his folks for wanting you to spend your summers with them."

"You probably knew my dad better than anyone since the two of you became close friends in college and stayed close even after you pursued your different careers."

Cameron nodded and with his eyes twinkling, he told her, "One big difference between us . . . he loved to ski and I was no good at it."

"I remember that," she said with a wide grin. "But, I think you would know the answer to something that has always puzzled me." They all looked at her expectantly. "I was told that my folks met in college but my mother quit school when they married. Did she work to help him get through architectural school? How did they manage?"

Jean set plates of strawberry shortcake before them and then picked up the coffee pot from the sideboard to refill their cups to go with dessert. As she moved from one to the other, it gave Cameron a chance to sit quietly and consider how to phrase his answer. He had never cared much for Lillian, who hadn't given her husband and daughter much love and finally left them for a reason Kate and Jake probably didn't know—that is, for another man. He also knew that Lillian had done nothing to help James through school.

They waited expectantly for Cameron to continue.

"Your dad worked all through college because he didn't want his folks to pay all his expenses. When he decided to become an architect, they insisted that he let them pay for everything so he could concentrate on his studies."

Kate listened intently in between bites of the irresistible short-cake.

"They loved him so much that whatever he wanted to do with his life was okay," Cameron continued. "Of course, they would have liked it if he could have taken over the ranch, but as he grew up he had suffered with terrible allergies to most everything on the ranch." He smiled at Kate. "They were so proud of your dad."

"Oh yes, they told me that. They even said they were proud of me, but I don't know what for." Someone would have reassured her but she went on too quickly, "Were they happy when he married my mother?"

Jake and Jean exchanged a glance, seeing that Kate had asked a hard question. Jean already knew how her husband felt. Kate's grandmother and Jake's mother had been close friends so Jake knew his mother hadn't taken to Lillian either.

Cameron was cautious when he replied to her direct question. "I can't speak for what they thought about the marriage but as I said, they wanted the best for their only son." He paused before he added, "I'm sure you know better than anyone how they felt when your mother left you and your dad."

"I guess I was so mad at her that I didn't pay much attention to what anyone else was thinking. But now that we're talking about it, I don't remember my grandparents ever saying anything mean about my mother. They would tell me not to be bitter and to be glad I had my dad."

Jake put his hand over Kate's. "I'm sure we all know that was a tough time for you. I never did meet your dad but your grandparents were as kindhearted as anyone could be." He squeezed her hand and teased, "Do you need help eating all that cake?" he asked, lightening the mood.

They finished their meal and Kate helped Jean with the dishes, then they joined the men who were visiting in the living room.

Later, as they were lying in bed, Kate said, "I still don't know how Grandma and Granddad felt about my parents getting married."

"Well, Katie, I suspect that even if they weren't too happy about the marriage, they were delighted with who came to them as a consequence of that marriage."

"I'm glad you said that. Maybe I should think of that and forget that she abandoned me. I wouldn't even be here if they hadn't married."

He held her close and whispered, "Actually, I'm right happy that your mom and dad married—they saved me from being a crotchety ol' bachelor."

———•———

After breakfast the next morning, Jake and Kate went with Cameron to his office where Cameron discussed what investments Kate had and what dividends were being paid. Kate and Jake signed the papers necessary to have everything in both names. They were able to complete their business in time for a late lunch. On the way to lunch, they stopped at the bank where Kate had her accounts so Jake's name could be added to them too.

As they waited for the waitress to bring their food, Jake again brought up the unwelcome subject of Kate's mother. "Kate told me about Lillian calling. It isn't up to me but I wish Kate would let you give her mother our whereabouts the next time she calls."

Kate put up a hand before Cameron could respond. "Okay, if she wants to come see us, tell her where we live," she said resignedly. "But she can't call because as you know we don't have a telephone."

Cameron smiled. "I'm glad you've had a change of heart, Kate. We all understand how abandoned you must have felt but your mother is getting on in years and maybe she's sorry she left you."

"Well, that's what Jake thinks, too, so I guess I should show her some consideration."

Soon after lunch, Kate and Jake drove to Saratoga for an overnight stay. Jessie, Danny, and Abby were so excited to see their Uncle Jake and Aunt Kate, they nearly bowled them over with their exuberant greetings.

They were standing in the fenced yard admiring the abundance of petunias, sweet peas, and hollyhocks when Jesse and Mary Anne came out to join them.

"Jake told me that this ranch house was built by his mother's parents," Kate said. "It must be old but it certainly is a beautiful house." She studied the two-story stone house with a wide front porch on the east side.

"It was covered with a kind of stucco at first. Our folks did quite a lot of remodeling and added the siding and stonework to the outside and modernized the house inside," Jesse explained, with family pride in his voice. "The tongue and groove ceiling wood is original, just like the hardwood floors."

Kate turned to Mary Anne. "Of course, the Bunkhouse is wonderful too, but it's good you can be here where you have more room and the kids can go to school."

Mary Anne laughed. "You're right. Trying to keep up with three different grades was getting too much for me." She sobered. "They need to be with other kids for the rest of their schooling and they do like that. They're in 4-H and band. All things we didn't have at the upper ranch."

"You two seem to be okay with changing places. Was it hard?" Kate asked, addressing Jake and Jesse.

"Not for me," Jake said nonchalantly.

"Not for me, either," replied his twin brother. "We mostly grew up here, but liked the other ranch when we moved up there, so we've lived on both and like them pretty much equally."

While doing up the supper dishes, Kate answered Mary Anne's endless questions about living so far from town, the ranching operations, the Bunkhouse, and the neighbors in the valley.

"I'm happy for you, Kate," Mary Anne said before they went to join the others in the living room. "Our mother-in-law speaks highly of you and she's pleased to see Jake settled down and content."

"You and I are blessed to have Mother McClary in our lives. She and Dad must have been apprehensive about Jake marrying a woman who had been married before. They probably wondered if he'd made another bad choice. They worried so about him marrying Laurie."

"After getting to know you they realized Jake had found his true love."

"Thanks for saying that. I have to tell you it's a thrill every time one of your kids call me Aunt Kate. David's nieces and nephews were warned by their grandmother not to refer to me as their aunt."

"How sad and difficult it must have been for you. But you're part of our family now and the kids think you're wonderful. They like all the attention you give them." She smiled warmly at her sister-in-law.

"I hope you'll bring the kids up to our ranch before school starts," Kate said, giving Mary Anne a hug.

"We'd love to if we can get away. We'll be haying for several weeks, though."

———•———

On their way home, Jake stopped at the bank in Rock Springs so they could deposit part of the money they'd brought with them from Denver. He suggested they put the rest in their bank in Pinedale. Kate agreed to that as well, thinking it would go into the ranch account. But she was wrong.

"This money isn't going into the ranch account." He placated her by adding, "We don't need it now but we'll know where it is when we need to use some of it."

Kate could see clearly that her money wouldn't be paying for any electricity or telephone lines. She let it go for the time being.

They started for the ranch. "You know Don and Marie Martin will be coming to the ranch in a couple of weeks," Jake said. "They've come every summer for several years to help with the haying. She cooks and he works in the field. Brad, their son, comes, too."

"Yes, I remember," Kate murmured.

"Marie doesn't really like anyone in her kitchen."

"So what am I supposed to do? To tell the truth, I'm not crazy about having someone in *my* kitchen."

"Hold on. I was hoping you'd be willing to work in the hay field."

Kate was rendered speechless by Jake's proposal.

"You can drive a rake. We have a gentle team—you'll get along good with Star and Baldy." She recovered from her disbelief and in her excitement interrupted Jake. "Are you teasing me? Do you really want me to work in the field?"

"Yes, I do. What do you say?"

"I would love it. Will Marie make the bread and churn the butter? And wash the separator and . . .?"

Jake put his hand on Kate's knee. "Whoa. She does all that. She's doesn't have much time to do any housekeeping but we don't worry about that during haying."

"Then I won't worry about it either. I've been wishing all summer I could be outside and helping with the work around the place. Not that I know much about driving a rake."

"You'll learn. I'll teach you, if I can keep Charlie away from you while I'm doing it. He fusses about you so much, I wonder if he thinks you really are his daughter."

"From the things he's said about him and Martha wanting children, I'm sure he's missed being a dad. We're family to him."

"Yeah, that's how it is, and we're lucky to have him on the ranch. Not all ranchhands are so dependable or willing to be snowed in all winter."

"He's so easygoing about everything. That's what I love about him."

"A few years of putting up with me alone out there might have changed his mind about staying. Since you're with us, I don't need to worry about losing him. I'm lucky he's not twenty years younger."

Kate laughed and stifled a yawn. "Are we there yet?"

"Nope, we have to drive through several more miles of sagebrush," Jake said, grinning.

Just before they turned down the lane on the way to the ranch buildings, Kate said, "I saw some poles set along the county road as I went to town the other day. Are those poles for the telephone line?"

"I'm sure they are," Jake said nonchalantly. "We *might* have a telephone by fall but I don't think they'll get here with the electricity until next year."

Kate poked him in the ribs and then planted a kiss on his cheek. "I wish the money we put in the bank could be so mixed up with yours that you wouldn't know who's paying for all this luxury."

"I know who's paying for it. We are . . . or have you forgotten that we're partners?"

"I haven't forgotten. I just wish I was having my way about using *our* money for ranch expenses."

"That's not hard. You have your way about everything, including me." His smile resonated through her whole being. She snuggled next to him and hugged his arm.

"Glad to be home, Mrs. McClary?"

"Yes I am, Mr. McClary."

They set to work unloading everything from the car and greeted Charlie who came out to help.

"Sure is lonesome around here when you two are gone. I'm glad you're home."

Kate smiled. "You said that the last time we were gone," she said. "I'm glad you miss us. We had a good trip but my heart is in this home."

"I thought it was 'home is where the heart is,'" Charlie said.

"That too," Kate replied, lacing her arm through Charlie's as they made their way to the Bunkhouse.

# Chapter Ten

**After Jake** told her how much work and slow going it would be to gather the cattle off the desert and start them toward the mountains, Kate decided to skip the first part of the move. She fixed a lunch for Jake and Charlie and watched them ride down the lane to the county road. They would be meeting up with riders from two other ranches, and Kate wondered if any of the women would be along. The Dixon and Holden cattle ran on a different allotment and she suspected that both wives went along when their husbands moved the herds.

When the men had the cattle ready to start for the mountains, Kate hurried with the breakfast dishes and was ready by the time Jake had her horse saddled. They met up with the cattle association foreman and several other riders. She and Jake rode at the tail end. "They seem to know where they're going," Kate said, after they'd ridden a while. "It doesn't take as much hard riding as I thought . . . or was led to believe," she said, looking askance at Jake.

"When they know they're headed for summer pasture, the old cows move up the trail to the forest without much herding because they've been there before and they like it up there. The others follow along." Jake yelled "Yah" and moved behind a couple of cows trying to graze some grass along the trail. "By the end of the day, the calves will be tired and lookin' for their mamas. It takes a while for all of 'em to mother up."

They dismounted for a rest and to eat the lunch that Kate had prepared for all the riders. The sandwiches she had put together with ground roast beef mixed with some sandwich spread brought appreciative comments from everyone. "I like riding but it felt good to be off this horse for a while," Kate told Jake as he held Misty for her to get back in the saddle.

"You'll be sore tonight. Might need some of that Absorbine."

"You wish," she replied, remembering how he had applied the liniment to her the year before.

They left the cattle along the trail and rode back home in time to do the chores. Jake watched Kate get off her horse. "You're right," she said. "My legs are sore . . . in fact they feel kinda raw."

"Too raw for Absorbine?" Jake asked without laughing. He could see she was hurting. "I'll take Misty. You go on up to the house. When I get in I'll start a fire."

Kate ate a bowl of the stew she'd made in anticipation of a long day. Jake insisted she go to bed early and suggested that she should only go riding the next day if she wanted to. He assured her that he and Charlie could handle the dishes.

The next morning Kate begged off going back to the trail, giving the men details of all she had to do. "Besides, I think several short rides are in order before I try another long day in the saddle," she confessed.

"We expected that, didn't we, Charlie," Jake said, giving her a kiss. "This breeze is going to make the day pretty cool and you've already seen how dusty it is following the cattle along the trail. It'll be a long day today. We'll be back late tonight. It takes a while for the forest ranger to count the cattle onto the forest. I just hope he'll be there when we get to the gate." Jake fastened the snaps on his chaps and said, "Can you put the calf in with the milk cow this evening then we won't have to milk when we get home?"

"I'll do that. Mrs. Cowley and I are good friends and she knows I'm not going to milk her."

"Take it easy today," Charlie cautioned.

*I intend to,* she thought, watching them go out the kitchen door.

———◆———

A few days after the cattle drive was finished, Jake mentioned they needed to clean the bunkhouse.

Kate bristled at the suggestion. "So you think the Bunkhouse needs cleaning?" she said defensively, her lips tightening.

"Now don't get all huffy. It's mostly dusty and could use some airing out. We washed up all the bedding last fall after the boys left."

"Oh, you mean the bunkhouse where the hay hands sleep. I thought you were telling me I'm a poor housekeeper."

"I saw those sparks fly," he said, giving her a broad smile. "But we do need to get the bunkhouse ready. Don and Marie will stay in the extra bedroom here in the house but Brad will stay in the bunkhouse. He has a friend Casey who will come right away. The other hands will start coming sometime next week."

The bunkhouse was swept, dusted, and smelling fresh by Wednesday when the young fellow named Casey arrived. "I've been driving one of the sweeps for a couple of years now, but I got promoted," he said, puffing out his chest. "I get to help the boss mow this year."

Privately, Kate wondered if that was a promotion but if he thought so, that was fine with her.

Jake and Kate left Casey to settle into the bunkhouse and strolled back to the house.

"Tell me again what everyone will be doing," Kate said. "It's so hard to keep track."

"Carl and Rick, a couple of high school boys, will be coming to work. Marie's husband, Don, and Carl will sweep. You and Rick will rake. Brad will stack and Charlie will drive the plunger. Casey and I will drive the mowers. Brad's a good hand. When he came last year, he told me he'd been helping Jesse in the hayfield since he was a freshman in high school. He's a sophomore in college this year but still wants to hay."

"I guess you can't ask for a better crew."

Since Jake had told Kate she could work in the hayfield, she'd hardly thought about having Marie take over her kitchen. The day Marie and Don Martin were to arrive, though, Kate was washing the breakfast dishes when she remembered that Marie didn't like anyone in her kitchen. *I hope she's not bossy. I like my kitchen clean and everything in its proper place so Marie had better keep it that way.*

Her thoughts were interrupted when Jake opened the door and motioned for Don and Marie to come in. Jake made the introductions.

"Would you like some coffee?" Kate asked, as Jake went out to get some firewood.

"Thank you, that would be great," Marie answered graciously.

Kate was immediately taken with the couple. She especially liked Marie whose smile reached her blue eyes. Light brown soft curls and her no-wrinkles creamy complexion added to Kate's impression of a gentle motherly type. Don's easy smile and sturdy build, his brown hair turning gray, and calloused hands made Kate realize that the two of them complemented each other perfectly.

Don sipped his coffee. "This is good coffee, Mrs. McClary."

"It's Kate . . . do call me Kate, and I hope you don't mind if I call you Don and Marie."

Just then a tall, good looking young man came in with Jake. Both had a load of firewood in their arms.

"This is Brad," Jake said. "He's Don and Marie's youngest son."

"How do you do, Mrs. McClary? I'm glad to meet you. Sorry I can't shake your hand." He waited for Jake to dump his armload of kindling into the wood box then Brad dropped his load on top.

Kate noticed right away that Brad had gotten the best of each of his parents. With blue eyes like his mother and hair the color Don's had been, he resembled both of them. He especially inherited their friendliness. When he came to the table, Kate offered him a cup of coffee.

"No, thanks. I'm not much of a coffee drinker but I could sure use a glass of water."

Kate started to rise from her chair. "Please don't get up," he said. "I can get it myself."

"Brad says he wants to stack this year," Jake said. "And I was glad to hear it since Wally isn't coming. It's great to have him step up and fill that spot."

"Don't you mean 'climb up'?" Brad said with a grin.

It took Kate a moment to realize why they had laughed at his remark. *Of course, he'll be climbing up on haystacks all during haying season.*

———•———

Don and Brad helped Jake and Charlie get machinery ready, then they all worked horses on a wagon for a week. They were enjoying Marie's chicken-fried steak, baked potatoes, and homemade bread when Jake addressed Don and Brad.

"We still need to work some horses this afternoon. It always takes ol' Dutch a while to decide he'll do his job. Most of the others have tamed down pretty good. We'll use the same ones that worked last year."

Don nodded. Jake had told Kate he was a top hand with horses.

"I hope the others get here by morning," Jake said. He tipped his head toward Casey. "Casey and I mowed the northeast meadow so that can be raked in the morning."

"If they don't get here in time, do you want me to rake in the morning?" Brad asked.

"Sure, that will help a lot." He extended his hand toward Kate. "We have a new ranchhand this year. Kate is going to rake too. We can be sure the field will be clean when she gets through."

Kate's cheeks flushed. "I'm looking forward to it but don't listen to him," she managed to say. "I'm new at this so when he complains that I messed up, remind him of what he just said."

———•———

Kate came to the mudroom dressed in jeans and a long sleeved cotton shirt, as Jake had suggested she wear, along with sturdy leather shoes. "Keep this on all the time," he cautioned as he handed her a wide brimmed hat. "We don't want you sunburned. And put some of this Bag Balm on your lips. It will keep your lips from getting dry and cracked." He grinned and added, "I don't like to kiss cracked lips."

"It's a good thing this is a new can of Bag Balm. I've seen you use the one in the barn on the milk cow's teats," she said, wrinkling her nose.

"It's a staple around the ranch—good for a lot of things." He laughed at the grimace on her face.

Rick and Carl arrived. Brad and Charlie helped harness Rick's and Kate's teams, and then Brad drove his pickup ahead to show Rick where to start raking. Charlie drove Kate's rake team to the field.

They spent some time with Jake showing Kate everything about driving the rake. By noontime, haying was in full swing and the hay was being stacked. Kate thoroughly enjoyed driving the horses and raking hay, but it bothered her when she missed some, so she felt obliged go back and get it. When she caught up and had a few moments, she watched Charlie drive the team to push the hay up over the beaver slide stacker. She had seen her grandfather do that many times and she was always fascinated by how he stopped the team at the right moment to throw the hay over the top. Charlie was just as good at the job.

By sundown, Kate was raking hay as if she'd been doing it for years.

Jake told her so that night as they were getting ready for bed. "Need some Absorbine tonight?" he asked when she mentioned that her arms ached.

"I do. It helped last year."

"Last year I didn't get to do as good a job as I could of."

"Now I'm giving you a second chance," she said, remembering how his touch had turned to a caress. She had called him a big bad wolf but that hadn't kept him from planting a kiss on her temple. On this night she offered no protest and welcomed his touch and all the loving he gave her.

 **CHAPTER ELEVEN**

**During haying,** Marie prepared a hearty breakfast and then cooked a meat and potatoes dinner and supper for the hungry crew. She usually had pie, cake, or cobbler for dessert. Sometimes cookies and fruit served as dessert following supper.

After working in the hayfield the first day, Kate had gotten up from her place at the supper table and picked up two serving bowls to take to the kitchen, but Marie had stopped her. "No, that's my job. Besides, the boys bring most everything to the kitchen."

Kate had welcomed the chance to rest but when Jake joined her on the couch that evening, she told him she was tired but it didn't seem natural to have Marie do the dishes and wash the separator.

"Why do you fret so much? Brad helps his mom with the dishes. That young man is going to make some lucky girl a great husband."

"I guess you're right."

Everything else went smoothly until Rick's team spooked one afternoon and he was thrown off his rake.

At supper that evening, everyone had something to say about the runaway.

"I thought you told me that Pete and Dan were a gentle team," Rick said pointedly to Jake. "And, you didn't tell me Pete bites."

Jake grimaced. "Oh, yeah, I forgot about that," he replied jovially.

Don added his two cents. "Well, I was impressed, Rick. I was afraid you were hurt when you went off that rake, but you jumped right up and managed to talk those horses into slowing down so you could get a hold of 'em."

Rick grinned his thanks to Don. "I never did know what scared 'em. We don't have snakes around here so it might have been a gopher. We were pretty close to the ditch when the horses took off."

"Whatever it was, you did a good job, Rick," Jake said, at last praising him.

———•———

Marie proved to be more than an excellent cook. She was as fastidious as Kate when it came to keeping a clean kitchen, and Kate didn't hold back telling her so. "I sure appreciate coming in to a meal I didn't have to fix myself," Kate told her one morning. She gave Marie a wide smile. "To tell the truth, I was surprised that you like this old wood stove as much as I do. I'm not sure many women these days would be willing to cook if they didn't have a gas or electric cook stove."

Marie was heating water to wash the breakfast dishes. "I learned to cook on a wood stove so I'm glad for the chance to use one." She gave Kate an amused smile. "I also grew up washing a separator."

"Guess I better get going for another day of haying. Thanks again for all you're doing."

She started out the door then turned back and said, "Marie, don't worry about washing the tea towels. I'll do that first thing in the morning so they can hang on the line."

"Thanks, I have plenty of towels and I want to bake pies today so that will help."

When Kate got out of the pickup, Don was hooking up her team while Charlie and Brad moved the stacker into a new stackyard. Before long, the haystack was up ten or twelve feet high. She was near the stackyard when she saw that Charlie's plunger was stopped at the base of the beaver slide. When she realized Charlie wasn't with his team she sensed something was wrong. Even Don's team was standing with the reins wrapped around the lever. Charlie came running to stop her team. "Come quick. Brad fell and we need you to see if he's all right."

With her heart pounding, Kate leapt over the plunger pole and ran to the other side of the stack where Don hovered over Brad's still body. "What happened?" she asked, dreading an answer.

"The corner gave way where Brad was standing and he fell off the stack," Don said worriedly.

Kate lifted Brad's eyelid and recognized signs of a concussion. "He must have hit his head," she said without realizing she was scaring Don even more. She took Brad's wrist and calculated his pulse, then checked his breathing. Gently she moved her fingers all around his head. Brad moaned and in another minute he opened his eyes. She turned to Don. "He's coming to."

Charlie knelt next to Don, his brow furrowed with worry.

"We don't want to move him until we're sure nothing is broken," Kate said.

Soon Brad was trying to sit up, but Kate told him to lie still. She moved her hands over his legs and arms and asked where he was hurting.

His eyes were dilated. When Kate asked if he had a headache, he indicated no but put a hand up to his head. Kate wasn't sure he was thinking clearly.

She turned to Charlie. "I think you'd better drive the pickup over and tell Jake we need him."

A few minutes later, Jake jumped out of the truck and joined them at Brad's side.

Kate was filled with anxiety but spoke calmly to the others. "I think he has a concussion but there doesn't seem to be anything broken. I want to take him in for some x-rays to be sure."

Jake and Don helped Brad stand and get into the pickup. He didn't appear to be disoriented but he was too quiet for Kate's comfort. She climbed into the pickup next to him, and with Don in the back Jake drove them to the house. Jake helped Brad into the back seat of the car. Jake instructed Don and Marie to get in with him and the five of them headed for the clinic in Pinedale.

The doctor confirmed Kate's diagnosis of a concussion and said he thought Brad would be okay after some rest. The x-rays didn't show any broken bones but the doctor told Kate confidentially that he couldn't rule out that Brad might have hurt his back. She promised to let him know if anything was amiss.

Jake did the stacking for the next two days. By then Brad insisted he was fine and needed to get back to work. They all breathed a sigh of relief and rejoiced that there didn't seem to be any lasting effects of the accident.

Rick's runaway and Brad's accident all in a period of two weeks made Kate nervous. Jake tried to reassure her when he said, "I'm thankful no one was hurt seriously and none of them are careless."

———•———

They finished haying the first week of September. By then Kate and Marie had become close friends. At their final breakfast, Jake said they hoped to see all of them again next year.

Rick embarrassed Kate when he said, "You drive a mean rake so I'm sure we'll be seeing you in the hayfield next year."

Marie added, "And we all think the boss is one lucky man."

Everyone applauded as Kate covered her mouth, hoping to ward off the threatening tears.

She and Jake stood on the porch, waving goodbye as the pickups drove away.

"I love haying season, Jake," she said softly.

"Most people think it's long and tiresome. It's just like you to think it's fun." He tightened his arm around her. "At the time, I couldn't imagine that finding you in a snow bank could turn out to be the best thing that ever happened to me."

"God is good, huh."

# Chapter Twelve

**In the two weeks** after they finished haying, Kate caught up on household chores and supposed she ought to be taking inventory of what they had on hand before they went to town for winter supplies. However, she was finding it hard to concentrate.

Finally her anxiety prompted her to confront Jake with what worried her. He was reading a paper that had come in the mail when Kate sat down in one of the recliners. He set the newspaper on the table and took up a magazine.

"Jake, we need to talk about something."

He looked at her without saying anything but didn't open the magazine.

"We've been fortunate that we haven't had a more dire emergency during the past two winters, but ever since Brad fell off the haystack, I can't help thinking about something happening and we won't be able to get out of here."

Jake's mouth worked for a few seconds before he said, "Look, in what you call a dire emergency, we could ski out, or pull a toboggan if we needed to."

"I don't see that as a very good solution. Consider how we would feel if Charlie got really sick and we couldn't get him to a doctor or hospital." When Jake didn't respond, she went on, "Surely, we could buy . . ."

"Whoa, if you're going to suggest a snowplow, it is simply not possible. We haven't even shipped yet. Besides, whatever we get for the steers wouldn't be enough to buy a plow that could do the job."

"Money is not the issue and you know it!" She got up and went to the kitchen.

A few minutes later, Jake found her sitting on a stool at the counter near tears.

"Kate, don't fret. We've always managed just like everyone else who has been snowed in here. But if it will make you feel better, I have an idea that should take care of the situation. Just leave it to me, okay?" He bent and kissed her on her unresponsive cheek.

Even Charlie felt the tension around the house after a couple of days. One Monday morning he and Jake were digging a posthole when he asked, "Jake, is Kate feeling okay? She's awfully quiet and seems worried."

Jake glanced up from tamping dirt around the post. "She's mad at me because I won't go out and buy a big snowplow. She's so sure someone around here is going to get deathly ill or have a disastrous accident after we get snowed in for the winter."

Charlie didn't say anything for a minute. Finally, he said in a low voice, "She has a point."

Jake drew in a deep breath. "Well, I haven't told her yet but I intend to see about buying a couple of snowmachines when I go to town on Saturday. That way, we could drive out to the county road. Handy to get the mail, too."

"Too bad we can't park the pickup out at the road."

"That's an idea. I don't know if it would ever start out there in the weather, but I'll think about that."

"Of course, they don't plow the county road this far out," Charlie said quietly.

That didn't elicit a comment from Jake so Charlie kept his thoughts to himself.

Things hadn't changed by the middle of the week. Frustrated, Kate got out of the Bunkhouse to walk a bit. As she started down the lane, she heard one of the horses make a noise that sounded like a sneeze or snort. She looked toward the corral and saw that Misty and Buck were in among the work horses. *Good time to talk to my horse*, she thought. She passed Charlie working on the door to the chicken house.

"What are you up to, Charlie?"

"Just putting a new hinge on this door. The other one wasn't holding the door tight. Out for a walk on this nice Indian summer day?"

"I see that Misty is in the corral so I thought I'd pet her a bit. I could use the currycomb on her. She likes that."

"It's in the tack room. I think Jake is in there, putting new reins on his bridle."

Jake spoke when she came in through the door. "Hi, there. Come sit a while." He indicated a wooden box they used for a seat.

"No thank you, I just came to get a comb for Misty," she said coolly. She picked up the currycomb and went right back out the door.

The other horses stood around as if they'd like a good combing, too, but Kate's arm was feeling the strain so she hooked the currycomb in a niche of the fence and put her cheek next to Misty's. "Maybe we'll go for a ride tomorrow, how about that?"

The small gate in the fence of the pasture just beyond the corral caught Kate's eye. It provided a shortcut to the old homestead cabin in the meadow a little northeast of the barn. She opened the latch to the corral gate to let herself out into the pasture. The pull on the gate to swing wide, caught her by surprise. It slipped from her grasp so she grabbed for a pole and felt a piercing sliver slice the palm of her hand. She let go of the gate and it swung clear around, where it stopped at the corral fence. In spite of the wrenching pain in her hand, she hurried to bring it back, but it was too late. All of the horses were crowding through the gate before she could close it.

Jake heard the pounding of the horses' feet and stepped to the door of the barn to see what was happening. "Kate," he yelled, "what the hell are you doing?" He stomped over to where she was trying to bring the heavy gate back in place. "Leave it open, damn it. We have to get the horses back in the corral."

"I'm sorry, the gate . . ." she tried to explain, near tears. She could feel how enraged he was. "I'll go after them," she said, weakly, letting the gate go and starting out into the pasture.

"Get back here! You've done enough damage. Go on back to the house." His face was twisted with anger.

Kate headed for the Bunkhouse, and only after she saw Jake leave the corral with a bucket of oats and a bridle hanging from his shoulder did she take a good look at her hand. She figured that the splinter must have gone in at least an inch. It was big and it hurt a lot.

Washing her hands with plenty of soap and hot water intensified the pain. She sterilized a needle in the flame of a match and sat down where the light was good from the south window in the living room. A few minutes later, she gave up trying to remove the sliver. The wood broke off every time she managed to catch a piece with the needle. On top of that, it was awkward trying to work with her left hand.

She started for the kitchen to get some hydrogen peroxide from a corner cabinet. As she passed the dining room window, she looked toward the barn. Jake was astride Misty and was driving the rest of the horses into the corral.

His outburst alarmed her. She'd seen Jake mad about a few things but none of his anger had been directed at her like it was just then. For the first time since she and Jake had gotten married, she was afraid. Being upset with him about money and his lack of concern about their safety during the winter was one thing. But his swearing and raging at her for an innocent mistake left her frightened and miserable.

In spite of the pain in her hand and the ache in her heart, she set about warming the roast and vegetables from the day before for their supper. Gingerly, she opened a can of pears and set out cookies for dessert.

Jake and Charlie did the chores before they came in. She and Jake hadn't greeted each other warmly for the past several days so she was glad he didn't say anything. She had everything on the table by the time they'd washed up.

She said grace and passed the food but didn't eat much. After finishing her pears, she got up from the table, picked up a serving dish in her left hand, and started around Jake. He caught her by her right hand and she let out a near scream.

"What the hell . . .?" Before she could move, he turned her hand gently to see what had caused her to cry out. "Oh, for heaven's sake, Kate. How'd you do that?"

Charlie was craning his neck to see. "Katie, what happened?"

Kate choked back a sob. "I tried to catch the gate and this huge sliver went into my hand. I haven't been able to get it out. It broke off so what's left is in deep."

Jake studied her reddened palm and the slight swelling where the wood was embedded in her hand.

"Let's clean it as best we can and then we'll see if we can get that out." He looked up to see Kate trying to compose herself. "I'm sorry, I didn't know this is what caused you to let go of the gate."

Jake and Charlie sat Kate down where the light was best in the west window and Jake took her hand. A needle and tweezers failed to get a hold on the splinter.

"There are some surgical scissors in the black bag," Kate said. "You'll have to cut the skin to get a hold on the splinter."

"I think we'd better go find a doctor to do this . . ." Jake began.

Kate stopped him. "No, try cutting it out."

Water was at a boil in the teakettle. Jake sterilized the small but sharp scissors he found in the bag. When he approached her again, he said, "I don't know, Kate. This might make everything worse."

"Do it anyway," she said emphatically.

They had a hard time keeping her hand in the light with all three heads clustered together. Kate lifted her head and looked away and said calmly, "Go ahead. It won't hurt any more than it does now."

He held her hand over a basin so Charlie could pour warm water to wash away the blood. Twice, she had to tell Jake to cut the skin deeper and open it so he could get to the piece of wood. Reluctantly, he finally cut deep enough to see where the sliver was solid enough to attempt getting it out.

Jake and Charlie were both holding their breath when Jake finally clamped the tweezers tight on the splinter and was able to pull it out.

They all breathed a sigh of relief but Jake hadn't forgotten about the possibility of infection. "Don't you think we'd better get you a tetanus shot and have a doctor see to this?"

"No, my tetanus shot is current and I'll disinfect this with hydrogen peroxide."

"I'll get it," Charlie said, and headed for the kitchen.

When they had cleaned and bandaged her hand, both men insisted that they would take care of everything so she could rest.

Kate looked in the black bag for something to ease the pain. Most medications in the bag were outdated but she decided a couple of aspirin would help. Exhausted she fell into bed, unsure of how much sleep she would get.

As they were washing up the supper dishes, Charlie confronted Jake about what happened. "You know, Jake, I heard you yell at Kate about leaving that gate open. It clearly upset her. But I had no idea she got that terrible splinter in her hand or I would have gone after her."

"Yeah, I know," Jake said, wringing out the dish rag. "I didn't know it either."

"It rankles me to hear you talk like that to Kate," Charlie said slowly, with an edge to his words. "You were awful hard on her. I wanted to knock you on your ear, but of course I can't compete with your strength. It's pretty darn hard to stop horses from running out a gate like that. She sure didn't do that on purpose." He hung up his towel and left before Jake could answer.

Jake just stood there, knowing Charlie was right. He headed for bed. Kate appeared to be asleep when he slipped in beside her, yet he couldn't help but wonder if she was just pretending in order to avoid speaking with him.

# CHAPTER THIRTEEN

**On Saturday,** Jake went to town alone, armed with a list of things Kate wanted him to pick up. When he brought in the groceries late in the afternoon, she didn't ask about his day in town, and he didn't offer anything. Her avoiding him indicated that she wasn't near ready to voice her fear that his rage could put a wedge in their relationship. Even though he'd been concerned about her injured hand, he didn't seem the least bit worried about what could happen to their future. And thinking about being snowed in again only fueled her already high anxiety.

Jake came in from the barn one sunny afternoon and found Kate sitting on the front porch reading a magazine. He opened the screen door cautiously. "Want some company?" he asked.

"Sure," she replied, without much enthusiasm.

Jake had intended to sit in the other rocker when something caught his eye. He pulled Kate to her feet, causing her to drop what she had been reading. "Look," he said, pointing toward the end of the lane.

Kate could barely make out the two trucks, one with a crane, just inside the gate. "What are they doing there?"

"See what that crane is attached to?"

"It's a pole. You mean the electricity is about here?" she asked, her voice rising.

"Close," he said, tapping her head playfully. "That's a telephone pole. We're going to have a telephone pretty soon. How 'bout that?"

They sat down. Jake decided not to disturb the pleasant atmosphere with the frank talk he had meant to have with Kate. "I see you had a letter in the mail the other day from Margo. How is she doing?"

"She's fine. Excited to let me know that she's expecting the end of March."

"That's nice," Jake said noncommittally.

For a while they watched what was going on at the end of the lane. Finally Kate stood up and said the bread should be ready to take out of the oven. A few minutes later she started for the porch again, but when she saw Jake sitting with his elbows on his knees and his head lowered into his hands, she resisted a momentary urge to go to him and went back into the kitchen.

They went to Mass in Pinedale on Sunday. On the way, Charlie commented about the progress of the telephone line, but didn't have much else to say. Even during their brunch in town, none of them spoke a lot.

On Monday morning Kate heard the rumbling of a big truck pulling into their driveway. She stepped out the door of the mudroom and watched as Jake directed the driver to a spot where they could unload two snowmachines. The truck was halfway back down the lane when Jake called her to come and check them out.

"What do ya think?" he asked when she'd had a chance to look them over. "Won't they be handy to go out for the mail?" When she didn't answer, he added, "And for anytime we need to get out of here."

"They're nice, all right." She smiled but she was thinking that getting to the county road that wasn't plowed didn't really make much sense. They could do that much with skis.

During the week, Kate kept a close watch on the men and their trucks as they moved closer to the Bunkhouse. She saw when the last pole had been set and watched while the workers attached the telephone line to the house. She was gazing out the window when a man drove up in a telephone company pickup. He stopped and waited for Jake who was coming from the barn. They spoke for a few minutes before the man picked up a telephone from the front seat of his truck and followed Jake to the house.

Jake introduced Kate and asked where they should put the phone. She hadn't thought about that yet so the question got her a bit flustered.

"Well, I don't know. Maybe the kitchen would be best, but then again we might want it in the living room. No," she finally decided, "I think the dining room. It's more central to all the rooms."

The phone man set about getting the line into the house and before long he had the wire connected to a black tabletop dial telephone on a small table under the window in the dining room. When he was done he handed Jake a piece of paper. "This will be your phone number, and your rings will be two shorts and one long. I guess you know this is a party line with the two families west of here."

Jake chuckled. "Guess we'd better not say anything we don't want the neighbors to hear, huh?"

"Won't you stay for dinner?" Kate asked. "I've made a goulash and there's plenty of it."

"My wife is expecting me, but thanks anyway," the man said, gathering his tools. "Your telephone is all set up and I've tested it." He handed Kate a phone book and told her to call him if they had any trouble with their new phone.

Charlie came through the kitchen door just as the telephone man was leaving. He'd been putting in a new fence post north of the house and hadn't seen all the activity, although he knew the telephone line was near completion.

"Look, Charlie, we have a telephone and it works," Kate said with a lift in her voice the men hadn't heard for many days.

"That's great. Sorta connects us to the outside world, doesn't it?"

After supper, Jake suggested they try out the new phone. "I'm sure Mom will be glad to know about it and I'd like to talk to them anyway."

Kate searched for the number in a small phone book she had put together with the names and addresses of their friends and family. She called it out to Jake and he fumbled with the dial a time or two before he heard the rings.

"I'm so excited to know you have a phone," Maureen said immediately.

"We're not used to having one but we're glad that we'll be able to keep in touch with you and Dad," Jake replied. "I just hope Kate doesn't duck her duties around here and start gossiping with all the neighbors," he said teasingly.

Kate took the phone from Jake, "I hope you know he's kidding. Actually, I'll make sure he doesn't listen in when the neighbors get a call." After several minutes of visiting, Kate promised to call regularly. "Give our love to Dad," she said before hanging up.

Jake had been sitting at the dining room table watching Kate. When she finished, he said, "I think it must have been easier when you could just tell the operator who you wanted to call. To tell the truth, my fingers get caught in those little circles."

Kate looked serious. "Well, we won't want to call for no reason. Long distance phone calls can get expensive."

"Around here, it's long distance to anywhere except the neighbors. Somehow, I don't think you're apt to run up our phone bill."

She shrugged. "No, it will be good to have the telephone but I'm not inclined to use one for just visiting."

It seemed an opportune moment for Jake to talk things over with Kate and ease the tension between them. "Kate, I know you didn't let the horses out on purpose and I'm really sorry that you got hurt."

She glanced at him and sensed that he wanted to talk but she didn't say anything. He continued. "Something's really wrong and I wish you'd tell me what it is."

She stared at him. *Does he really not know?*

He waited while she gathered her thoughts . . . and the courage to be forthright.

"The truth is, Jake. I'm scared."

Jake frowned in disbelief. "Scared?"

"Scared of what happened when I let the horses get out of the corral. You got every bit as angry then as you were the day you told me I was snowed in here." She looked down at her hands clenched together in her lap. "I'll never forget how you hated me that day."

He'd been leaning forward, wanting to clear things between them. Now he sat back and thought over what she had just said. After a moment he asked in dismay, "Did you just tell me you're scared of *me?*"

Tears burned in the back of her eyes but she managed to say, "Maybe I don't really belong here . . ." She swallowed hard and tears trickled down her cheek before she realized that Jake had gone down on one knee next to her chair.

"Don't ever say or even think that!" he said, placing a finger under her chin so she would look at him and then took her hands in his. "I'm sorry. I shouldn't have yelled at you. I guess I act before I think, but I can't stand to hear you say you don't belong here."

Kate bit her lower lip in an attempt to stop from crying.

"This is your home, and I need you here with me. I love you with all my heart."

Kate was moved by Jake's heartfelt words and the worried expression he displayed. "I love you, too, more than I can say," she reassured him. "I just can't believe I upset you so much that you would swear at me with such angry words. It scares me and makes me think you're sorry you married me."

Jake stood up, pulled her into his arms, and said tenderly, "I probably ought to be sorry about a lot of things, but there's one thing I *am not sorry* about and that's marrying you."

After a few minutes, Kate pulled back and looked into Jake's eyes. "Thank you, my love. I needed to know everything is okay between us."

"It is now," he whispered.

The change in atmosphere didn't escape Charlie when they sat down to have supper. "Thank you, Lord, for blessing our happy home," Jake added to the usual grace they always said. Charlie looked from one to the other and saw them exchange smiles.

———•———

Jake and Charlie spent the next few weeks repairing fences, mending harnesses, and fencing stackyards. When it came time to bring the cattle home from the forest, Kate went along as often as she could, helping to move their cattle into a pasture after Jake and Charlie separated their cattle from the other ranchers' herds.

Weaning the calves made Kate's heart ache as the mothers called from the pasture to their babies who were penned up in a corral. Late one evening Jake found her standing on the front porch. "What are you doing out here?" he asked. "You'll catch a cold."

With her arms close to her chest she looked toward the pen of milling calves. "I hate to hear those young ones and their mamas bawling for each other."

Jake wrapped his arms around her and put his cheek on hers.

"I don't know how you can sleep through it—they're all grieving so," she said.

"You're softhearted," he said close to her ear. "It's necessary. And, they do get used to being separated. Those mamas are already carrying their new babies so feeding the older ones would be too much for them. Besides, the calves can do okay on their own now."

Thinking about the cows and their calves being separated got Kate to pondering her own separation from her mother. She mentioned it to Jake later as they were getting ready for bed.

"I don't know why but I keep thinking about my mother leaving me. She didn't seem sad like those mama cows."

"You don't know what was going through her mind. I suspect she felt it was something she had to do. And she probably thought you'd be better off with your dad."

Kate frowned.

"Naturally you felt deserted," he hastened to add. "Not knowing why she left has to be difficult, even now."

She shrugged. "Oh well, it's all in the past. It's kinda strange though, we haven't heard any more from Cameron about her wanting to find me. Maybe she changed her mind."

Kate was getting into bed when the phone rang. Two shorts and a long. It took a few seconds for them to register that it was their ring.

"I'll get it," Jake said. He went in and picked up the receiver. When he returned he said, "It was Jesse . . . wondering when we're going to ship."

His words fell on deaf ears, as Kate was already fast asleep.

"I was hoping the trucks would be here for the yearlings today," Jake said to Charlie the next morning. "When I called the company yesterday, Glen said they can't get here until day after tomorrow. I guess everyone else is shipping too."

Charlie looked around. "Where's Katie?"

"She wasn't feeling well so I told her to stay in bed for a while."

"What's wrong with her?"

"Don't know. Just said her stomach was upset."

Charlie made a harrumph and poured himself a cup of coffee, then sat down and waited for Jake to finish frying the bacon.

Charlie said, "Probably a good thing we'll be around all morning to check up on our patient in there."

Kate was so tired that she welcomed the chance to stay in bed. By midmorning she was feeling better and told the men to go about their business. The following morning, however, Jake and Charlie had gone to do the chores and she was feeling queasy again. She told herself she didn't have the luxury of resting this time and went to the cabinet where they kept some medicines and pulled out the Pepto-Bismol. When they came in she had breakfast almost ready and things were back to normal.

# Chapter Fourteen

**At dinner** that day, Jake explained that he'd be going along when the trucks came to haul their steers to the railroad. Kate looked at him with a question in mind. "I thought you had to drive the cattle to the railroad. Grandpa used to tell me that he had to spend several days getting his cattle to somewhere down by Rock Springs and then he went with his cows on the train to Omaha to sell them."

"Years ago they did make a cattle drive to ship and if they hadn't consigned their cattle, they would go to market, usually to Omaha. But we've had trucks to haul them for about twenty years now." Thinking about the cattle drives, Jake added, "I rode on a few of those drives. Sometimes it was a long day getting from one watering place to the next one . . . and camping out wasn't all that much fun either. It seems like the days were rainy or dusty. We had snow sometimes, too, so it could be plenty cold. I'm glad to send them out on a cattle truck."

Kate got up to clear the table. "I'm sure it wasn't easy but I wish I could have gone along just once."

Jake shook his head and looked at Charlie. "She probably would have thought it was fun. We could have given her the job of driving the chuck wagon."

"Oh no, I would have punched cows all the way."

Several days later, after Jake returned from taking the yearlings to market, he told Kate he would saddle Misty so she could ride out with the men to cut out the culls. He explained that these were the cows that hadn't calved or were getting old.

When they had the cattle gathered and ready to be worked, Kate sat on her horse where Jake had told her to help hold the cattle in the corner of the pasture. She was fascinated by how Jake and his horse moved together, working a cow out of the herd to where Charlie was at a gate, ready to drive each one into another field. When Jake finished, they put the culls in a holding pen where there was a loading chute. He let Kate know that a cattle truck would be coming for them the next day. He'd be going to the sale barn in Lander and asked her to go along.

"Oh, yes, I do want to go. I can hardly wait to see what goes on at a sale barn."

"Well, be ready when they get the truck loaded tomorrow and we'll be on our way."

Kate had her morning chores done and had finished getting herself ready before the truck got there so when it came, she went to the corral to watch the men load the cattle truck. When she climbed into the pickup with Jake, he whistled and said, "Wow, Levi's and cowboy boots look good on you."

"Thank you. I'm glad to have a chance to wear this western shirt and the handsome vest you gave me for Christmas. You look good too, cowboy."

As they drove along, Jake told Kate some history of the area. She was fascinated by stories of the courageous men and women who homesteaded and about men who worked so hard to build a ditch that kept washing out. He pointed out where the Oregon Trail crossed the road. He told her about some of the hardships endured by mail carriers and explained that the ghost towns of South Pass City and Atlantic City were once thriving communities during the gold rush days. When they reached Red Canyon, Kate mentioned she had passed by there several times and was always in awe of the magnificence of the deep valley. By the time they reached Lander, they assured each other it had been a fun trip.

They'd seen several pens of cattle sold before theirs were driven into the ring. "I've never seen anything like this," Kate exclaimed as she sat next to Jake. It amused him to see her so fascinated by the bidding and arena men calling out a new bid to the fast-talking auctioneer.

Their day out together left Kate more contented than she'd been for weeks. It quite surprised her that she didn't have the anxiety about being snowbound that had plagued her earlier. She hugged Jake's arm as he was driving them home and she said, "This was a special day. Thanks for taking me with you."

He patted her thigh and said, "I'm glad you enjoyed it. I liked it too."

While the men were finishing up the fall work, Kate was thinking about winter and the nausea she was now feeling nearly every morning. So far, she had managed to hide from Jake the symptoms she was experiencing, but one evening when they had settled into bed and he was raining kisses and caresses on her, she stopped him.

"We need to talk," she said, suppressing a smile.

"Sounds serious. If it's about the electricity not getting here, don't give up. I know they won't make it this fall but we ought to get it first thing next spring."

She put her fingers to his lips. "It's not about electricity or the ranch or anything like that. It's about this baby," she replied, her happiness bubbling over.

Jake's eyes widened. "Are you sure?" He could hardly contain himself as he sat up and placed a hand on her stomach.

"I hardly dared to believe it myself, but yes."

"You're really sure about this?"

"I'm sure. I just need to check with a doctor. I really liked Dr. Welsh in Jackson. We ought to make an appointment before we're stuck here with the snow and can't get out."

"You call him in the morning." Jake held her gingerly, but with such love that she snuggled against him.

The next day, Kate spoke to Cindy, the receptionist, at the obstetrician's office. "We have to drive about 120 miles from the ranch to Jackson, so we probably can't get there much before eleven," she told Cindy. They set the appointment for one o'clock.

"We haven't met but I'm anxious to get to know you," Cindy said. "All the doctors say you're an excellent nurse. Oh, before I forget. Congratulations."

"Thanks, I look forward to meeting you, too," Kate said.

Kate hung up and hurried to the barn to find Jake. "Tomorrow at one," she told him as soon as she could catch her breath. "I can hardly believe this is happening."

Jake gave her a quick kiss and grinned when he said, "Just when will we meet this little miracle?"

She counted on her fingers. "By my calculations, it will be the first week in July."

Jake scratched his head. "Bad timing. Now, I'll have to find another hay hand."

At breakfast the next morning, Jake told Charlie, "Take it easy today. We need to go to Jackson and you can come with us if you want."

Charlie thought about it for a minute. "There's not much to do today, I might as well go along."

In Jackson, they dropped Charlie off at a store to buy some new overshoes and told him they would pick him up later.

At the doctor's office, Kate's diagnosis was confirmed. He suggested a follow-up in a few weeks.

"We might be snowed in before then with all the snow that's expected," Kate said. "But, I'll keep in touch by phone and call you for an appointment as soon as the roads open."

"Make sure you do. In the meantime, I'll make out a prescription for enough vitamins to see you through."

Jake and Kate couldn't wait to tell Charlie their news. On the way back to the ranch, Jake, trying to sound natural, spoke up. "Kate has something to tell you, Charlie."

Charlie looked over at Kate with a puzzled expression.

"We're going to need a grandpa around here come next July," she said. "We think that ought to be you."

His eyes lit up and a grin as big as the Wyoming sky spread across his face. "I figured something must be up when you two left me off this morning without a word about where you were headed."

"Well, we wanted to be sure before we said anything," Jake answered.

Charlie shook his head in amazement. "Congratulations you two. This is going to be one lucky baby."

In a letter to Maureen, Kate wrote that Jake and Charlie would hardly let her do anything. *I finally told them that women have been having babies since Adam and Eve, and that I'm fine. They don't mind me, of course, but I love all their attention. P.S. When Jake found out that we're going to have this baby during haying season, he said that was bad timing. I told him maybe it would rain and he'd have the day off. Just between us, he is so delighted that I don't think having the baby during haying is going to upset him.*

The winter passed much like the two previous years as far as the feeding and other work went. Jake had told Kate not to bother with a traditional Thanksgiving dinner, but she would have none of it. They had turkey with all the trimmings and mincemeat pie for dessert, a favorite of Charlie's. Two weeks later, on a sunny Wyoming day, Jake and Charlie showed up with a Christmas tree in tow. They hadn't even asked her to go along.

"No more going out in the cold even if it's not quite as bad as last year," Jake told her.

Neither Jake nor Charlie could stop her from helping to decorate the tree though.

"You two do the higher decorations. I'll do the lower ones . . . then I'll check to see if you got everything spaced right," she said, trying to keep a straight face.

"Bossy, isn't she," Jake whispered to Charlie but loud enough for Kate to hear.

The tree developed into a thing of beauty and they all stood back to look it over. Charlie was first to speak. "We're quite good at this," and the other two quickly agreed.

On Christmas Eve, they watched as she read the tag on a beautifully wrapped package: For Mother and Elizabeth John . . . from Jake and Charlie. They had talked about names for the baby, and Charlie had suggested Elizabeth John . . . *until we know if you are having a cowboy or a cowgirl* . . . was his rationalization. Carefully, Kate opened the package and took time to fold the paper and put paper and ribbon on a pile she'd started. It drove the men crazy but she wanted to savor this special moment. Cradled inside the box was everything a mother would need for a newborn baby: blankets, undershirts, and nightgowns with drawstrings at the bottom, tiny socks, and at least two dozen diapers.

Jake dug to the bottom and held up a small piece of cotton cloth. "We don't know what this is for, but it looks like it might come in handy."

Kate laughed. "It's a burp rag so you and Charlie won't have spit-up all over your shoulder when you burp the baby."

"Oooohhh, I see."

As was becoming customary, everyone had ordered gifts from Montgomery Ward or Sears & Roebuck, and several times this year, Jake had carried packages from the mailbox to the house on his snowmachine. There were boxes from Jesse and Mary Anne and gifts from Mom and Dad McClary.

This year, Charlie read *The Christmas Story* as a fitting end to the last Christmas they'd be spending as a threesome. New Year's Eve dancing was subdued compared to their usual celebration. Both men asked Kate for a couple of waltzes, then insisted they play poker so she wouldn't get too tired. During a hand, Charlie spoke up, "Jake, didn't I warn you that if you taught Kate to play poker and we all bet with money, she'd end up owning the ranch?"

Jake winked at Kate. "She managed that without playing poker. I guess I'm lucky I got to stay."

"No, I'm lucky I got to stay," Kate replied.

It was Charlie's turn. "I'm lucky you both stayed."

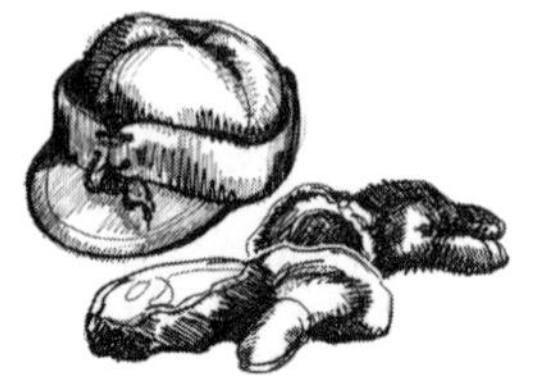

# Chapter Fifteen

**For the first time** since she'd come to the ranch, Kate found herself getting bored. She always had meals ready on time and did what needed to be done in the house before the men got in from feeding, but without being able to help with some of the outside chores, she had a lot of extra time on her hands. Jake and Charlie fretted about her doing laundry, while she insisted she wasn't doing anything to hurt the baby or herself. They fussed about her having to reach up to hang sheets on the line that Jake had strung from one wall to the other in the laundry room. So she always managed to have that done before they came back from feeding. Kate used the two drying racks they had found in town the previous fall to hang the rest of the laundry.

Even with reading books she found in the den, darning socks, or doing crocheting and knitting, Kate felt restless. When the maternity clothes she ordered from a catalog overcrowded the closet in their room, she made up her mind to move some of her clothes into the closet of Jake's previous bedroom. There she found a box that was filled to the brim with material for sewing. She looked at the treadle sewing machine along the bedroom wall. She'd never thought about sewing or making anything before, but she had watched her grandmother sew on a machine much like this one. She opened it up and seeing that it was threaded, she sat down and attempted to sew together two small swatches of material.

At dinner she mentioned what she had done and how frustrated she'd become when the machine wouldn't go or it took a spurt and went too fast.

"I'll teach you how to sew," Charlie promised, surprising both Kate and Jake.

"Since when do you sew?" Jake asked.

"Martha taught me years ago."

"Well, I'll be darned. You mean I could have asked you to sew me up some duds all of this time?"

"Right. That's why I've kept it a secret all this time."

Kate started to clear the dishes, anxious for her first sewing lesson. "Never you mind, Jake. As soon as I get the hang of it, I'll make you a new shirt."

"Get going, you two, I'll finish up here," Jake offered.

"First thing we need to do is oil this machine," Charlie said as soon as he and Kate sat down together. To her surprise, he found a can of oil in a drawer. He oiled the bobbin case and squirted oil into several small holes, then picked up the fabric she used earlier and sewed a straight line across it. With a little coaxing, he got her to try sewing a seam.

"Lower the needle into the material, then turn the wheel just enough to get the needle going in and out. Keep it going by steady pedaling with both feet."

The fabric got caught up a couple of times. Kate heaved a sigh. "I think I'm all thumbs."

"Just practice a bit and you'll be a regular seamstress," he encouraged her.

Kate stuck with it and gradually felt more comfortable. "Thanks. I think I'm going to like this."

"There are some flour sacks in your pile there on the bed." She handed him one. "Practice doing a small hem like this," Charlie said. He showed her how to fold over the edge twice to make a narrow hem. "Put it under the needle, lower the foot, and be sure your needle is in the material before you start the stitching." He sewed to a corner, showed her how to miter the corner and stitched along another side.

After dinner the next day, Kate brought in two newly hemmed tea towels to show them. "The first one is pretty crooked but look at this one."

"I knew you could do it," Charlie said.

Jake whistled. "Well, what d'ya know . . . another talent of yours just turned up."

"Why, does that surprise you, Mr. McClary?"

"Not a bit. When do I get my new shirt?"

"Be patient. I'm not sure I should have promised you a shirt. It took me an hour to hem a tea towel."

It wasn't long before she showed Jake and Charlie the baby blanket she had made as well as several sheets for the crib. But she wasn't quite up to the task of making a shirt for Jake or a dress from a pattern she found in the fabric box.

---

Kate wrinkled her nose at the smell of some foods, but overall the pregnancy was a pleasant experience. Jake often commented that her pregnancy made her even more beautiful than usual.

Once in a great while on a warm day, the men would let her ride along when they went to feed. Picking up a fork to pitch hay on or off the sled was out of the question, but they did let her drive the team now and then, especially when they were forking hay off the sled on the feed line. The snow was just as deep as the previous year—at least three feet of snow on the level—so that Jake and Charlie had long days and hard work. Most days, Kate read a lot, sewed, played the piano, or baked something special. Even though it was routine, she was hardly ever bored again and the months passed quickly.

By the time calving season came around, Kate was well along in her pregnancy and as much as she wanted to go out with Jake on his night rounds to check the heifers, he wouldn't hear of it. "Not in your condition," he kept repeating.

Exasperated after hearing it one too many times, she stood in front of him with her fists on her hips. "I'm not an invalid so don't tell me I can't do something because of my condition. I'm healthy and the baby seems to be just fine."

"Honey, don't get so upset. That can't be good in your . . ."

Kate stopped him with a glare.

He wrapped his arms around her. "I can hardly get close anymore. You're getting so fat."

"Wait a couple of months if you think this is fat." They laughed, but Kate cautioned again, "Don't say 'in my condition' anymore, you hear?"

Jake nodded. "Yes ma'am."

The men were busy day and night with baby calves being born. When they were in the house, if Kate so much as lifted a stew pot, one of them insisted on doing it for her. Most evenings after supper they sent her off to sit in front of the fireplace, saying they would do the dishes and wash the milk bucket. But she was adamant when it came to feeding the several calves that had to be brought to the house to get warmed. She loved taking care of them.

By the second week of May, the snow had melted enough that they could get out from the ranch and schedule a checkup for Kate in Jackson.

"I guess a hundred years ago, no one thought it necessary for regular checkups during a pregnancy but I have to admit that going months without seeing a doctor kinda goes against my better judgment as a nurse," Kate said as they left the ranch gate on their way to Jackson. "I'm thankful nothing went wrong."

Actually, Dr. Welsh told her he was pleased to see her looking so well and the baby in good health. "But," he said with raised brows, "let's not skip your checkups next time."

"Thanks, Dr. Welsh. I just hope there is a next time. My past pregnancy went well. Getting pregnant seems to be the problem."

"That may be, but frankly I wouldn't be surprised to see you back next year with the same symptoms."

Jake and Kate left the doctor's office in high spirits with firm orders to be back in two weeks. By June he wanted to see her every week. Jake had winced at that but hadn't offered any protest. He told Kate there was just too much at stake. "We'll make the time," he assured her.

———•———

"How come we were able to get out this soon?" Kate asked on their way back to the Bunkhouse. "I seem to remember the road being really muddy this time last year. The gravel you hauled for the road last summer must have helped."

"We pushed it a bit this year, but thankfully we were able to get out. We usually don't try until the road is dry—saves making so many ruts. But, I was getting worried about you needing a check-up with the doctor."

"Well, see, the report was very good and it won't be long now."

Kate went along to brandings at the Peterson's, Dixon's, and Holden's with instructions from Jake not to overdo. Theirs was next in line. Jake suggested he call Marie to cook the dinner for the branding crew the following Wednesday. "It's too much for you with the baby due in five weeks," he said. "The doctor said you're fine but cooking for a branding crew is not a good thing for a woman in . . ."

Kate scowled at him.

". . . for a woman about to have a baby."

"I already called Marie. She offered weeks ago to come for branding or anything else if we needed her."

"You haven't missed a beat. Is this how it's going to go with the rest of the kids we'll be having?"

"Let's hope so," Kate said, smiling up at Jake.

The three other women arrived on branding day, and all of them were glad to see Kate and Marie again.

"Have you picked out names for your baby?" Jackie Peterson asked when they were cleaning up after dinner.

"We've thought of some, but I think we're going to have to see the baby to know what name fits," Kate answered.

"I hope you have a boy first," said Janie Holden. "A little girl likes having a big brother."

Marie chimed in, "Even so, at a young age, a girl will help out with the babies."

Kate thought to herself how all this talk was so immaterial. She and Jake didn't care if the baby was a boy or a girl, as long as it was healthy. They were just anxious for it to arrive.

Brad Martin had come in time for branding and stayed to help with getting the cattle out on the desert. Then he and Charlie dragged the meadows, irrigated, and took care of the stock but Brad always stepped in to help out in the house when they came in for meals. Most of the time he did the supper dishes so Kate could rest.

# Chapter Sixteen

**Kate nudged Jake** just before dawn on the fifteenth of June. "Jake," she said anxiously, "I just had a contraction."

He rubbed the sleep from his eyes. "Do you think it's false labor, like the last time?"

"No, I know the baby is early but this is it." Kate reached for her robe at the end of the bed. "We should start for Jackson right away."

Jake sat bolt upright. He lit the lamp and dressed in record time. Kate's urgency had him in a state. He didn't know whether to help her, tell Charlie they were leaving, or get the car out of the garage. Kate tried to calm him down while trying to evaluate the stage of labor she was in. She called the hospital and asked that her doctor be alerted. They'd be on their way in a few minutes but it would take two and a half or three hours to get there since they had quite a ways to go before they got to the highway, she told the nurse. Kate had another contraction before they left, but then it was twenty minutes before she had another. She was surprised at its intensity and when it subsided she was sure they were not making the drive to the hospital for false labor.

Kate had seen some anxious fathers-to-be, but Jake McClary was about the most apprehensive and fretful man she'd dealt with as a nurse. He asked her a dozen times if she was all right and how close her contractions were. And she asked him just as many times to slow down around the curves. After coming out of one contraction, with shortness of breath, and trying not to alarm him, she said, "Jake, you'll have to stop, the baby is coming."

"Oh, no! Are you sure? We still have twenty miles to go," he said, disbelief in his voice.

"I'm sure," she replied firmly.

Jake pulled into a parking area on the side of the road in Hoback Canyon. He was out of the car and had the back door open as Kate was taking deep breaths to ride out another contraction. "Look in my black bag. Put on the rubber gloves," she said when she could speak.

"Oh Lord, I can't do this," he said, while fumbling for the gloves.

"Jake, do what I tell you. You've delivered a lot of baby calves so you can do this, I guarantee."

"I know," he stammered, "but this is *not the same thing*." Just then he saw the baby's head appear.

"Okay, I'm going to push on this next contraction," Kate said, taking in a deep breath and gripping the edges of her pillows.

Jake hardly had time to assess what his wife was saying before the baby came and there was an infant girl in his hands.

"Pass her to me and give me a towel from the bag," Kate said. She spread a blanket over her stomach, reached for the baby, and covered the infant before she cleaned the mouth and nose. The baby let out a gusty cry. Kate breathed a sigh of relief. She cut the cord and made the baby comfortable while Jake kept busy with the afterbirth and cleaning up. When he finally could take a good look at the newborn, the expression on his face was so emotional that Kate thought he was going to cry. "Is she all right? Will she be warm enough?" he asked.

"She's fine. Let's get on to the hospital. I'm a mess, you know."

Jake pulled up to the back door of the big log hospital in the middle of town and rushed inside. Kate's doctor and a nurse greeted him, while an orderly sped through the door with a gurney.

Later, when Kate and the baby were settled in a room and resting comfortably, Jake hovered over them, showering them both with kisses. He watched as Kate helped the baby learn to nurse. Their little girl soon responded to the instinctive urge to suckle but after a few minutes she tired of the effort and fell asleep.

"Are you ready to hold her?" Kate asked.

She watched as Jake held the tiny brown haired baby in his arms and adored the precious addition to their family. Then Kate said a prayer aloud, "Thank you, God, for our little girl. Please keep her safe always."

Jake said thoughtfully, "Now, I know what people mean when they call the birth of a baby a miracle." He looked at Kate. "Did you do all this? Make these pretty little eyes to see and a mouth that soon learns to eat."

"No, we did the easy part. God did the hard part. But you're right, God gave us a miracle."

"Didn't take long to fall in love with this little miracle." Jake shook his head slowly. "She's so perfect."

A few minutes later Jake said he thought the baby needed a diaper change. When Kate said to hand her a diaper, he said, "I'll do it." Kate was quite astounded to see how well he managed his first experience with a messy diaper.

"I think you'd better call Charlie. He'll be wondering if we got here in time," Kate finally suggested.

"Right. I'll give Mom and Jesse a call too." He gave the baby to Kate and said, "Maybe we had better decide what we are going to name her so I can tell them. Did we decide for sure on Molly Maureen?"

"We both like the name and it seems to suit her, so it's fine with me. They will want the details, too, so tell them she weighs six pounds and eleven ounces." Kate grinned and asked, "Are you going to tell them you delivered our baby?"

"Sure, I think *we* did just fine delivering our baby." He put on his cowboy hat and started out the door. "Just for the record, next time we are going to get to the hospital on time."

Charlie assured Jake that everything was fine at home and he shouldn't worry about a thing. "Everything's fine here. You just stay there with Kate getting to know that little Molly. I like that name, by the way."

A few of the nurses and doctors whom Kate had known when she worked at the hospital came by over the next few days to see her and the baby. One of the nurses confided to Kate. "We're all envious. You have such a handsome husband and, of course, Molly is a little doll." They admired the baby together and the nurse said, "We'll miss you. Do stop by when you come to Jackson again."

The doctor said she and the baby could be released on the morning of the third day so Jake shopped for the groceries Kate asked him to buy and then he went to the hospital to get Kate and Molly. They picked up what they needed for the baby and started for the ranch. Charlie was waiting for them at the gate.

"Well, Grandpa, what do you think?" Jake asked when he opened the car door for Kate. She held the baby so Charlie could see her.

"She is without a doubt the prettiest baby girl I've ever seen."

Charlie picked up some of the groceries in one arm and Kate's hospital bag in the other. "I can hardly stand it when you two go off somewhere."

Kate carried the baby. Jake had his arms full with baby paraphernalia. Charlie followed Kate inside, watching her every step.

Jake set the baby's things on the dining room table. "Hey, I think we completely forgot about one important thing."

"What?" Kate and Charlie asked in chorus.

"Where is Molly going to sleep?"

"We can always use a dresser drawer until we get a crib," Kate suggested.

Charlie cleared his throat. "I don't know much about babies but I do know they need a place to sleep." He led them into Jake and Kate's bedroom and pointed to the corner. There stood a beautiful walnut wood cradle.

The sight of it took Kate's breath away. "Oh my goodness, wherever did you get that?"

"My nephew Chet makes furniture so I custom-ordered one for my first grandchild," Charlie said, beaming with pride. "It was ready the day you two went to the hospital. I called Chet and he met me in Rawlins with it."

"Thank you," Jake said with genuine warmth in his voice. "That's a very special gift."

Kate handed the baby to Jake and gave Charlie a hug. "Well, we might as well start making good use of it." She folded a baby blanket over the pad in the cradle and motioned for Jake to put Molly in it. They all watched her sleep for a few minutes, marveling at the precious infant before them.

They heard Brad come in so Jake stepped out of the bedroom and told him to come meet their new member of the household. After greeting Jake and Kate, he took a good look at Molly and congratulated them on their darling baby.

After a while, Charlie said, "Supper's ready. Let's eat. I cooked a pork roast. I just finished the gravy for the mashed potatoes. And," he said directly to Kate, "I know you like applesauce with the pork so I cooked up some apples from the cellar."

Kate took a deep breath. "It smells wonderful and we'd better eat before Molly wakes and wants to eat too."

They complimented Charlie on preparing such a fine meal for them and Kate got up to clear the table. Charlie put up a hand, "Just a minute, we have some dessert. You sit, I'll get it," he said as he headed for the kitchen.

"Warm vanilla pudding with cream?" Jake exclaimed. "You outdid yourself, Charlie."

"Well, that's the only kind I found in the storeroom and it looked easy—just add milk to whatever is in the box and cook it a while."

After supper, Kate looked in on Molly and then headed for the living room. She was surprised to see a new swivel rocker sitting in front of the fireplace. Jake and Charlie came in from the kitchen.

"I see you brought the chair home," Jake said to Charlie.

"When you called and said it should have arrived, I went to town and it was at the freight office."

Kate walked over to the rocker and smoothed her hands over the maroon velour. "Where did you get it?" she asked. "It sure looks nice with the other furniture in this room."

Jake said, "I ordered it from Montgomery Ward. We thought you ought to have a rocking chair now, with nursing the baby and all."

"Oh, you two!" She sat in the rocker and purred with delight. "All right then, whichever one of you is holding the baby can go ahead and rock her in this comfy chair."

"Did you hear that, Jake?" Charlie said. "Katie's given us permission to use the rocker."

Kate got up. "Here, try it out, Charlie."

"We're sure gonna have a lot of fun with little Molly around," Charlie sighed, grinning as he swiveled and rocked in the new chair.

# Chapter Seventeen

**While Jake and Kate** were at the hospital in Jackson, the electric company finished bringing poles and lines to the ranch yard. Immediately, the men Jake had hired to wire the house and other buildings for electricity came and set to work. With electricians moving about, Kate hardly knew where to go to nurse the baby in private. And it meant there were always at least two more people for dinner. Whenever Kate was in the middle of preparing a meal or cleaning up, it seemed Molly needed attention. Brad helped Jake and Charlie drive the cattle to summer pasture and they were also busy irrigating and getting machinery ready for haying. They all took over in the evening so Kate could take care of the baby.

One morning as she was burping Molly, she heard a truck pulling into the yard. She walked over to the window and saw a rig carrying a huge propane tank. Jake came riding up about that time and directed the driver to a place where he wanted the tank to be set down. Kate dreaded having one more worker in and out of the house but this one left before dinner.

The baby was crying when Jake came in. Kate was near tears trying to calm Molly down and set the table. A pile of dirty clothes was in a heap on the floor in the mudroom.

"You'll have to finish getting the men fed," she snapped. "I've got to nurse and change the baby." With that she left him standing in the kitchen.

Everyone had eaten and gone back to work by the time the baby was settled in the cradle. Kate made sure Molly was asleep before tiptoeing out of the bedroom.

Jake took a plate from the warming oven just as Kate slipped in and sat down at the counter. "I kept your food warm," he said. "Stay there and I'll do the dishes."

"While you're at it, would you mind heating enough water to wash the diapers?"

She ate, did the washing, and had the diapers hanging on the line by the time Molly began to fuss.

Before the service men left, Jake called Kate into the kitchen where he and one of the electricians waited. "Watch this," Jake said. He flipped the switch that turned on an overhead light with a glass bowl cover.

Kate had already inspected all the overhead light fixtures, but this was the first time she'd seen one of the lights come on. "We've been waiting for this moment. I am so pleased," she said.

The electrician picked up a tool belt to leave.

"Thank you," Jake said, shaking the workman's hand.

The man tipped his hat to Kate. "I hope you enjoy having electricity." He left to join his partner in the pickup.

It was about five o'clock when Kate saw the last of the pickups leave. She heaved a sigh of relief. "Thank goodness," she said aloud. It would just be Jake, Charlie, and Brad for supper.

Jake stole up behind Kate, startling her. "The diapers are dry but I guess you'd better fold them," he said. "I'm sure I wouldn't get 'em right."

She turned and saw the basket of diapers he'd brought in from the line.

"Where do you want the basket?" he asked.

"Set it by the couch." She followed Jake into the living room. He sat down on the couch, leaving enough room for the diapers as she folded and stacked them. "I've hardly seen you all day. What's gotten done with all these men coming and going?"

"The electricity is finished. I had them put in plenty of plug-ins for whatever appliances we want."

"I can't wait until it's done," Kate said. "It makes me cranky with all the hustle and bustle." She shot Jake an apologetic look. "Molly has been fussy and I have so much milk that I was miserable today, and there was a lot to do."

"Things will get easier," Jake said. "I'm glad the plumber finished puttin' in the hot water pipes. They cleaned up things pretty good, but I know you'll want it all done right so I'll do that tomorrow. Of course, there will be more cleaning after the hot water heater is installed but that will be a while. They have to put in the gas lines and the man who hooks up the hot water heater is booked solid, but he said he would come as soon as he can."

"Maybe we can both do the cleaning," she offered. After a pause, Kate asked, "Jake, isn't this costing a lot?"

"Well, I haven't got the bills yet, but I expect it will be quite a bit."

"We can get some money from our special account. I . . ."

"We could but we don't need to," Jake interrupted. "The cattle buyer was here yesterday and he offered a good price . . . better than last year, so we'll do okay."

When supper was over, Jake separated and washed the milk bucket while Kate fed Molly and put her in her cradle. Jake came in to gaze at his daughter.

"Let's turn in early tonight," Kate suggested. "You must be tired too. I can't remember ever being so exhausted."

"No wonder. This little miss keeps you up half the night. How long do these three or four hours between feedings last?"

"I don't know. Jeremy never slept through the night, but I only had to get up once most nights."

The phone ringing startled them.

"Was that our ring?" Kate asked.

"Yes, but I'll get it."

Jake went to answer the phone.

She heard Jake say, "It's for you." Kate couldn't imagine who would be calling her.

"It's Cameron Wyatt," Jake said, handing her the telephone. "He's calling to congratulate us."

Cameron and Jean had gotten the announcement a couple of days earlier. With his usual concern, he asked Kate how she was feeling and how things were on the ranch.

"It's a busy time with summer work and the new baby," Kate said. "But we're managing. Jake and Charlie are a big help most of the time."

Then Cameron delivered the bombshell. "I don't know how you're going to feel about this, but your mother came to see me this afternoon. She wanted to know where you live. She wants to see you."

Kate took a deep breath to compose herself.

He continued. "I haven't told her that you're living on the ranch, or that you're married. I wanted to talk to you first."

"It's hard to believe that she's asking about me. We haven't been in touch for such a long time. I couldn't even let her know about David and Jeremy."

"I know."

"I'd like to call you back, Cameron. I want to ask Jake what he thinks."

"Sure," he said before they told each other goodbye.

"What did Cameron want?" Jake asked when they had settled in bed. "I heard you say you wanted to talk to me about something."

"Mother went to see him this afternoon and she wants to come to see me."

"So, what'd you tell him?"

"That we need to talk it over. You've already said what you think, but I still don't want to see her."

Jake raised himself up and supported his head on one elbow. "One thing's for sure. She's persistent about wanting to see you. Don't you at least want to know why?"

"I suppose I'm a bit curious."

"Well, it's up to you. I'm okay by it either way. But think about it. Someday you might regret not letting her see her granddaughter."

Kate tried calling Cameron first thing in the morning, but someone else was on the party line. She finally reached him just as Jake and Charlie were coming in from doing chores. "Jake says it's okay with him if she comes," Kate told Cameron. "He thinks she ought to meet her granddaughter. By the way, is her husband with her?"

"Yes, he is. Kind of a stuffed shirt to my way of thinking, but that's none of my business. Have you ever met him?"

"No, and as for myself, I don't really care to see either of them but I have to admit I'm wondering *why* she wants to see me."

"Now's your chance to find out, I guess."

Kate said, "If you'll write it down, I'll give you directions on how to get here. She came to the Orland Place a few times. Tell her to watch for the sign that says McClary Ranch and turn in there."

They finished the conversation and Kate shook her head in disbelief.

Jake said, "I think we just need to wait and see what she has to say."

"You're too generous. We need to make arrangements for Molly's baptism and with everything going on here and so much to do before haying, I think this is darned inconsiderate," Kate said. She wasn't going to give in easily.

Jake just let her rant.

"You'd think she would . . ." Kate forced an exasperated breath and added, "I'm surprised she called Cameron. I don't think she ever cared much for him." She paused and added thoughtfully, "Probably because Dad and Cameron were best friends."

"You're cute when you get all worked up," Jake said, folding her in his arms.

Kate scowled. "I forgot to tell you that someone else was using the line when I wanted to call Cameron this morning. Since I could hear them talking when I picked up the phone, it made me conscious of the fact that they could listen in when we're on the line."

"We have good neighbors. I'm sure they respect our privacy as we do theirs."

"I hope no one heard me talking to Cameron. What would they say?"

"Don't worry, it's no one's business. Besides, they have their own lives."

Kate wasn't the least bit convinced, but she let it drop.

Cameron called back the next morning and passed on the information that Lillian and her husband would be at the ranch in two days' time.

When the men came in for dinner, Kate told Jake the plan. "They couldn't come at a busier time, unless they waited for haying to be in full swing," she said with disgust.

Jake didn't say anything.

Charlie shrugged. "No use in getting all worked up. If Martha were here, she'd look your mother straight in the eye and ask her how she could have deserted a sweet daughter like you."

"You're such a dear, Charlie. I wish your Martha were here now. From all that you've told me about her, she'd definitely know what to do about this situation."

— · —

The following day, Kate could hardly keep her mind off of her mother's impending visit. Did Lillian really want to make amends as Jake suggested? Could she really feel remorse for having left Kate? Did Lillian's husband have a hand in their sudden visit? Questions nagged at her, but one thing remained constant, and that was the hurt she still felt at her mother's biting words to Kate's father: "You're the one who wanted children so you can have custody of the brat." Those may not have been the exact words, but it didn't matter. The fact that she'd be facing her mother again after all these years had opened an old wound.

Kate's preoccupation with her own thoughts didn't go unnoticed. "You're awful quiet," Jake said, looking up from a magazine.

"Just enjoying nursing Molly."

"You're fretting about your mother coming, aren't you?"

Kate drew in a breath. "You're either very perceptive or you know me too well. But you're right . . . I can't for the life of me figure out why she's coming here."

"Maybe getting older has given her a nudge to set her life in order. Maybe she has cancer or survived a stroke and wants to make things right before she dies."

"That would be just like her . . . selfish to the bitter end. Sorry, I'm just not happy about her coming here."

"Don't let it bother you so much. Charlie and Molly and I will be here right by your side. Whatever her motives are, we'll find out tomorrow."

"I know you're right, but I'm feeling all the old rage and sense of being rejected that I felt back then."

Jake knelt down on one knee next to Kate and the baby and took Kate's hand. "You have Molly and me now. You'll never be rejected again." He gave her his smile that always went straight to her heart.

She squeezed his hand and gave him back a weak smile. "Thanks."

Jake stood up. "Remember, this is your home and if it upsets you too much to have that woman come, I'll send them both on their way. There's no use losing sleep over her and the stuffed shirt."

The image of a tall pompous man in a three piece gray suit, with an air of self-importance and gesturing with his walking stick, popped into Kate's head and she let out a giggle.

"What's that for?"

"I just pictured the stuffed shirt pointing his cane at you and saying, 'See here, my good man.'"

Jake chuckled, amused at her description of Lillian's husband. Now that Kate's mood had lightened he waved her off and went to do some of the cleaning.

Kate put the baby on her shoulder to burp and thought about how blessed she was to have Jake and the baby, not to mention his family who cared for all of them. She mentally added Charlie to her list of blessings. He counted them as family and adored Molly. Still, all the talk and thinking about the next day didn't entirely wipe away Kate's anxiety and resentment against the woman who was her mother, if in name only.

True to his word, Jake set about cleaning up wood chips and dusting wherever electrical plug-ins and fixture wires had been installed. Kate put Molly in her cradle after she finished feeding and changing her, then she asked Jake which room needed cleaning.

"You can help me finish the kitchen. After that I think it's all done." He handed her a damp rag and went back to sweeping bits of wood into a dust pan.

Wiping around the plates of the plug-ins and light switches didn't take long. As she finished, Kate chuckled at a thought. "I wonder what my mother will say when she sees that we have electricity but no appliances. When she came to Grandma's house, she complained all the time about how inconvenient it was that they had no electricity. It was bad enough that they didn't have a telephone. And she loathed the outhouse."

"Then she should be glad we have a toilet in the house," Jake said.

"Maybe, but I almost wish we still had the outhouse. Just while she's here, of course."

"Easy there, darlin'. You're pretty hard on that woman. Don't forget, we decided to give her the benefit of the doubt."

"I'll try. I do want her to see how much I love our life on the ranch, and I want her to see how happy I am."

"That's my girl." He went out the door and was back in a few minutes with an armload of wood for the kitchen stove. "Anything else you need to get ready for our company?"

"Patience . . . and for you to help me keep my mouth shut."

"That's easy." He gave her a lingering kiss on the lips. "Anytime you feel tempted to say what you really think, give me the signal and I'll do that again."

"You're the limit, you know that." They shared a good laugh, which left Kate a little less uneasy about what was to transpire the next day.

# Chapter Eighteen

**It was almost** five o'clock in the afternoon the next day, when Buster, who didn't bark often, began barking. Kate got up from the rocker and saw a big touring car coming down the lane. She put Molly in her cradle and went back to the window in the dining room and waited. She prayed to the Lord to give her strength.

When the Cadillac stopped at the gate, Jake rode up on his horse. He got off and wrapped the reins around the top pole of the fence, greeting and shaking hands with the two visitors. He motioned for them to follow him into the Bunkhouse. A burst of resentment rose up in Kate seeing Jake so hospitable, like he was saying hello to familiar neighbors and welcoming them into their home.

Kate had time to study her mother and Lillian's husband as they walked to the house. Lillian's dark hair was fashioned in the familiar roll at the back of her head. She hadn't changed much, just looked older. Her husband was a distinguished looking fellow, who looked at lot like she had imagined—minus the cane. He was at least a head taller than Lillian.

Jake opened the kitchen door. "Kate, our visitors are here," he called out.

When she entered, her mother stood there and looked at Kate as if she'd seen a ghost. They both kept a polite distance. "Come in," Kate said, mustering as much warmth in her voice as she could. She turned her attention to the staid man standing next to her mother. "I don't believe we've met."

She shook hands with him and cast a momentary glance at Jake who was standing a little behind the couple. Jake's barely perceptible wink let Kate know he knew what she was thinking—that her description of the man earlier was right on.

Lillian slipped her hand through the crook of her husband's arm. "This is my husband, Grayson Crawford. He's quite overcome by the long distance we've come over these awful roads. We can't fathom how you travel them."

Jake shifted from one foot to the other. "Well, we usually travel them in a pickup. They weren't really made for a Cadillac," he said lightly.

Kate directed the two to the small sofa in the living room and sat down in the wing-back chair nearby. Jake moved an ottoman next to her and took hold of her hand.

"How far did you come today?" Kate asked.

"We got into Denver day before yesterday and stayed in Casper last night. We followed the directions Cameron gave us, otherwise I would never have remembered how to get here," Lillian said.

As yet, Grayson hadn't said a word beyond "I'm pleased to meet you," which he said to Kate when they first came in. The covert glances that Lillian cast at him now and then didn't go unnoticed by Kate.

Jake said, "I see you have a Nevada license on your car. Where do you live in Nevada?"

"We live in Reno. Of course, we travel extensively, but that is our home base," Grayson answered.

This time, Jake caught the disapproving look that Lillian sent to Grayson.

"I need to attend to supper," Kate said. "The men will be coming in before long. Jake will show you where to put your things."

"We didn't see any cows as we came in. Don't you raise cows?" Lillian asked.

"Oh, yes, we raise cattle and horses. The cattle are on the summer pasture so hay can grow on the meadows. We'll bring them home in the fall after we've put up the hay."

Grayson finally spoke up. "I've never been on a ranch before. Lillian said when she visited the ranch, she always had to watch where she stepped. Animals leave such a mess."

Jake tipped his head and looked down at his boot. "I guess that doesn't bother us. We happen to be very fond of our animals."

Lillian hurried to change the subject. "Cameron said you only recently put in a telephone. I can't imagine being without a telephone. Another thing that was terribly inconvenient at my former husband's parents' place was that they didn't even have electricity. I'm glad to see that you have that, at least."

"Well, we've only had electricity for a few days so we're not quite used to it. We usually go to bed when it gets dark and get up when it gets light—don't need much electricity for that."

Grayson sniffed. "It seems to me that you are quite out of touch with the modern world out here."

Jake stood up and said, "Shall we bring your things in?"

The three of them went to the car. Jake watched as Grayson and Lillian set out a half dozen cases from the trunk and back seat. He put a small satchel under his arm and picked up two big suitcases and headed for the house. The couple followed with the rest of their luggage. Jake led them to the bedroom then left them to deal with where to put everything and went to wash up for supper.

The table was set, and Charlie and Brad were helping Kate get everything on the table when Lillian came into the kitchen. Kate introduced them and both men took food to the dining room and were out of earshot, when Lillian said to Kate, "You do just like your grandmother used to do . . . everything is so informal, even allowing the hired help to eat at the same table with you."

Kate didn't reply, taking it as criticism. It was all too familiar—the way her mother used to speak to her.

"Crawford and I prefer twin beds," Lillian continued. "Would you mind putting us in another room?"

This amused Kate and she suppressed a smile. "We don't have twin beds and we don't have another room either."

"Oh, that's a shame," her mother replied.

"We do have some twin beds in the bunkhouse where the help stays if you'd rather be out there. You'd have more privacy, but Brad has one of the rooms."

"I don't think that would work very well."

"Well, Brad could come in here and you'd have it all to yourself. There's no running water and no bathroom, though. The outhouse is behind the cabin." Kate was enjoying herself.

"No thanks, we'll manage," Lillian said resignedly.

Charlie pumped cold water and filled the glasses. He handed two to Crawford, who had come in to the kitchen. "Here, you can take these into the dining room. We usually don't have coffee in the evening but if you want some, the coffee is on the stove." He didn't mention that it had been sitting there all day.

At the table, Jake said the blessing. Afterward he did his best to keep up the conversation. "Charlie lives here with us and Brad helps in the summer. He came early to help drag the meadows."

"Bradley, is it?" Lillian asked. "Where do you live in the winter?"

"I'll be a junior at the University of Wyoming in Laramie. I'm majoring in Animal Husbandry and wish I could live on a ranch like this all the time. I'll want to find a job in agriculture when I finish college."

"That's nice," Lillian said. "Of course, you don't want to spend all your time in a place as isolated as this ranch. You'd never find a nice young woman to court around here."

Jake grinned and winked at Kate. "Oh, I don't know, I did."

Lillian glanced at Kate speculatively but didn't respond.

They had passed the food and Kate was about to take the breadbasket to the kitchen for more bread when Jake said, "I'll do it, sweetheart."

It was Charlie who spoke into an uneasy silence. "Brad and I checked the ditches in that upper field. The place that washed out last year seems to be holding. We fixed a couple of other places that needed more sod so they all look good."

"Thanks, I appreciate you doing all that," Jake said.

Brad complimented Kate on a good supper and asked if anyone else wanted a glass of milk as he got up to go to the kitchen.

They had nearly finished supper when Molly began crying.

"I'll take care of her, you folks go on and visit," Charlie said, scooting his chair back. Kate glanced at her mother and guessed what her mother would think of a hired hand tending to the baby.

Lillian gave Crawford a feigned look of enthusiasm. "Finally we get to see that grandchild Cameron told us about."

Brad shooed everyone out of the kitchen saying he would do the dishes and then wash the milk bucket and strainer after he milked the cow. Jake and Kate guided Lillian and Crawford into the living room. Molly was asleep on Charlie's shoulder.

"How old is the baby?" Lillian asked. "And, what's her name? It is a girl, isn't it?"

"She's two weeks old and her name is Molly. I would have let you know but I didn't know how to contact you."

"Life has had its challenges for me, you must understand that."

"I was married before," Kate said pointedly, ignoring her mother's reply. "My husband, David, and I had a son, Jeremy. He was four months old when David and Jeremy were killed in an accident. I wanted to let you know, but I couldn't reach you then either."

"I'm sorry to hear that," Lillian said, with a frown. "I had no idea."

"I came back here and found Jake and this beautiful ranch."

"You must miss the city. It's so isolated here. As I remember, the winters are terribly long and the snow is too deep to travel. How do you manage?"

"You're right about the weather, but I love it here and we manage quite well."

"We don't mind being snowed in," Jake said. "This winter will be different because we have a telephone. Last week the electric company finished bringing power this far up the valley, but we don't have anything that uses electricity yet."

"You have no washer or dryer? What a hard life. I would never have lived like this."

An uncomfortable silence hung over the room. Charlie continued to rock Molly and wished silently the socializing would end soon.

"There's an overhead light in your bedroom but no lamp by your bed," Jake told their guests. "Until we have time to buy some electrical fixtures, that's all we have. There's a bathroom down the hall. Right now, all we have is cold water in there. We don't have a hot water heater so we heat water on the kitchen stove. Or the water in the reservoir at the side of the stove is usually hot enough to wash up."

"It's all quite primitive for people like us, but we'll make the best of it," Grayson said. Lillian was taken aback by her husband's sudden assertion, but she beamed back at him and nodded her approval.

Kate went over and took the baby from Charlie. "I'd better change Molly and nurse her," she said, bidding everyone goodnight.

———•———

Later, Kate snuggled in bed next to Jake. He ran his fingers through her hair. "Well, what do you think?" he asked.

Kate stifled a giggle. "I *know* they don't like sleeping in the same bed. They didn't want to move to the bunkhouse where *hired men have lived, for heaven's sake,* and they don't like to eat with the help."

"I could see that. They were quite appalled to see Brad and Charlie helping with supper. And then Charlie is so comfortable in our house, and taking care of Molly too. They didn't seem too smitten with our baby either."

"I don't know what to think about why they've come here, but I think your theories are all wrong."

"I still wonder if she might be sick or something," he added half-heartedly. "She doesn't have a very healthy look. She's kind of pale and her skin is pretty wrinkled for someone who has probably used every trick to ward off looking old."

"I just wonder how long they intend to stay."

"A couple of days of no hot water and our primitive ways ought to be enough for them." He turned her face to his so he could kiss her. "I sure do love you," he whispered.

Kate and the men had eaten breakfast and they'd gone out to work before Lillian and Grayson showed up. Kate was in the milk room washing the separator. When she heard them, she called out, "There's coffee on the stove. I'll fix some pancakes for you when I'm done here."

Kate finished in the milk room. She came to the kitchen and poked some kindling in the stove then moved the griddle to the hot side.

"We don't want a pancake. A piece of toast is fine for us," Lillian said.

Kate sliced some bread and let it toast on the griddle while she poured their cups of coffee. She gave each a plate with two slices of toast. Butter and jam were already on the table. "I have juice if you want some," Kate offered.

"No, this is fine. We don't eat much breakfast," Grayson said.

After they finished, Kate suggested they might want to take a walk to see the beautiful valley while she nursed the baby. They weren't gone long. The rest of the morning they spent reading magazines and looking through a photo album with pictures of Kate, David, and Jeremy.

They ate a hearty dinner and seemed to genuinely like Kate's meat, carrot, onion, and potato casserole with mushroom gravy. They sat in the living room and read most of the afternoon, but seemed anxious to get to their room soon after supper.

"She could have helped with a few things around here," Jake said when they were alone again and cleaning up the kitchen.

"I warned you that Mother wasn't likely to offer any help. She never did," Kate replied.

"It's amazing you turned out the way you did, given you came from that unthankful woman."

"Right, I think you're beginning to see the reality of what I was accustomed to in my early life."

"Honey, I'm so proud of the way you're handling this situation. I hope they don't intend to overstay their welcome with us. I fear you might run out of patience."

"You fear right. But it's your job to keep me in line, remember," Kate teased.

# CHAPTER NINETEEN

**Grayson** shut their bedroom door for the night and grumbled to Lillian. "This is damned inconvenient. The only bathroom is down the hall, the water's cold and there's no shower."

"I tend to think that this ranch is a prosperous one in spite of the lack of amenities," Lillian commented. She turned down the bed covers and sat down to take off her shoes.

"Your first husband's parents lived this way?"

"Worse. There was no toilet, just an outhouse."

"I'll be glad to get back to Reno. I wish you'd hurry up and ask for what brought us to this desolate place."

"Don't push me. I wasn't sure what our reception would be. Kate is distant but doesn't seem to mind us being here," Lillian mused. "What do you think of Jake?"

"Decent fellow. I've never met a rancher before but he seems to be taking good care of your daughter."

"I wouldn't call it that when she has to cook and clean without any conveniences or household help. I'm surprised they even have a toilet in the house."

"If she has as much money as you think she has, I can't understand why they don't modernize this place. It's hard to believe that they just got electricity around here."

"Kate is just like her father. He made good money, but he managed it on his own terms. I survived on the pittance of an allowance he gave me and had to hire a lawyer to get any kind of a settlement when we divorced." Shivering, Lillian pulled the covers up to her chin. "I'm sure Kate has a tight rein on all the money she inherited and probably decides what to spend it on."

Grayson was deep in his own thoughts. "I wonder if Charlie is a relative. He certainly makes himself at home."

"I should hope Kate wouldn't let a hired man tend to the baby. Maybe he's related to Jake somehow."

———•———

Kate was standing at the counter kneading bread dough when Lillian came into the kitchen the next morning without Grayson tagging along behind her. She sat on a stool nearby and watched Kate use the heels of her hands to push down on the dough.

"Aren't you afraid you'll strain your back doing that?" her mother asked.

Kate folded the dough in half. "No, Mother, as long as I keep my arms stretched out like this and don't hunch over."

"You're lucky Molly doesn't fuss much," Lillian said, trying to keep a conversation going.

"It's no wonder. She has Jake, Charlie, and me right there if she starts to cry. She's got those two men wrapped around her little finger." Kate nodded toward the stove. "I think there is a cup or two of coffee left if you want some."

"No thanks, I had two cups for breakfast. Do you always make such a big breakfast?"

"I sure do. The men work hard and sometimes they're late getting in for dinner so they need a good breakfast."

"Dinner?"

"On ranches, usually the noon meal is dinner and the night meal is supper."

"Seems backward, but then I never understood the ranching way of life."

Neither of them spoke while Kate formed the loaves and placed them in the pans.

Finally Lillian said, "I need to ask a favor."

Kate looked her mother. "Yes, what's that?"

"I hate to ask but we're in dire straits. Grayson made a bad investment and we are really strapped for money to live on right now."

Kate held the tea kettle still for several seconds then poured the hot water into the basin so she could wash her hands. She set the kettle back on the stove and turned to look at her mother, waiting for what she was beginning to suspect her mother would say.

Lillian lowered her eyes from Kate's gaze and went on, "I know you inherited a large sum from your father. I was meant to have his life insurance but he changed everything to your name to spite me. Your grandmother must have left you a lot too. When she sold the ranch she would have given you all that she had. Kate, I *am* your mother and we have no one else to turn to."

Kate was stunned by her mother's boldness. "How much do you need?" she asked, hiding her reaction.

"Well, fifty thousand would set us right again, I think."

"I'll talk to Jake about it," Kate said, absorbing the further shock.

"I wish you wouldn't."

"Of course I'll talk to Jake. It's his money, too, and I would never do anything behind his back."

Lillian smiled for the simple reason that Kate hadn't turned her down outright.

But Kate had no intention of giving Lillian and Grayson any money. "I inherited money from my late husband also, but I'm careful with my money."

Lillian didn't care for the mean-spiritedness of Kate's words. "Sorry I had to ask you. It's a very uncomfortable position for me to be in. And Grayson too."

———•———

"Well, the mystery is solved," Kate told Jake as she crawled into bed next to him that night.

"The mystery?"

"Yes, the answer to why my mother and Grayson came here. She asked me for money today. It seems Grayson lost their money in a bad investment and they're penniless to hear her tell it."

"How much money does she want?"

"Wait till you hear this. Fifty thousand dollars!"

"She's got a lot of nerve," Jake said, clearly taken aback.

"She knows I inherited the insurance money from Dad, and

assumes I got money from my grandmother after she sold the ranch. I'm sure she's figured out I sold Dad's business and the house. She must think I'm a wealthy woman."

"Did you tell her I married you for your money so you don't have any now?"

Kate poked him in the ribs.

"Kate, I don't want you to say or do anything about the money. I'll take care of it."

"Suits me. I don't think we ought to give them anything. So what if it makes her mad. She doesn't give a hoot about me, just the money. Besides, I've seen her mad before . . . the time she came back after Dad died expecting to get the insurance money."

The next morning after breakfast Jake came into the Bunkhouse just as Lillian and Grayson were sitting down at the dining room table to have coffee and toast. He and Kate took their usual seats at the table. Grayson commented on the weather and bemoaned the fact that the mosquitoes were terrible.

Jake drew in a breath. "I understand you need money. I've decided to give you some."

Grayson cast a glance at Lillian who was about to say something. He plainly wanted her to keep quiet.

Jake took Kate's hand and looked at Lillian. "I owe you something. You brought this beautiful woman into the world, and I'm blessed to have her as my wife. That's without doubt." He pulled an envelope from his shirt pocket and handed it to Lillian. "You can take this check and cash it at the bank in Rock Springs. I'll call the manager to let him know you're coming."

She took the envelope and put it in her purse as she murmured, "Thank you, we are grateful to you."

Then Jake turned to Grayson. "I think you ought to find a new line of work, Mr. Crawford."

"I beg your pardon," he sputtered.

Matter-of-factly, Jake said, "Gambling doesn't pay very well. And if you really need to cut back, that fancy Cadillac could be traded in for something much more economical."

Grayson pulled at his shirt collar. "I'll keep it in mind."

Jake stood up and leaned over to kiss Kate. "I've got to get to work." When he got to the door he turned around. "By the way, don't come back for more money. That's all you'll be getting."

"Thank you," Lillian murmured into the unbearably silent atmosphere.

Soon after Jake left, Lillian and Grayson stood up. "We'll get our things and be on our way," she said to Kate. "We appreciate the money and your hospitality. It's good to know you're happy with your life."

Jake came back in to help carry their things to the car. He shook hands with both of them, knowing that they would have preferred avoiding that gesture or even seeing him again. Kate put out her hand to Grayson, who returned a cool handshake, probably not wanting to appear ungrateful for the money. Before climbing into the Cadillac, Lillian gave her daughter an awkward hug. Kate reciprocated with a quick peck on her mother's cheek.

As soon as the car took off down the lane, Jake and Kate started for the house. Kate turned to Jake who held her firmly by his side. "How much money did you give them?"

"Not nearly what they asked for, but you'll pester me until I tell you, right?"

"Okay, so . . ."

"Twenty-five thousand."

"That's no small sum, Mr. McClary."

Jake looked thoughtful but couldn't stifle a wicked grin. "I figure you're worth at least that much."

Kate slapped his arm lightly. "So how'd you know Grayson was a gambler?"

"I gambled on it. They live in Reno . . . they usually 'travel extensively' and now they're broke. He didn't deny it when I called him a gambler, which means I won the bet I had with myself."

"You're incorrigible, you know that? But, I love you anyway."

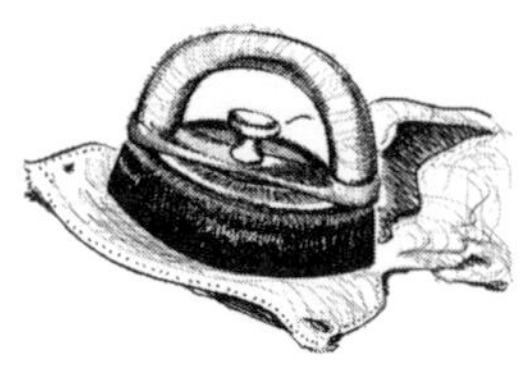

# Chapter Twenty

**The next morning** at breakfast, Charlie wasted no time in bringing up the subject of Lillian and Grayson's visit. "Funny thing, Mr. Crawford asked me if I'm related to Jake. I told him no, I'm the hired man."

"I bet that got a rise out of him," Jake said, passing the butter to Brad.

"He said he had no idea that a hired man would be living in the same house with the family, so he and Katie's mother assumed I was a relative."

"Sounds like my mother talking," Kate said.

Charlie took a sip of his coffee. "Golly, it never occurred to me that you might not like having the hired man livin' in your house."

"I never think of you as the hired man," Kate said. "You should have told him that you *are* related. You're Molly's grandpa and you're my father now."

"Guess that makes you my father-in-law," Jake said, laughing and setting the others to laughing too.

Kate could see that Jake's wisecrack tickled Charlie. She turned her attention to Brad. "You and your folks are like family, too. Just because you stay in the ranch bunkhouse doesn't mean you couldn't stay in this house if you wanted to."

"Thanks, but I'm perfectly happy in the bunkhouse. Your ranch is like a second home to me. I'm just glad I always get to come for the summer."

Charlie looked at Kate. "Anyway, your mother and Mr. Crawford didn't stay long."

Kate and Jake looked at each other, trying to decide how much information they should divulge. Jake spoke first. "They were just passing through. Wanted to see the baby."

That evening after Kate had gotten Molly settled in her cradle, Jake and Kate sat down in the living room.

"Thanks for not letting on about the real reason my mother and Grayson came to the ranch," Kate said.

"There was no purpose to it. Besides, it would've irked Charlie to no end."

"Grayson had no right grilling Charlie the way he did. They're a perfect match, my mother and Grayson. I saw how she treated her housekeeper when I was growing up."

"Truth is, you have to feel sorry for people like that."

"You're right. Having money and being rich makes them happy, I suppose. They must have really been down on their luck."

"They were desperate enough to come asking for money from you."

Jake took off his boots and picked up the kerosene lamp they used instead of the bright overhead light.

"I'm rich and it has nothing to do with money," Kate said.

"Me too, sweetheart."

———•———

Kate was hanging up a full load of laundry on the clothesline when Jake came riding in from the field. They reached the back door about the same time. "Are you through irrigating?" Kate asked.

"I'll go out later on this afternoon after we make arrangements for Molly's baptism on Sunday. I need to call Father Malone again and be sure he plans to do it this Sunday. Then I'll call Jesse and Mary Anne to make sure they are set to meet us in Rock Springs."

"I'm sure Charlie will want to go with us," Kate said. "Before Molly came, we could hardly get him to leave this place. She's given him a new lease on life."

"Yep, he takes his 'grandfather' job seriously."

"I wish your mom and dad could be there, but it's too far and it would be impossible for your dad to make the trip."

"It's too bad, but Mom agrees that it's important to have Molly baptized as soon as possible. We've had so much going on and we're behind already, but this baptism comes first." Jake added, "It was good of Brad to say he'll take care of things while we're gone."

Packing what they needed to stay in Rock Springs had Kate in a tizzy. Jake's white shirt was wrinkled from being in a crowded closet for several weeks so Kate had to clean the top of the stove and heat the irons, praying that none of them left a black mark on his best shirt. Then, to her dismay, she couldn't find a dress that fit. She hadn't given much thought to the few but significant pounds she had left over from pregnancy. She had to stop and tend the baby in the middle of all her preparations. It was late Friday afternoon when she finally had everything in a suitcase for Jake and her. She still hadn't gathered all the things she had to take along for the baby and put that chore off until morning.

"Well, good lord, do we need to take all this stuff just to go to town?" Jake exclaimed when she had everything stacked by the door at eleven o'clock the next day. "We're only staying two nights," he went on as he grabbed a bag of baby things and picked up a heavy suitcase. Kate was nursing the baby and smiled with a shrug of her shoulders.

They were on their way after a quick lunch of sandwiches and milk. By the time they got to Rock Springs a couple of hours later, it was time to meet with Father Malone. Jesse, Mary Anne, and the kids met them at the motel where they got acquainted with Molly. Everyone was happy but Molly, who slept fitfully and curled up as if her stomach hurt. "I guess it was the chocolate cake," Kate told Jake when Molly cried again during the night. "I didn't stop to think even though I know chocolate bothers some breastfed babies."

"Get some sleep, I'll walk with her and maybe she'll settle down," Jake said. It took a while but finally Molly slept so he could put her down between them on the bed. It was only a couple of hours later that she wanted to eat again. Kate sat in the uncomfortable chair to nurse the baby and they were still there when Jake woke about six and said, "We'd better get ready." He grinned at Kate and teased, "Can you remember the last time we had a good night's sleep?"

Kate got up, feeling stiff from sitting in the awkward chair, and put the baby on the bed so she could shower and dress. In the lobby, they met Charlie who was well rested and ready to go. Even with their early start, it was all Jake could do to get them to the church on time. Jesse greeted them on the steps outside and said they had kept seats at the front for all of them.

The priest finished his homily and called the family up to the altar. They all gathered around the baptismal font, glad to see that Molly was quiet in Mary Anne's arms. With Jesse holding one little hand, she was anointed and made a member of the Church. Only the cool water on her forehead brought a surprised cry that subsided after a moment. After the baby had been christened Molly Maureen McClary and Mass was over, they went to have brunch at a nice restaurant. Abby scarcely took time to eat, insisting she'd rather hold the baby.

Later, Jesse and Mary Anne said they needed to start for home because they were already in the middle of their haying season. Jake and Kate understood, but they would stay another night because they needed to shop for provisions for their haying crew. At the grocery store on Monday morning, Charlie, sitting in the back seat, said, "Molly is asleep so I'll stay here with her and you two can get the groceries."

"Thanks, Charlie. It won't take us long."

They were on their way home when Jake said, "I suppose we should have shopped for some electrical appliances while we were in town. Do you know what you need, besides an electric iron?"

"We don't need to buy an iron. There's too much to do right now. Let's wait until after haying," she said wearily. "I can hardly remember what it was like to have all those electrical conveniences anyway."

———•———

The summer of 1960 had been unusual and full of events up to now, including the unlikely visit of her mother and Grayson, who Kate refused to think of as her stepfather. It had been a trying time so Jake suggested that they take time for something special on the second Sunday in July.

Jake said he wanted to take Kate to the DeSmet Mass in Daniel, a few miles west of Pinedale on the road to Jackson. He explained that Mass would be said on the hill overlooking the beautiful Daniel valley. "It's where Father DeSmet said the first Mass in Wyoming with Indians and mountain men in the congregation."

"I know, I've been to the DeSmet Mass but it was a long time ago," she replied.

Kate was excited to go but weary by the time she had the baby fed and they were on their way. After the service, she told Jake, "The river winding its way through the willows down in the valley and the Mass wide open under the blue sky was so meaningful. I wouldn't be surprised if all of heaven was watching."

Jake scratched the back of his neck. "The mosquitoes liked it, too."

They decided that after Mass they would take in the Green River Rendezvous at the pageant setting on top of the hill above Pinedale. On the way, Jake mentioned that until this year, the pageant had been performed at Daniel, not far from the original Rendezvous location. "They needed more space so it's been moved to an area behind the rodeo grounds where people can sit on bleachers and see the whole show. Rendezvous is a county tradition with local people as the entire cast," he explained.

"I remember that," Kate said. "Grandma and Granddad took me to Rendezvous several times. They liked the show but they also enjoyed seeing many of their friends there. Granddad called it the last hoo-rah before haying."

Jake chuckled. "Sounds like your granddad. We didn't go every year but I've seen it many times. It sure tells the history of the mountain men and how they traded their furs for things they needed to get through another year."

Molly slept through the presentation even though the story was narrated over a microphone and the whooping of Indians and mountain men was usually enough to wake the dead. Even the rattling of tug chains and rolling of the wagons bringing colorful cloths that the Indian women snatched up right away, and whiskey that the men fought over, didn't disturb the little miss, so Kate enjoyed the show.

Jake knew some of the people who portrayed mountain men, wagon drivers, or Indians. But he didn't recognize any of the young people who rode hell bent for leather through the arena riding bareback and with only a chinstrap on their horses. There was a collective gasp from the audience when one young Indian went flying off her horse. Luckily someone caught her horse and she was back on and riding at a full run again in moments.

After the rendezvous they could anticipate what the next few weeks would demand of them. They were glad to see Don and Marie come right away and set to work as if they'd been there the whole time.

Many of the workhorses had been out on the desert most of the spring and early summer. Jake and Brad set out to run them in so they could work the horses for a while before putting them on haying machinery. On their first run, they found one frisky bunch and soon had the horses running through the lane toward the corral. Kate watched from the front porch and saw Jake dismount and close the gate. Controlling horses that hadn't been worked in months scared Kate. Remembering the runaway from the summer before, she prayed there wouldn't be any injuries this year.

Kate had realized early on that Jake and Charlie were good with horses. She had seen both of them talking to the animals and approaching the wild ones carefully, especially when they were carrying a rope or halter. She'd never seen either of them hit a horse with anything more than a rein and even that was a gentle slap to keep them moving. Jake had told her that his dad taught his boys to treat animals right. "After all," he'd say, "you expect them to work for you and be gentle so you have to treat them the same way." Charlie once commented that it was their good fortune that Don and Brad had the same respect for their horses.

Jake and Brad worked several teams over the next few days. They were usually out early and got back in late. One morning they set out to hook up one of the desert horses they called Joe with their gentle workhorse Major on a wagon. After they caught Joe without much trouble and he stood still while being harnessed, Jake said, "These two work good together. We'll put them on a sweep." They led the horses to the wagon. Jake hooked the line to his bridle and threw it across Major's back. He picked up the tongue and hooked the neck yokes while both horses stood patiently. Jake placed his hand on Joe's rump and reached around with his other hand for the tug so he could attach it to the singletree but he dropped the chain. Without warning, Joe kicked and caught Jake's shin.

"Damn it!"

Alarmed, Brad asked anxiously, "You okay?"

"I think so, but maybe you could hook that tug from your side."

Brad reached behind Major and fastened the chain while Jake hooked the one on the outside. Then Brad climbed onto the wagon and waited for Jake. "Let's see that leg," he said as soon as Jake sat down on the wagon seat.

Jake pulled up his pant leg. A four-inch cut was bleeding and had started to coagulate.

"I'll pull around to the house and you can get Kate to bandage that for you," Brad said.

"It's not that bad," Jake protested.

"You at least need to get it cleaned out."

Brad waited until Jake went in the mudroom door, then he started the team down the lane. He got back about twenty minutes later, unharnessed the horses, and went to check on Jake.

Kate had cleaned and bandaged the cut. Jake was lying on the couch with his leg up. She was in the kitchen holding a fussy Molly and trying to set the table.

"I'll take her," Brad told Kate.  He glanced in the living room. "Is Jake okay?"

"It's not a very deep cut, but I wanted him to stay off it until we see that it has stopped bleeding."

"Jake was so close that the horse couldn't land a hard kick, but it was enough to clip Jake's leg." Brad carried Molly with him to the living room.

Jake sat up on the edge of the couch. "I'm fine," he said. "It isn't a bad cut and Kate fixed me right up. It could have been a lot worse. He could have broken my shin bone."

"I didn't have any problem unhooking his tugs. We've worked him several times the last few days and he was okay."

"He's not mean. I startled him when I dropped the chain."

Molly began to fidget. Brad handed her over to Jake.

"The rest of the crew should be here by next Thursday," Jake continued. "We'll start on the east fields so I'll shut the water off right away so the meadows can dry. It sure has been a big help having you here."

"Happy to oblige."

"I can't believe how many logs you and Charlie have brought in and sawed. You two chopped a lot of kindling for the kitchen stove to boot. We appreciate it."

Over the next few days, Kate checked Jake's leg often enough to be sure he didn't have an infection. It healed nicely, and Jake told Brad and Charlie that was because he had an excellent nurse.

Charlie was quick to comment. "We already knew that."

———•———

"Oh, thank goodness," Kate exclaimed when Jake came in to tell them the gas company men had arrived and would have gas lines to the house and ready for the water heater to be installed the next day. "No more heating water to do the dishes, Marie. Isn't that wonderful?"

"Now, I have to go to town and I want you to go with me," Jake told Kate.

"Right now?"

"Right now."

In town, Jake carried Molly as they shopped for what few groceries they needed. Jake handed the baby to Kate, signed the charge slip, and loaded everything in the back of the pickup. "I need to stop at the hardware store," Jake told her when they were in the truck.

"That's fine. You go in. I need to nurse Molly."

"That'll have to wait a few minutes. I want you to come with me."

Jake carried Molly and led Kate through the store to the large appliances department. "Now, which do you want first? A refrigerator or the washer and dryer? We don't have room for everything in the pickup."

"Do we have room for a washer and a dryer? That's what I need the most," Kate said, excitedly.

"With all those diapers you wash, I'd say that's the best choice. You pick 'em out."

When Kate had chosen what she wanted and the new machines were loaded into the pickup, Jake said they'd come to town again soon to pick out a fridge.

"No need until spring. I'm not used to having one anyway," Kate said.

"Good," Jake replied with a lilt in his voice. "You've cost this outfit a lot of money already."

"Are you complaining Mr. McClary?"

"No. But we do need to get a refrigerator, too. Maybe we can do that before I start mowing next week. Marie might appreciate that."

# Chapter Twenty-One

**The washer and dryer** were hooked up in no time. Jake said they'd better get a refrigerator and a freezer so they went back to town to buy them. When they were all set up and working, Jake told the ladies to have fun with the new appliances, but he needed to get out and start mowing hay.

Kate commented that she was glad to have the refrigerator and freezer.

"The meat house is built right over the creek, so the provisions stay cool and we haven't had much trouble, but I'd hate to have anything spoil."

"The steer that Jake butchered the other day is still hanging in the meat house," Marie said. "If we all help, we should be able to get the beef cut up and in the freezer right away."

Jake and Carl began mowing in the furthest field from the Bunkhouse. As she had in the past, Marie offered to take lunch out to the crew everyday. One morning, Kate insisted on going with her and taking Molly. Not only that, she wanted to drive the pickup, so Marie held the baby.

"Finally I get to hold her," Marie said, beaming. "If you're not feeding her or she's asleep, Jake or Charlie thinks she needs to be held." They crossed a ditch that tossed them in one direction and then another.

"It's amazing how a household changes when there's a baby around," Kate said.

She pulled up close to where the hay was being stacked and at a spot where they could sit and eat, shaded by the stack. "Ooh, I like this sweet smell of new mown hay," Kate said to Jake when she sat down where he was holding the baby and eating with one hand.

Marie had kept the food as hot as she could with towels wrapped around the roaster filled with sliced roast beef and vegetables. Along with homemade rolls, lemonade, and cookies, everyone ate their fill. The hay hands kept telling Marie they sure liked her meal. "And, it's a treat to have ice cubes in the lemonade," Brad told Kate.

"Thanks to our new freezer," she responded.

The mosquitoes and horseflies were thick. Swatting them away was an effort. "Watch that Molly doesn't get any bites," Jake said.

Charlie sauntered over and offered his advice. "You ought to carry some calamine lotion or something with you when you bring Molly out."

"You guys need to relax about this baby," Kate said. "I'm sure she's fine. We've been watching her closely. She'll be ready for a nap after this outing."

The crew set everything from the meal in the pickup and went back to work.

On the way back to the house, Kate told Marie, "I enjoy having you here. Sometimes I miss having a woman around to talk to. You're good company."

"I like it out here. I love the mountains that surround this valley. We can't see anything but mountains on any side except to the west. I think we could see the Wyoming Range if there weren't a few hills between here and there."

"I know," Kate responded. "I like seeing the sun come up over the mountain here and then being able to see sunsets way over there," she said, pointing. "I feel very blessed to live in such a beautiful spot."

"Even with all these mosquitoes?" Marie asked with a wide smile.

"Well, I feel sorry for the horses, having to constantly switch their tails and throw their heads around to fight them off." She slowed for the ditch. "I was complaining about the mosquitoes the other day and Jake said I should just be glad that they leave when it gets cold." She paused then added, "And that comes soon enough. It surprises me when the morning temperatures are between thirty and forty above. Last year, that happened in August. By the way, do you and Don take some time off to get away after haying?"

"We usually go to the other side of the state for a few days. We have a daughter, Kathryn, her husband, and our two grandchildren who live in Sheridan so we like to go there and we also visit my sister in Thermopolis. Kathryn went to the university and met Jason who was from Sheridan. They live on a ranch up there. I'm hoping Brad will settle down closer to home."

They rode along for a while, each in their own thoughts. Kate made a quick laugh.

"Something funny?" Marie asked.

"I was just thinking how you were browning the roast in the kitchen this morning. I usually think of it as my kitchen. Before you came last year Jake told me you don't like someone in the kitchen when you're doing the cooking."

"Does it bother you that I'm in your kitchen?" Marie asked.

"No, it doesn't. You're a wonderful cook. But I couldn't work with some women in my kitchen. Not everyone is as particular about keeping things washed up and having the food ready on time. You and I seem to like things done about the same way."

Marie smiled at Kate. "I have to admit that last year when Jake asked me to cook for your hay crew, I wondered what you would be like."

Kate laughed. "Did Jake tell you I was bossy?"

"No. He told me we'd get along just fine, but he was going to have you work in the field so I'd have the kitchen to myself."

"Little Molly here put a damper on that for this year," Kate replied cheerfully.

"Anyway, you're sure not bossy. I've always liked cooking for hay crews, and you and Jake have made me feel comfortable, even though I have pretty much taken over your kitchen."

Later that afternoon, Marie and Kate worked together to get supper ready for the men. Marie poured a pot of cooked macaroni into a colander while Kate stirred the meat and onions in a cast iron skillet. She added canned tomatoes to the mixture and then set down the mixing spoon. She washed her hands and hung up the towel. "I need to wash a load of diapers, then I'm going to get Molly fed before the crew arrives," Kate said. "Doing the laundry is easy now. I still like to hang the towels and sheets outside, but the diapers are a lot softer when they are dried in the dryer. Not having those two appliances for so long makes me really appreciate the convenience now."

"I know what you mean," Marie said, stirring the goulash.

—•—

The mosquitoes were even fiercer in the evenings. Even so, sometimes Kate left Molly with Marie or Charlie in the house and went to the shop where Jake was grinding sickles for the mowing machines. It was the only time they had to themselves until the day it rained.

For two days, the crew lounged around, napped, or played cards. The rain finally stopped during the afternoon of the second day, but the fields were still too wet the next morning so everyone had to wait another day to put up hay again.

Jake was getting antsy and asked Kate to go with him to Pinedale to the implement store. She was relieved to get a break and in thirty minutes, she was ready with a list of things she needed to buy at the grocery store. She put a few diapers in a sack, picked up Molly, and wrapped a light blanket around her.

On the way out of the ranch they slid around on the muddy road. Jake drove carefully but a couple of times he barely missed going into the ditch.

"This mud is as bad as the snow that got me stuck that day," Kate said.

Jake nodded his head but was too busy to engage in a lot of talk. He gunned the engine to pull out of a deep mud hole and Kate drew in a quick breath and brought her fist to her mouth, making Jake grimace and pinch his lips together.

"Sorry," she said, "I thought sure we were getting stuck."

She was relieved when they reached the graveled county road and the rest was easy going. In town, Jake kept the baby in the truck while Kate shopped for groceries. When he went into the implement store for some parts for the haying machinery, she stayed in the truck with Molly.

A week later, when one of the rakes needed a part, Jake went to the Bunkhouse and asked Kate to go to town for the part he needed. By the time haying was over, she'd gone the eighty-mile round trip for parts three times. The clerks in the stores called her by name and automatically wrote out a charge ticket. On the way home she thought how pleasurable it was getting to know some of the people in town. The time it took and driving so many miles made Kate more aware of how isolated they really were from people and town.

The last time Kate brought home parts for Jake, he met her at the yard gate and looked in the back of the pickup to make sure it was what he needed for the mowing machine. She said the baby was asleep and asked him to take Molly into the house.

He laid Molly in the cradle and slipped out quietly. Kate came from the kitchen where she left the groceries she brought from town. She was carrying two glasses.

"Let's go out on the porch and drink this lemonade Marie made," Kate suggested.

"Okay, I had to come in early so we have a little time before everyone comes for supper."

They sat on the lowest step and sipped the cool drink.

"How was your trip to town?"

"I enjoyed the drive and went to the implement store first. I had to feed Molly before I went to the store for some laundry soap and some fresh fruit and vegetables. At the grocery store, I met Julie that we know from church, and she suggested that we have a Coke so we went to the café and had a nice visit. Molly was good through all that but I had to stop on the way home and nurse her again."

She put on a frown. "Did I sign up for this go-fer job?"

"My love, you signed up to be this rancher's wife and being the go-fer was in the fine print."

"Hmmm, there seems to be a lot of fine print in that contract. You forgot to mention that you have lots of mosquitoes and horse-flies, too." She slapped one of the pests on the back of her hand. "Before I forget, I hope we can get some tall sagebrush growing here before long."

"I guess I signed my contract without reading the fine print that said I had to plant sagebrush in the yard."

"That's right, my love," she said.

Before long they could hear Molly's soft cries. Kate went to tend to her. She sat in the kitchen nursing the baby while Marie cut the bread for supper. "What do you think Jake said when I told him I wanted him to plant some sagebrush in the yard?" she asked.

"I suspect he said something like, 'All that sagebrush out there and you want some in the yard?' Or he told you he's too busy to plant sagebrush and you should do it yourself."

"That's about it. 'For heaven's sake' were his exact words. He said ranchers don't plant sagebrush. They might have to grub it to grow something else, but they don't plant it."

Marie laughed out loud. "I can just hear him expounding about that. My Don probably would have flat out refused to do such a thing."

"He told me that Mary Anne didn't have sagebrush but she had a nice yard. I wonder how she had the time."

"She spent a lot of time with it when I was here in the summers. Like everyone around these parts she missed the lilacs when a frost kept them from blooming. One year she planted a rose bush, but I don't think it ever had a bloom on it. She was always glad to see the wild roses start to bloom in her yard."

"Did they ever plant a garden?" Kate asked.

"They did, but only for root vegetables like carrots and beets. She always had green onions, lettuce, and radishes. They usually had potatoes for late summer and some to put in the cellar for winter."

"My grandmother had a garden and she must have had good soil and a protected spot because she raised those same things. She told me once that she wished she could raise corn and tomatoes, but the season here is way too short for things like that."

———•———

When haying season ended Kate was of two minds; whether she would miss everyone or if she would enjoy peace and quiet. The extra hands had worked hard and even helped Jake and Charlie get the machinery stored for the winter. They always expressed their appreciation for the fine meals and good company. Having Marie around was an added benefit and joy. They had a special steak dinner with ice cream and cookies for dessert for their last meal together.

"I'm sure glad you got that fancy refrigerator with a freezer section," Charlie said to Kate. "I do like ice cream."

While saying goodbye to Marie and Don and the rest of the crew, Kate suspected that she was going to miss all of them. On the other hand, the prospect of having Jake, Charlie, and Molly the only kindred spirits in her midst was the kind of contentment she looked forward to.

The morning after the crew left, Kate brought up the unwanted subject of planting sagebrush in the yard.

Jake raised an eyebrow. "Why don't you just walk out on the prairie . . ."

"I was wonderin' when you'd get around to that again," Charlie said quietly.

"What will she think of next?" Jake asked rhetorically.

Charlie scratched his ear. "I don't know, but she did say somethin' about fixing up that old cabin on the other side of the barn."

Kate stifled a laugh. "It was in the fine print, if you read that part."

"I don't think I should have ever said anything about fine print in our marriage vows. It gets me in a lot of trouble."

"But you did say, 'I do,'" Charlie said to Jake with a sideways glance.

"I know."

The next day, Jake came in with some sagebrush planted in a big galvanized tub. He set it down in the living room and said to Kate, "Okay, you keep this in the house all winter and if it grows, I'll plant it outside next spring."

"Will it grow like that?" Kate asked skeptically.

"I don't know. I never planted sagebrush before."

"Thank you," Kate gushed and gave him a kiss.

"What I won't do for a kiss," he said wryly. "Life used to be so quiet and peaceful around here."

"Won't it be nice to have that tangy odor in the house now?"

"You better still like the smell of sagebrush by spring," he retorted. "I think it will be more pungent than tangy. I can smell it already." With that, he headed for the door.

Soon afterwards, Jake and Kate, toting Molly, went to Jackson for an overnight stay to have their medical checkups and to do some shopping. Kate was looking at toasters in the small appliances section of the general store. Jake called to her down the aisle, "Do you want one of these coffee pots, a percolator or whatever they're called?"

"No thanks. That is, unless you do. For myself, I prefer our cowboy coffee."

"Suits me," he answered.

They moved on to choose an electric iron and put it in their cart. Then Kate looked over the selection of mixers and finally settled on a Sunbeam Mixmaster. "I know these glass bowls are all right, but I'd rather have stainless steel bowls," she said.

"Get metal bowls, too, if you want some."

They ended up with a hand mixer and three lamps added to their purchases.

"That's enough for now," Kate said, tired of shopping.

"What about the toaster?"

"Since you're standing in front of them, pick one. They all look about the same."

"This says it can be set for light to dark toast and the toast will pop up when it's ready," he said, reading about it on the box. "Isn't that what a toaster is supposed to do? Do you want the white one or the black one?"

"White, please."

He set it in the cart among the rest of the appliances.

They paid the bill and loaded everything in the back of the pickup.

On the way home, Jake asked teasingly, "Have you noticed that pungent smell in the house lately? I think it's coming from sage-brush."

Kate nodded and replied, "It's nice, isn't it?"

"It's pretty strong."

# Chapter Twenty-Two

**Having** the new appliances gave Kate time for reading, sewing, or crocheting an afghan or two for Christmas presents. On most days she did laundry in the mornings and crocheted in the afternoons while Molly was asleep. By suppertime she had put sheets back on the beds and had the towels and baby clothes folded and put away.

"It's sure nice to settle down to a routine again," Kate told Jake.

"You don't have the routine you're used to, but that's the trade-off, I guess."

"You're right, I don't know why I said that." She took hold of Molly's tiny hand where the baby was perched in a little seat they had placed on the table. They liked having her with them while they ate. Her constant cooing and playing kept them entertained.

Later, Kate and Jake got comfortable on the couch in front of the fireplace. "Will the cows be down soon?" she asked.

"I haven't seen any sign of snow, not even in the mountains. I think we'll go gather them pretty soon. I'm sure the Forest Service will want them off since it's so dry." He coiled a strand of her hair around his finger.

"It's early, isn't it?"

"Earlier than usual but a lot depends on the weather. I wish you could go along to bring the cattle home. But, you've found yourself another job."

"I like my new job. Someday I'll get to go with you again." She snuggled up next to Jake.

"I wonder how your mother and Grayson are making out. Do you suppose he's had a lucky streak and they're up again?"

"I doubt we'll ever know. She isn't apt to get in touch a second time, and I'm almost positive that he won't come around unless he's found another occupation."

"It's good you've got a sense of humor about it all. Hindsight is 20/20 or something like that."

"I feel sorry for them. They're missing the important things in life. My parents were married in the church but she never became a Catholic."

"They don't seem much like church-going people, which reminds me, we'll go to Mass on Sunday."

"I hope we can go for a few weeks yet, with the snow so slow coming."

———•———

By Thanksgiving there had been only one snowstorm, leaving just a few inches of powder. One day in the middle of December as the men were coming in from doing chores, Charlie asked Jake, "Do you suppose this is a natural cycle? I sure thought we'd have a foot or more by now. I can hardly believe we're still feeding with a wagon and that the cattle can still graze. It makes feeding easier but I'd hate to see a winter with no more snow than this."

"I don't think the mountains are getting much either. If this holds out, there'll be no irrigating water next summer."

"That's not a happy thought," Kate piped up.

"At least this weather will make it easier to get a tree. Do you and Molly want to go along tomorrow?"

"Yes, I can dress her warm enough."

Molly flapped her little arms.

Charlie let out a chortle. "I think she's trying to tell us she wants to go."

The following day was sunny and a little warmer than it had been all week. After the cattle were fed they went to bring in a tree. Because there wasn't much snow, Charlie was able to drive the horses deeper into the woods.

Jake jumped off the wagon. "I think this one will do," he said, starting for his axe.

Kate shook her head. "The branches are too ragged on the side of that one. We need a special tree for Molly's first Christmas."

"Alright, let's keep lookin' then."

The one they chose was smaller than they'd had before but it was perfectly formed, and Jake cut it down with ease. They headed back to the Bunkhouse for a later than usual dinner.

When the tree was set up that evening, everyone was too tired to do any decorating. By dinner the next day Kate hadn't made much headway with it either. She had the decorations out and realized they had forgotten to buy lights for the tree this year. When she mentioned that to Jake, he told her they weren't used to Christmas lights anyway.

Molly's presents took up most of the space around the bottom of the tree. After the gifts were opened on Christmas Eve, Kate took a look through the assortment of clothes that Mother McClary and Mary Anne had sent.

"She didn't pay much attention to all those toys and clothes," Charlie commented. "I don't think she even cares that you got her a snowsuit and boots. What she liked best were the boxes and wrapping paper."

"Yeah, just think of all the money we could have saved," Jake kidded.

"She'll grow out of some of them pretty fast, but we won't have to buy clothes for her for a few months," Kate said. She held up the tiny denims Charlie had found for Molly. "These little Levi's are darling. Who would have thought they made them so small. They might not fit for a while, but she'll wear the warm pajamas right away. Thanks, Charlie."

By tradition, Charlie read the Christmas story. By the time he finished, Molly had fallen asleep so Jake put her in her crib. Kate went to the piano, Jake tuned his guitar, and they sang Christmas carols until Molly woke up fussing and hungry.

Jake reported that it was twenty below already and went to put more wood on the fire. Everyone went to bed, contented with their good life, and happy that they had spent Molly's very first Christmas together.

———◆———

By the end of January, twenty-four inches of snow had fallen, nowhere near the usual amount. Jake and Charlie were becoming increasingly concerned. By calving time there still wasn't a lot of snow, which made the routine of checking the cows day and night a bit easier for them.

They were already weary from all the feeding, calving, and chores when three of their calves needed treatment for scours. Jake, who had anticipated the possibility of the disease, was prepared with the medicine and kept each cow and her calf in a stall where they could watch their feeding and treat them. Quickly, they got the calves well and taking their mothers' milk again.

Finally a big snowstorm in the middle of May put down two feet of wet snow. Even though it began to melt soon, the moisture was a boon to the lack of water. Kate was worried about the shortage of hay, but Jake assured her they had enough left from the previous winter to tide them over the next winter even if hay was short. His words eased her concern until she overheard him telling Charlie that he'd hate to sell down the herd. They'd just have to wait and see.

With branding season on the horizon, Kate felt pressured to be getting through with her spring cleaning. "When will we brand?" she finally asked Jake.

"We'll be last again this year, but the Petersons want this Saturday. Do you want to go?"

"Sure, I'll be glad to see the ladies again. I'll call Jackie and see if I can take anything."

When it came time to brand at the McClary ranch, their calves were big and healthy. The year before, when Rick and Carl left at the end of haying season, they asked if they could come to help out when Jake had his branding. Everyone was glad to see them. Strong as the two young men were, they had their hands full wrestling the big calves. One kicked Rick rather hard, giving him a limp for a while.

The neighbor women brought salads and desserts. Kate had the rolls in the pans by the time they got there and everything else was done except the last minute cutting of the roast, which Jake would do.

After branding was over and the crew left, Kate said to Jake, "I guess you'll be cooking Rocky Mountain oysters for breakfast in the morning, huh?"

"Only if you'll help me," he replied, knowing full well she wasn't about to.

"Well, what's next around here then?" Kate asked.

"Cliff is coming to shoe the saddle horses on Tuesday. Then Brad's coming to help drag the meadows. Charlie and I will irrigate with what water we can get. The creeks are full now so we need to use it while we can."

Before long, it was time to turn the cattle out on the desert. Kate watched the men drive them down the lane while Buster kept any stragglers together with the herd. Wistfully, she longed to go with them.

At supper that evening, Charlie told Kate, "I'm glad there was a little green grass showing up out there. That snowstorm sure helped and the rain last week didn't hurt either."

The fifteenth of June was a bright sunny day and Molly had been toddling around the house for the last couple of weeks. Kate gathered the ingredients to make a birthday cake and was ready to mix the shortening and sugar when she realized it would be easier using the mixer. She was so used to doing such things by hand that she often forgot to use one of her handy appliances. Today, the noise of the mixer brought Molly to the kitchen to investigate and she was underfoot until she was ready to play again.

"Hey, Molly," Jake called to her after he dumped an armload of kindling in the wood box. She looked up from some blocks and put her arms up for him to pick her up. "Come see what Mama made for you," he said.

Molly squealed with delight when she saw the frosted cake decorated with sprinkles and one candle in the middle of it. After they'd eaten supper and Kate put a piece of cake on her highchair, Molly made crumbs of the whole thing and only took a couple of bites of her first birthday cake.

Kate asked about the irrigating.

"We don't have the water we usually do but it's shaping up better than I thought," Jake said. "Can't say I mind an easy winter now and then but we sure needed more snow than we got last winter."

"Grandpa always said ranching is a gamble. Good years and bad years, good prices or poor pay for good cows."

"How do you remember all that?" Charlie asked.

"My grandpa was a wise man and he was always telling me things about ranch life. Grandma taught me how she kept her man happy. I had good teachers."

"Apparently you were a good student," Jake said. "Look how happy you're keeping me."

"Katie, you've learned the ways of being a rancher and adapted to a whole new way of life," Charlie said. "It must be a lot different than what you knew back in Kansas City. Jake and I are both proud of you."

"I knew you would learn to love this life, but you were so danged slow about signing up for this job," Jake said.

"Don't be a wise guy. If it weren't for Charlie I might still be a nurse back in Jackson and you'd still be a miserable something or other. It's a good thing Charlie scared us like he did. It made us both realize what we really wanted."

"Maybe that's what they mean when they say love is blind." Charlie stood up to clear the table. "I was beginning to think you both needed glasses."

Molly, who up until now had been playing with her cake, cooed "Dada." She had spilled her milk and had the milk and cake in a glob.

Kate washed Molly's hands and swiped at her face as Molly tried to avoid the wet rag. When Kate decided she had most of the goop off, she took off Molly's bib and lifted her from her high chair. "What a mess you've made," Kate said, pretending to scold.

Molly wobbled toward Jake who was holding out his arms to her.

"She'll be walking better any day now," Kate said with a mother's pride in her voice. Later, Molly's new doll and a cuddly teddy bear kept her occupied while the grownups finished the day's work.

———•———

Brad arrived at the ranch soon after he got home from college. He couldn't believe how much Molly had grown and would have taken her from Kate but she clouded up when she saw this stranger coming close.

"It'll take a while but she'll get used to you," Kate said. "Jake told me your folks would be coming before long. I'm anxious to see them."

"They're looking forward to getting here and seeing the baby, too."

Kate was in the yard with Jake when they spotted two trucks coming down the lane. Each one carried a tractor. "Are those yours?" she asked.

"They're ours, partner. We'll use these two for mowing and another small Cat is coming for the plunger."

"Cat?"

"Caterpillar," he grinned. "I hope we can manage to get tractors for the rakes and sweeps by next year. Until then, I'm glad we still have hands that can drive horses." He walked out to where the two trucks had pulled up, with the drivers waiting for instructions on where to unload.

She wasn't surprised to learn that Charlie knew about the tractors. But something was bothering her and she didn't say ten words during supper or while they did up the dishes.

Kate found Jake reading in the living room after she put Molly to bed.

"Come here and sit down," he motioned.

She sat stiffly next to him.

"What's the matter? You've been tightlipped all afternoon."

Kate looked up to the mantle. "I'm mad because you won't buy the machinery you need. Everyone in the county is using tractors to put up the hay. They even feed with tractors."

Jake opened his mouth to speak but Kate cut him off.

"*We* have plenty of money and you're too stubborn to use it. You say I'm a partner, but you sure don't treat me like one. Your pride won't let you accept the money I've already given for this ranch."

"I guess you're right, it's just that . . ."

Kate was on a roll. "I can't believe it. You do without things you need when you could make things easier for the men if you'd just buy it. It's foolish for us not to be using the money my family gave me."

"As the head of the family it's my job to provide for you and Molly. I'm not used to taking money from a woman."

"Well, get used to it."

Jake put up his hands. "All right, all right. But it's too late to buy more machinery this year. To tell the truth, I like using horses but come next spring you and I will go buy tractors and whatever else you think we need."

"You can start with buying a snowplow this fall."

Jake shook his head in amazement. "What made you think of that?"

"You work darn hard to open the road for us and when it gets to be too much you have to quit. I can barely take watching you."

"Yeah, it's something I've thought about a lot. But it would take a very big plow to keep our road open all winter, not to mention the time it would take to clear the road." When she didn't say anything, he added, "We might have to build us a bigger barn one of these days to put all this equipment in. Are you satisfied?"

Kate gave him one of her Cheshire cat grins.

---

Jake came in the next day from irrigating and found Kate folding diapers in the laundry room. "We won't start haying for a couple of weeks. This would be a good time for us to get away for a few days."

"Get away? I can hardly believe my ears."

"Charlie and Brad can take care of everything. Besides, Don and Marie should be here tomorrow or the next day."

"Where are we going?"

"I want to see the folks. Dad seems to be doing good, but Mom doesn't want to leave him alone to come here and they both want to see Molly."

"That's great. When do we leave?"

"Tomorrow."

"Tomorrow? It doesn't give me much time to get ready."

"It's warm there so you won't need much."

"I suppose I have a few summer clothes. I haven't worn short sleeves and shorts since I moved in with mosquitoes. At least you're easy, since you wear pretty much the same thing all year. We can buy you some shorts when we get there."

"I don't think so," he said wryly.

Naturally she knew her rancher husband wouldn't be caught dead in a pair of shorts.

# Chapter Twenty-Three

**Jake finished** changing the oil on Kate's Buick just as Marie and Don were driving up the road in their pickup. Kate came out with Molly and suitcases in tow.

"I'm glad you got here before we left," Kate told Marie. "We'll be gone about a week so if you need anything in the way of food supplies, send Brad or Charlie to the grocery store in Pinedale where we've got a charge account for the ranch."

"I doubt I'll need anything. There's always plenty around here. Have a good time and give Maureen and Dan our best." Marie bent down and patted Molly's cheek. "Bye, bye, sweetheart."

Jake had washed up while Kate was getting Molly settled in the back seat of the car. He loaded up the trunk and then came around to the front. "I hope you have some room in here, the trunk is packed and I can hardly shut the door. Do we really need to take all this stuff?"

"'Fraid so. I'm sure we'll use all of Molly's things and I put in everything you and I might need."

"A razor, toothbrush, and a change of clothes are enough for me."

"We need overnight bags if we're going to stay in a motel going down and coming back. It'll be enough having to wash diapers while we're on the road."

"Just don't buy anything while we're gone. We won't have room for one more toy."

"Yes, Mast..." Kate began and quickly took it back at his scowl. As they turned onto the county road, Kate heaved a sigh. "I hope I remembered everything."

They made a stop in Rock Springs where Jake had reluctantly agreed to take some money out of Kate's savings account for their trip. Molly fussed at lunch because Kate insisted on spoon-feeding her. Neither she nor Jake had the patience to let her feed herself and make a mess.

By the time they checked into a motel in southern Utah, they were done in.

"I'll go get us hamburgers at a drive-in," Jake offered. "I'm not too crazy about taking Molly to a restaurant again."

"That's fine with me. I've got some baby food with us." Molly was used to food Kate cooked and mashed up for her, so getting her to eat the Gerber's was a challenge. At last, they got Molly situated in the bed between them and she slept through the night. Jake was up by five and they were on their way after a quick breakfast.

When they arrived in Phoenix, Mother McClary met them at her apartment door. She was delighted to see them and marveled at how her granddaughter was growing. "We must get over to see Grandpa so he can get to know Molly," she said. "He doesn't look forward to much these days but he really perked up when I told him you all were coming."

Kate offered to help with supper before they headed out.

"Mix this salad and we'll be ready. I've put together a simple casserole. I don't cook much anymore and I miss having milk and cream like we had on the ranch."

They ate hurriedly and were on their way in no time.

Maureen sat in the back seat with Molly. "Your coming means a lot to Dad and me, especially with how busy you are," she said.

"We know," Jake told her, glancing at his mother in the rear view mirror. "It means a lot to us, too."

"Molly is growing fast and we want her to get to know her grandparents," Kate said. "It's a priority for us."

Molly let out a loud and happy shriek.

"I swear she knows what we're talking about," Jake said.

They found Jake's dad in his room at the nursing home. Kate caught the look on Jake's face when he saw how his dad's health had deteriorated. Dan had been a strong and handsome man and now he appeared emaciated and weak. It hit Jake hard but he quickly greeted his father and introduced his daughter to him. Dan McClary's eyes lit up and became as wide as saucers when he took Molly into his arms. She took to him right away and let him hold her all the while they visited. The watch he wore absorbed her attention for the most part. She fiddled with it until he took it off and gave it to her to play with. When she became bored with that they played her favorite game.

Jake asked her what a cat says. "Meow, meow," she answered right away. They went through all the animals she knew, but the big surprise came when she pointed at her grandpa and grandma and called them by those names. When the clock struck ten, Molly was fast asleep in her grandfather's arms. He reluctantly handed her over to Jake and asked them to come back in the morning.

"You can't imagine what good that did for Dad," Maureen said as they rode back to her place. "He hasn't been that excited about anything for a long time."

"I think we wore him out, though," Jake said.

Kate agreed. "We need to watch that Molly doesn't get him too tired out."

"You need to spend as much time with him as you can. It's given him such a lift," Maureen said.

Although Maureen wanted Jake and Kate to do some sightseeing in Phoenix and offered to baby-sit Molly, they said they'd prefer to spend their time with Dan and her. From her smile, they could see that she was pleased. At naptime, Maureen rocked the baby, talking softly until Molly fell asleep, and then held her while she slept.

After three days, it was time for the long ride home. "Your mother treats me like a daughter," Kate said after they'd gotten underway. "She's what a mother should be."

"The kind of mother you are," Jake said quickly.

"She reminds me of my grandmother. Kind and thoughtful."

"I guess you got the message that Mom and Dad highly approve of our marriage." Jake's eyes were on the road, but there was no mistaking his teasing when he added, "She's told me a half dozen times how glad she is that I found you. Of course, I reminded her that you found me, you lucky girl."

"Not on purpose, you know," Kate replied, poking him in the ribs.

———•———

Jake and Kate took one look at Don and knew something was wrong. "What's the matter, Don?" Jake asked, as they carried the suitcases into the Bunkhouse.

"Charlie's sick. He has a fever and is aching all over. He said he'd had a bad tick bite not long ago. He might have tick fever, but we couldn't get him to go to the doctor. Maybe you can convince him."

Kate left Molly in the kitchen with Marie and went straight to Charlie's room. He gave her a weak smile and tried to return her squeeze when she took his hand. "Oh, Charlie, I'm sorry to see you feeling like this. I'll be back in a minute."

From the black doctor's bag she had stored in a closet, Kate found a thermometer and blood pressure cuff. She went back to Charlie's room and took his vital signs. "You're going to a doctor first thing in the morning."

"I don't think that's really necessary," he protested.

She gave him a stern look. "In the meantime, I'm going to try to get that fever down. You've probably had the chills, right?"

He nodded weakly.

"Have you had anything to eat?" she asked.

"A little soup, but I'm not hungry."

Kate gave him a sip of water and told him to rest.

Early the next morning Kate and Jake took Charlie to the doctor in Pinedale while Marie looked after Molly.

Charlie was lying on the exam table when the doctor delivered the news. "You have tick fever and you'll have to go to the hospital."

The three of them left for Jackson right away. It was dusk by the time they got him settled in a room. They hemmed and hawed about nothing until Charlie told them to get on their way and to watch out for animals along the road."

He didn't sound much better when Kate called the next morning. By the third day, he was sounding more like himself and said that the doctor told him he might be able to go home the next day. "I sure hate to put you to all this trouble. I should be home helping get ready for haying."

"Hush, Charlie, you just need to get well. We'll be glad to get you back home but you're going to stay in the house until you feel good again. Brad and Don are here to help Jake and they're taking care of everything."

"I don't feel of much use lately," he confided to Kate.

"Don't worry, we'll put you back to work. We miss you around here."

"I feel better already, just for hearin' that."

"I'll check in the morning to make sure you're being discharged, then Jake and I will be up to get you."

When Jake came in for dinner, Kate told him what she had learned. "I hope you can go tomorrow but if you can't, I'll go get him."

"I'll go. If you and Molly want to go, too, that's fine by me. But if you have things to do here, I can go alone."

"No, I want to go. We can get some fresh fruit and vegetables at the store while we're at it."

Charlie was in his room, dressed and waiting for them. He protested loudly when a nurse insisted that he had to ride to the car in a wheelchair.

"Hospital policy," she said firmly.

"Wait till my horse hears about this," he told her.

Jake and Kate cracked smiles, but the nurse was dead serious.

Back at the Bunkhouse everyone was glad to see him. Even as pale and weak as he was, Charlie was in a jovial mood. "I guess it does a man good to find out you can't take care of this place without me," he said.

Kate made it clear that he was to rest up a few more days to be sure he didn't have a setback.

Haying started in earnest the last week in July and once again Kate longed to be in the field. Her only compensation was that she and Marie got to take dinner to the men when they were in the far fields. The crew teased Jake and Carl about having things soft, riding on a tractor.

Rick had a summer job in town and had suggested that Jake hire Derek, a junior in high school who lived in Pinedale. Jake was a bit skeptical because Derek had never driven a team before but decided to give the boy a job. The first thing Kate noticed about Derek was his hair. It was almost down to his shoulders and straggly looking, she decided.

Derek talked a lot about things he watched on TV, which kept Jake wondering what kind of a hand he had hired. But Derek put in three good days of raking before he had a runaway. Don was closest to Derek, who had fallen from the rake and was able to get to him. Don had Derek hold his own team on the sweep while he caught the runaways. Once Don had the team calmed down, Derek was able to get back to raking.

It turned out Derek was okay. Everyone expressed relief at supper.

"You wouldn't think they'd spook just because a little ol' rabbit ran out in front of 'em, but that's what happened," Derek said, amused.

By the last week in August haying was nearly finished.

"The hay was short, but we'll get by," Jake told Kate one night in bed. He pulled her close. "Luckily I know a lady who will lend me some money if I have to buy some hay."

"Quit that. If you have to buy hay, *we* have some money. That money is ours, not mine."

"Whoa, I'm just teasing you. We shouldn't have to buy hay anyhow. When we ship the steers, we'll have enough money."

"Thanks for telling me. A partner should know these things."

"The ranch is doing okay and my credit is good if we need to borrow money. I hate to use your money." He held up his hand to stem a protest. "I mean our money, but that ought to be for an emergency or for Molly going to college. I'm supposed to be taking care of you."

"I think the problem is that you can't accept money you haven't earned. Right?"

"Well, I guess if you want to analyze it like that, you're probably right."

"For gosh sakes, I only wish you'd remember that we're partners. Can you try?"

"I'll try," he said, nuzzling her neck. "Could you get closer?" he whispered.

"Not hardly," she whispered back.

# Chapter Twenty-Four

**Charlie** wasn't a complainer, yet Kate and Jake saw how tired he was by evening. The hay hands had the machinery stored and were leaving when Charlie told Kate, "I hate to see everyone leave 'cause we have a good crew. Now that they're leaving maybe I can do something useful around here."

"We're not worried about you not working," Kate said lightly. "We think you want to work too much. Everything is in good shape and maybe if you'd play Grandpa more, I could help Jake with some of the work. In fact, Molly is on the floor in the living room putting together one of her puzzles. Why don't you go sit in the rocker and keep an eye on her while I hang some clothes on the line?"

"Sure, I'll do that. Of course, I know what you and Jake are up to—giving me such easy jobs. Really, I'm feeling fine and I need to earn my keep around here. I haven't brought in a load of kindling all summer."

"You worked all during haying. You ought to rest while you can."

"Driving the cat on the plunger wasn't much work. I'll go check on Molly so you can get your laundry on the line."

"Thanks, Charlie."

When Kate finished, she looked in on Charlie and Molly. They were on the couch, both asleep and with a book about to fall off Charlie's lap. She smiled to herself and sat down in the rocker to enjoy the peace and quiet.

That evening, she was doing the supper dishes with Jake when she asked, "Do you think Brad will come back again? He's a senior this year."

"He'd like to, but he wants to go to vet school so he might be in school or working for a veterinarian next summer."

"He loves ranch life so much. I wish he could afford a ranch of his own."

"I'm sure he would be the best ranchhand that anyone could find but he'd want something of his own. Owning a ranch probably seems impossible for him. Maybe that's why he has decided to become a veterinarian. He loves animals, that's for sure."

Molly began crying from the living room where she was playing with her toys. "I hear your toddler calling you," Jake said.

"She's calling you, I can tell. How come she's mine when she cries and yours when she's happy?"

"That's the way kids are," he answered.

"I know, but right now she's calling you because I have to get the clothes off the line." Kate went for the clothes basket and Jake went to check on Molly who had dropped her doll behind the small sofa. She stopped crying when she saw her dad. He retrieved her doll and she was happy again.

———•———

Checking fences, mending harnesses, and going for firewood kept Jake and Charlie busy before the cattle needed to be brought back to the ranch. On the day they went to town for a load of grain, Kate made a list of groceries and other necessities they needed. Jake added to her list then showed her the last item.

"A radio?"

"Let's look for one of those machines that play eight-track tapes or whatever they're called."

"Oh my, aren't we getting uptown," she said wryly. She took the list from him and wrote down something else.

She wasn't surprised at his answer. "Snowplow? I don't think we'll have time to see about that today."

They bought groceries and other essentials then put everything in the truck.

"We should have left Molly home with Charlie. I spent half the time trying to keep track of her," Jake said.

It didn't take long to buy the radio and an eight-track player because there wasn't a large selection at the hardware store. On the way home, Kate said, "I hope we can get good reception on the radio. Have you ever tried one out here?"

"No, I haven't. Jesse had one, though. I remember him saying that the ranch seemed to be in line with a transmitter or airwaves or something."

"That's good. I almost suggested that we get one of those TVs in the store but then I thought we'd better see how the radio works first."

Jake cast a glance her way. "I hear there are some good westerns on the TV, but I'm not sure we want to know what else is going on in the world. I was reading in the paper the other day about all those hippies showing up in Jackson. Seems pretty strange to me."

"Mary Anne sees them in the park, playing their guitars. They dress different is all, and wear lots of beads and stuff," Kate said. "And believe in free love, whatever that means."

Jake laughed. "You ought to know what it means. Yours is free."

"That's not what hippies call free love and you know it," Kate retorted.

⸻ ◆ ⸻

Molly had fallen asleep on the way home. Getting her into her pajamas didn't keep her from going right back to sleep. Kate spent most of the next day organizing and putting things away. She'd been skeptical about the radio but Jake had tried it first thing when they got home the evening before and Kate listened to music and news all morning. She turned it off just before the men came in for dinner. When Jake asked if she'd tried the radio, she replied, "I had it on most of the morning but to tell the truth, I find the noise distracting. I guess I'm used to the silence around here and I never listened to one when I lived in the city. But," she added, "I think we will want to hear what is going on in the world."

"Maybe," was his only comment.

When it came time for roundup, Kate watched Jake and Charlie ride off to the mountains. Late September snow had started the old cows down the trail and most of the younger stock followed. Gathering the cattle and separating their cows from those of the other ranchers took several days. There was some back riding to do and one morning Jake insisted that Charlie take care of things at home while he went to look for strays.

By three o'clock that afternoon, Kate started to worry. Charlie had been splitting kindling. He came in with an armload and dumped the wood into the wood box, then found Kate in the living room where she was reading a book to Molly.

"I think I'll ride up the trail and see if Jake needs some help." He went out before she could stop him, but what he said had her even more frightened. The thought that they might not get back before dark filled her with anxiety.

At four-thirty she bundled herself and Molly in warm coats and went to gather the eggs. She turned the calf in with the milk cow so they wouldn't have to milk when they got back. Kate was in a real state of panic when the men weren't back by dark. She imagined the worst and put their supper in the warming oven, worrying that it wouldn't be fit to eat. When she finally heard them come in the mudroom door, she rushed out to find out what had happened.

"I was sick with worry. How did you get home in the dark?" she asked anxiously.

"The horses knew how to get here. Charlie met up with me about where we saw those elk that time and helped me move the cows down to the creek. We left them there so I'll go back in the morning. There were twenty-two head in a clearing where they had to come through a draw full of snow to get to the trail. It was slow going trying to get them to fight the snow through the draw, and it took quite a while to get them started home."

Kate put their supper on the table and after he ate his, Charlie went off to bed. Jake finished eating and poured a second cup of tea for himself. "Sorry to worry you, but there wasn't any way to let you know what was going on."

"All I could think of was that something had happened to you and then when Charlie went out, I was beside myself."

"All's well that ends well," Jake said nonchalantly, trying to ease her anxiety. "Just remember that I try to be careful."

The next day they had all the cows home and in the meadows.

Calves bawling in the weaning corral made Kate think about a calf she had helped Jake pull last spring. He was a big calf even then. She asked Jake if that calf would be going to market.

"No, we'll keep him with the others that we'll ship next fall. I bet he'll weigh over 550 pounds though. He had a good mama and he grew like a weed."

"I think I saw that calf in the corral the other day," Kate said. "I could see he was the biggest one there, if that's the same one."

"He's the same one."

"How do you know that? There's so many of them."

Jake shrugged. "They're like people. They've got their own look and sometimes their own personality, or cowality.

"Cowality?"

"Well, that's what I like to call it."

"I don't think that's a word but it fits so I'll let you by with it. But don't try to use it in Scrabble because I'll challenge you on it."

"Sure thing, but now I've got to go do the milking. So keep that thought for our next game."

Jake took the snowplow off the front of the truck then attached it to the Caterpillar and kept the yard plowed. He even managed to get through the lane with it. They shipped the cattle and went to town for winter supplies. By Thanksgiving they still used one team on the sled. When the men came in on Thanksgiving Day,

Kate said, "I wish one of you would get Molly out of my way. She keeps climbing on a chair and getting into things."

Molly didn't like the turkey but the mashed potatoes and gravy went down well. Also the Jell-O and candied yams. She was feeding herself well by now so when she wanted more of the sweet yams, Charlie dished up a small serving for her.

"Tanks, Gra-pa," she said, warming his heart.

Jake helped clear the table and then washed the dishes while Kate put the leftovers in the refrigerator.

"I think Molly needs a nap. Would you mind putting her down?"

"She and Charlie are playing in the other room. She won't like it if I take her away from him."

"You don't mind taking those baby calves away from their mamas. This is easier."

"Well, Molly likes me better than those calves do, you know."

Molly and Charlie were trying to keep a top spinning. She was tiring of the play and let Jake pick her up. "Let's go take a nap, pumpkin."

"No, Gra-pa," she shrieked.

"That's okay, sweetheart," Charlie said. "Grandpa's going to take a nap, too."

After they left the living room, Kate came in and picked up a book she'd been reading, but her mind wasn't on the story. For the last two weeks, she suspected she was pregnant again. A week or so later when she was certain that they were going to have a baby, she told Jake one evening just before he went out to milk the cow.

He caught her in a bear hug. "Make it a boy this time, okay?"

"If it's a boy, you made this baby a boy," she told him. "If it's a girl, that's your doing, too, you know."

"Whatever. The rest is your job."

"You'd better move. I'm making soup and some food makes me want to throw up."

Jake stepped back. "Just one thing you need to know. I'm not delivering this baby in the car," he said emphatically.

"You did okay the last time."

"I didn't have a choice with Molly but this time you're going to town before you go into labor."

"I'll try to remember that."

He kissed her on the nose. "Time for me to go see Mrs. Cowley."

After Jake left, Kate realized that it was all too quiet in the house. She left the soup simmering and went to see what Molly was up to. She found her sitting on the floor in the living room looking at a book she knew by heart after hearing it so many times. Kate sat in the rocker and watched her a while. Kate offered a silent prayer, thanking God for her good husband, their child, and the one to come.

Jake came rushing in after having been to the barn. "Kate, you need to go to the doctor. The road is passable but another snowstorm is coming and we're probably going to be snowed in."

"I'll call the doctor and get an appointment while we can still get out," she replied calmly. "I can ask him to prescribe some vitamins to get me through the winter."

The expression of dismay on Jake's face gave him an ashen look.

"I'm fine. I hardly have any morning sickness, and I can check blood pressure and heart rate right along. I'm sure we don't need to worry about it. You know, women have been having . . ."

"Babies since Adam and Eve. I know, you told me that before. I'm just worried about not getting out if something goes wrong."

"Don't borrow trouble, okay? You can always ski out and pull me on the toboggan. Doesn't that sound like fun?"

"Not really." He shook his head and went to do the separating.

The appointment was set for the day after tomorrow. Jake was relieved he wouldn't have to plow again for them to get out of the lane. They made the trip and got back home just in time. Had they waited any longer they wouldn't have gotten out, even with the snowplow on the Cat.

———•———

It was a hard winter from then on, but they'd been through hard winters before. Kate kept assuring Jake that she, Molly, and the expected baby were fine. In frequent phone calls to his mom, he gave blow-by-blow details of the developments.

When Kate had a chance to speak, she'd say, "It's the same as last time, Mom. They hardly let me do anything."

"Personally I'm glad Jake and Charlie are taking good care of you. It worries me too that you're snowed in and not under the doctor's care."

"I call him regularly and report everything so that isn't a problem, at least for me. You taught Jake well. He thinks just like you do," she said. "Give Dad our love," she always added before hanging up.

"Have you noticed?" Jake said one night as Kate was crawling into bed. "Molly chatters all the time and I only get about half of what she says, usually when she wants something."

"It isn't fair that she says daddy more than mommy, but I know why that happens."

"Oh?"

"Yes, you and Charlie give her everything she wants. I'm the one who has to discipline. You don't have to wash a mark off the wall or scold when she scatters her toys all over the place."

"I wonder how she'll react to a new baby."

"I don't know firsthand, but I've heard some children can be jealous when a new baby is born. I've also heard there are some who want to hold the baby a lot. I guess we'll just have to wait and see about Molly."

"I just thought of something," Jake said.

"What?" Kate said and yawned.

"You're going to have the baby at haying time. You know we don't have time during haying to be having a baby," he said half seriously.

"Well, you said that last time, too."

"I know, but Molly came early. She was due in July. This one is due in August so this baby is sure to come during haying."

"Like I said before, maybe it'll rain and you'll have the day off."

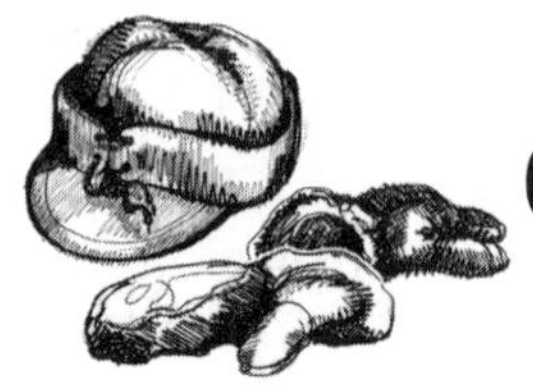

# Chapter Twenty-Five

**Christmas** in the winter of 1961 took on a new meaning for Charlie and the McClarys simply because Molly was curious about the decorated tree in the living room and she figured something special was going on. She had already opened one package from under the tree when Kate interrupted her baking to check on Molly one morning. Kate scolded but she also let Molly help rewrap Jake's shirt in a box. "Daddy will be so happy to see that you wrapped his package," she said, while watching Molly tape and re-tape the patched up wrapping paper.

Kate told Jake later that it was a full-time job keeping Molly from exploring all the packages and "accidentally" getting one open. Kate had ordered a Kodak from the Montgomery Ward catalog and when Christmas Eve arrived she took an entire roll of film, mostly of eighteen-month-old Molly squealing with delight as she opened each new package that brought forth a toy. Molly blithely tossed aside the clothes, but held tightly onto the doll that Charlie had given her as she sat on his lap while he read his favorite Christmas story to everyone.

When Molly was finally put to bed on Christmas Eve she suspected something was up. She'd seen her daddy open the phonograph and look for records in the shelves in the lower doors. As soon as they thought she was asleep, Jake turned the handle on the phonograph and started playing a waltz.

"Would you care to dance?" he asked Kate, extending his hand to help her up from where she was sitting in front of the fireplace.

"Keep the *Tennessee Waltz* record handy," Charlie said. "We won't let you get tired, but I sure would like a waltz or two."

"I'd be honored," Kate replied.

They stepped into the one, two, three rhythm with the ease that came with the practice they'd had doing those steps.

With a gentle squeeze, Jake released Kate as the music came to an end. Charlie caught their eye and gave a slight nod toward the bedroom. With a grin on his face and shaking his head, Jake went up the two steps to the landing. He picked up Molly and told Kate to wind up the phonograph again. Molly looked adoringly at her dad as he waltzed her around the room.

When it became obvious that she wasn't going to settle back in bed, they covered her and her doll on one end of the couch and she watched them dance until she fell asleep.

Kate reminded Jake and Charlie of the peach cobbler she had in the oven. Topped with thick cream it was always a real treat. Soon after they had dessert, Charlie said it was time for him to hit the hay. Jake and Kate sat on the floor looking over Molly's toys and trying out the miniature piano. Jake picked up a small bench that required using a little wooden hammer to pound pegs into slots.

"Just what she needs," Jake said half seriously. "Something that makes noise."

"At least it's not a whistle," Kate added.

Kate put the box of large-piece puzzles back under the tree and wondered aloud how long it would be until Molly had all the pieces mixed up. For his part, Jake speculated about where they were going to put so many stuffed animals. They sat quietly on the floor in the darkened room with their backs to the couch and Jake's arm around Kate until Jake said, "Let's go to bed."

Molly slept through Jake carrying her to her bed in his old room. She was still hugging her Christmas doll. Silently, he reflected on how blessed they were to have her, and then he tucked the covers around her and slipped out of the room.

———•———

Since the first of December, feeding the cattle had been a full-time job, and by January the snow was so deep it nearly covered the fence posts. Needing to feed more hay during the bitter cold, Jake and Charlie fretted about having enough hay to get through the winter. By late March, when they brought in the heifers for calving, the weather had warmed up some during the day, but the nights were still cold. Jake felt sure the hay supply would hold out, although they wouldn't have much left by the time they quit feeding.

Calves were coming fast during the middle of April. Charlie had the first night shift at the heifer barn and Jake relieved him before midnight every night.

Aware that Jake was trying to make things easier for Charlie, Kate said, "I hope Charlie's feeling okay. Those weeks of being sick last summer took a lot out of him."

"I worry about it, too, but he says he's fine. He's gotten cranky about me asking so often. It's good that the heifers are calving easily so far. We fed out the old hay first so their feed is good and they have plenty of water in the corral."

"That's a godsend."

Jake leaned over and gave Kate a kiss. "I'll be glad when you calve, too."

Amused, she eyed him warily. "Are you calling me an old cow?"

"Well, you're not exactly a heifer and I shouldn't say you're calving, but . . ."

"But you're a rancher . . . and I really don't know what to do with you."

"Just keep loving me like you do."

—•—

Spring brought a muddy mess. The weather had spells of wind and more light snow, but as soon as it turned warmer, the mudroom became almost unmanageable for Kate. She was grateful that Jake and Charlie took off their boots in the mudroom and didn't track dirt into the house. Otherwise life was as usual, the seasons dictating the expected activities.

Then in May, an early morning phone call disrupted their lives. Jake's dad had died during the night. With her voice cracking, Mother McClary told Jake that he had died peacefully. Sensing how distraught his mother was, Jake tried to calm her and then called his brother Jesse right away to make plans for their father's burial.

He told Kate he'd drive out to the road where Jesse would pick him up then he and Jesse would go together to Arizona. "You know Dad wanted to be buried here on the ranch, so we'll take Jesse's truck that's big enough to hold the casket. Mom wants to come, too, of course. We hope she'll want to stay in Wyoming for a while."

Kate began putting out some clothes for him. "How long do you expect to be gone?" she asked. Catching the look of sadness on his face she put her arms around him.

Jake wiped his eyes with the back of his hand. "I can't believe he's gone," he said, his voice trembling. "I hope we can be back by Monday. I hate to leave you so far out here with no way to get to a doctor."

"Don't worry, Charlie's here and I'll call you if there's an emergency."

He collected his thoughts. "I have a better idea. I'm going to have Charlie go with me out to the county road so he can bring the pickup back. I don't think you ought to try getting out of here with the car. He could get you out with the pickup."

"Quit fussing about me. We'll see Dr. Welsh when we can. You need to take care of your mother now."

"I'll call you when we get there. How we're going to get a grave dug at this time might be a problem, but Dad wanted to be buried next to his folks in our McClary cemetery up on the hill, so we'll manage to do it somehow."

He set his suitcase by the door. "It'll be this afternoon before Jesse can get here. I'd better call Father and set the time for the funeral, and I suppose I'd better call the men we want to serve as pallbearers," Jake said, thinking out loud, and making sure he did everything that needed to be done before he left.

That afternoon, Kate watched Jake maneuver the four-wheel-drive pickup down the muddy road. She lingered on the porch until she saw Charlie come back up the lane and drive to the other side of the house. She didn't hear him come in through the kitchen and living room to the porch.

"Do you want me to let the neighbors know that Dan passed away?" Charlie asked, startling her. "They'll want to know."

"Thanks, but Jake called Sam Peterson to be a pallbearer and the others that he wanted. I'm sure the word will get around."

"What about the priest?"

"Jake called him already. He'll be here when it's time."

Four-wheel-drive pickup trucks began showing up that evening. Everyone expressed their condolences. The women who arrived brought plenty of food with them, and the next morning, Steve Collier, a long time friend of both Jake and Jesse, brought a backhoe from his construction company in Pinedale. Kate greeted him at the door.

"I'm sorry about your loss," Steve said. "Thought I might be able to dig the grave."

"We appreciate that. Thanks for coming. Jake tried calling you before he left, but he missed you. Said I might need to call you later, so this is a big help."

"It's the least I can do for a fine man who was a good friend and one of the best ranchers around."

"Come on into the kitchen and have a cup of coffee. Charlie just put on a fresh pot."

She asked Charlie to show Steve where to dig the grave. "Maureen wants Dan's grave put next to his dad's. I'm sure you'll know where Steve should dig. I'd go with you but I wouldn't be any help."

Molly stood close by her mother, hugging her leg, unsettled by all the commotion and strangers coming into their house.

"Don't worry, Katie. We'll take care of it. Don't get yourself all worn out." Charlie nodded toward cakes and cookies on the counter. "With all the food everyone has been bringing, you don't need to cook anything for a while."

Kate smiled. "It's heartwarming how people gather around when someone has died."

"Folks around here have always been like that. They want to help make things easier."

Steve nodded in agreement. "My missus said she'd be by later with a couple of her homemade pies. I told her to come in the pickup. Your road is still muddy."

"It sure is," Charlie said. He turned to Kate. "We might be a while. There are several pickets on the fence around the graves that need repairing. All that snow during the winter did some damage." He bent down to talk to Molly. "Take care of your mama."

Molly put her little arms around Charlie's neck and gave him a hug.

Four days later, Kate spotted the truck coming up the lane, carrying Dan's casket. A gaunt looking Maureen slid over from the middle seat and with Jake's help she stepped down from the truck and made her way unsteadily up the stairs. Kate was on the porch holding Molly.

"I'm so sorry Dad is gone, but many loved ones met him at heaven's gate, I'm sure," Kate said. "He was a dear man and getting to know him was something I'll cherish forever." They hugged each other while wiping away tears.

Maureen swallowed hard. She glanced at Kate's swollen belly. "God took him home but He's sending us a new life. I wish Dan could have known this little one. He'll be watching, though."

Jake set down several suitcases. He kissed Kate and held her for a long moment. "I sure missed you and Molly." He looked down at his wife's belly and added, "You're sure getting fat."

Kate put her arm around Maureen's shoulder. "We have plenty of food here. As it's almost dinnertime, let's put out some things to eat."

Mary Anne and the kids arrived from Saratoga later that afternoon. She brought a variety of casseroles and put them in the already overstuffed refrigerator. Between that and the pantry, they were well stocked for several days of feeding whoever came to offer condolences. Mary Ann assured Kate that their family didn't mind staying in the bunkhouse, which Kate had gotten ready for them.

That night, Jake moved Molly's bed into his and Kate's room so Maureen could have the small bedroom. Molly thought that was really special, but it was hard to get her settled down when it was time for bed. Charlie told her bedtime stories until she fell asleep.

Jake and Jesse turned the couch around and moved chairs so they could all face each other. They talked over the funeral plans and visited for about an hour. Maureen said she wanted to go to bed. "It's been a long day," she told her family as they gathered around to tell her goodnight.

"Mom doesn't want to go back to Arizona for a while and would like to take care of Molly when you have the baby. Is that all right?" Jake whispered after they settled into bed.

"It's perfect," Kate said softly. "By then Molly will be accustomed to her and it'll be a relief to know she's taken care of."

"I thought you'd agree, but it never hurts to ask."

"I believe your mother is a saint."

"I know. So what does that make me?"

"Hmm, a son-of-a-saint, I guess." Kate had a hard time stifling a laugh at her own response.

"Shush," Jake said. "It won't be so funny if our little darling over there wakes up."

⬦

The Mass for Jake's dad at their small cemetery was well attended. An old horse Dan had ridden when he lived on the ranch stood outside the fenced burial grounds, as if paying his respects. The sight of him standing there with Dan's empty saddle on him saddened Kate. She couldn't hold back the tears, as the recollection of her grandfather's horse standing outside the gate of their ranch house for two days after his death filled Kate with sorrow. He too had worn an empty saddle.

After everyone had eaten and friends and neighbors had left, the McClary clan moved to the living room and spent time recalling the memories they had of Dan, as a father and a grandfather.

Jake perched himself on the arm of Kate's chair and stroked her hair. After a bit of coaxing, Molly sat on her grandmother's lap but didn't stay long. She scooted over to Charlie. Never one to intrude, he would have gone to his room, but everyone insisted he join them.

Some of the memories were humorous, like the time Dan caught Jake and Jesse smoking behind the barn. They didn't have cigarettes; they were smoking some kind of weeds that grew in back of the barn.

"Remember the time we managed to get a rope hanging from a rafter in the hay loft and we'd swing down and land in the hay?" Jesse asked Jake. "Dad scolded us and said it was a wonder one of us didn't fall down into a manger."

Jake chuckled. "We thought it was great fun but we missed a good chance to get hurt."

Kate and the others shook their heads in dismay. Maureen mentioned how little she really knew about their antics.

"We know, we didn't tell you everything," Jesse said with a wide grin. "We won't mention how many times Dad had to tell us to quit riding the milk cow's calf."

"I remember how you and Dad cheered us on when we roped at the rodeos," Jake said.

There were many thoughtful recollections, too, including how quick Dan was to help out neighbors and donate to good causes. Maureen told them of some of the good and bad times she and Dan had experienced in their long marriage. And of how precarious the money situation was when they decided to buy this ranch.

Both Jake and Jesse assured Maureen they were glad they had been given the good life of living on a ranch.

"You and Dad have been the best parents a couple of wayward boys could have," Jake said. "We decided a long time ago that you believed you could keep us out of trouble if you made us work all the time. Isn't that right, Jesse?"

Their lighthearted small talk and good memories made their grief easier to bear.

The beds in the bunkhouse were clean thanks to Jackie Peterson who had helped Kate get it ready. Jesse's family had opted to stay out there even though Charlie offered his room to Jesse and Mary Anne and said he'd stay in the bunkhouse with the kids. Soon Jesse's family headed off to bed.

Maureen found Kate in the kitchen preparing for the next morning. She sat at the counter and watched in silence as Kate set the breakfast table. As soon as Kate finished that, she made a pot of tea and brought a cup over to Maureen.

"Your grandparents were our best friends," Maureen said. "I miss them." Her voice was steady as she added, "I'm sure Dan and your granddad are already talking about the cattle business."

Kate was touched beyond belief by the great love this family had for each other and their neighbors. "I feel good knowing that."

Maureen looked thoughtful. "Dan and I had a wonderful life here. I'm so happy that you and Jake are taking good care of this beautiful ranch and that your children will grow up here."

Kate smiled. "I loved hearing all of you talking about your lives. You have a wonderful family."

"And we are blessed to have you now, too. It's good to see my Jake so happy."

"I'm glad that you'll stay with us a while. And if you want to live here permanently, that's fine with Jake and me."

"I appreciate the offer, dear, but I really don't relish spending winters being snowed in anymore. I have friends in Phoenix and we have good times together. You may have to put up with me during the summers, though. It gets hot in Arizona and I do love being on the ranch again."

***

The McClarys and their neighbors made it through their brandings as usual. Maureen was delighted to be a part of it. "I haven't been here for branding for the last six years," she commented to Kate. "I tried to have most everything for dinner done ahead because I usually vaccinated the calves. Of course, the neighbors all helped and it is a great time to visit with them."

Marie came to help Kate cook for the McClary's branding, and then she and Don came again the middle of June when Marie took over the kitchen for the summer.

"You don't know how glad I am to have you here," Kate told Marie. "Running after Molly at this stage of my pregnancy is about all I can manage."

Brad had come early and finished dragging meadows in time for irrigating. He also made a trip to Rock Springs to get a load of grain for horses, corn for the pigs, and enough chicken feed to last until fall. He planned on going back to vet school in Fort Collins, Colorado, in September, but promised Jake he'd be there every summer until he began working as a veterinarian.

Don and Charlie helped with irrigating and getting the machinery ready for haying. And everyone lent a hand when it came time to butcher a beef. They cut and wrapped the meat to put it in the freezer.

One night at supper Kate suggested they take in Chuckwagon Days in Big Piney on July 4th as well as DeSmet Mass in Daniel on the following Sunday.

"I don't think that's a good idea in your condition," Jake said.

"What do you mean 'in her condition'?" Maureen asked.

"Plus I'd like to go to Rendezvous in Pinedale," Kate said before Jake could get a word in edgewise. "I think Molly would have fun there."

Jake looked at Kate and then his mom. Maureen raised an eyebrow at her son. When he tried to say something Kate cut him off at the pass again.

"Jake and I like to go to the local rodeos. He knows so many of the cowboys, and we see people we never get to see any other time."

"But . . ." Jake began.

"No buts, Jake. We haven't taken your mom to anything except church since she's been here. The baby isn't due yet and it would be fun to join the festivities around the county before the baby comes."

"I agree," Maureen said. "You'll come with us won't you, Marie?"

"We've seen it all many times. Besides, we're not much for crowds anymore."

 **Chapter Twenty-Six**

**"What a marvelous tradition,"** Kate commented when they were on their way home after the rodeo during Chuckwagon Days in Big Piney. "Someone told me they've been having the parade, free barbecue, and rodeo on the 4th of July since the 1930s."

Maureen said it was true and then added that they usually took in Chuckwagon Days, the DeSmet Mass, and Rendezvous. "There was never time for any outings the rest of the summer."

Jake looked at Kate sitting next to him, with his mother on the other side of her. "I don't know about going to DeSmet and Rendezvous next weekend, Kate. You look worn out and I think it might be too much."

"Oh no," she put in quickly. "I don't want to miss those events. I'm tired, but between your mom and Marie, I'm somewhat a lady of leisure. Besides, you get to keep track of Molly, you lucky man."

He shook his head in mock exasperation. "Oh sure. I'm thinking I ought to keep her at home."

When Sunday arrived Jake was herding everyone into the Buick. "Hurry, we'll be late. We want to get to Daniel in plenty of time." He helped Kate get into the car. She was too excited about the day's coming events to indulge in self-pity about how uncomfortable she was.

At Mass, Kate was fascinated by the recounting of Father Pierre DeSmet's mission to the Indians and mountain men in this once wild land. The place where they stood looked out over the green valley, below the monument dedicated to the Jesuit priest who offered the first documented Mass in Wyoming. A wide blue sky dotted with cottony cumulus clouds completed the scene of serene beauty.

Once again, they enjoyed Rendezvous and the reenactment of how wagons of goods came from St. Louis and other points to meet the mountain men to trade for furs they had collected since the last rendezvous. Molly got most excited while watching Indian children dance and young folks race bareback through the arena. She was finally at an age where she could enjoy the festivities, which brought plenty of joy to the grownups. After a wearying day, it was a relief when she settled down on Charlie's lap in the back seat and fell asleep.

"Molly chatters all the time," Jake said.

"She got that from me," Kate said, then she yawned. "But I'm not complaining. It means she'll have no problem standing up for herself."

"You've raised her well," Maureen said. "Before you know it, she'll be racing through the arena bareback like those girls did today."

"I never saw a kid enjoy herself so much," Charlie added.

Jake looked around at his sleepy companions. "Well, we've done our share of running around. Enough, I'd say. We have work to do, you know."

"Yes, Master," Kate said saucily.

"You two never stop ribbing each other, do you?" Maureen asked.

"Keeps the marriage interesting," Jake said lightheartedly.

⸻ ◆ ⸻

When August rolled around, Kate felt she might have the baby sooner than expected, though she informed Jake there were still a few days before she'd be delivering. Not one to risk having to deliver their next baby in the car, he insisted they go to Jackson early. There were others around to take care of things on the ranch, he said.

On the way to town Kate didn't seem herself.

"Are you okay?" Jake asked.

"Yes, I'm fine."

"You're awfully quiet. Are you sure there's not something you want . . .?"

With that, Kate burst into tears. "I've been thinking about Molly. She's been with us every day." She pulled a handkerchief from her purse. "The one and only time I left Jeremy . . ."

"Honey, I see what you're getting at, but Molly is in good hands. Mom and Charlie will take care of her the same as you do."

"It's just that everyone I loved and who loved me died."

Keeping his eyes on the road, Jake put a hand on Kate's thigh. "You miss that little boy and I don't want you to stop missing him, but right now you need to think about the new baby who, by the way, I'm sure will be a little girl."

His lighthearted comment brought the response Jake had hoped for.

"Wanna bet?" Kate said, sniffling. "I think it'll be a boy."

"Okay, what do I win if it's not?"

"A new hat. You need one but you'll have to buy your own because it's going to be a boy."

Jake shook his head from side to side and squeezed her thigh. "Be sure it's a Stetson."

"I hope you're prepared to buy me a new pair of boots. And . . ."

"Oh no, that's enough—you like expensive boots. It's a longshot anyway."

They both laughed, and in a little while Kate was asleep against Jake's shoulder.

When they had settled into a motel near the hospital, Jake and Kate studied the local ads for a place to eat and chose the Wort Hotel. It was a romantic spot for them, having been the place they chose to have supper when Jake came from the ranch to see her the summer she worked as a nurse in the hospital.

"Do you remember the night we ate here and then went to the rodeo?" Jake asked once they were seated at a table.

"Yes, we had a great meal here, then walked around the square before going to the rodeo."

"Jesse and I roped calves at a lot of high school rodeos, including some here in Jackson. After high school we both got on the college rodeo team at the University of Wyoming. We competed against each other but cheered each other on at the same time."

"Which of you was best, do you think?"

"It's a toss-up. The truth is, neither of us were as good as our dad."

Kate asked Jake to move the table a few inches away from her and him so she could be more comfortable. She patted her belly. "I suppose you'll want this little boy to be a roper, too."

"I will if this *is* a little boy. But I'll teach this little girl to rope, just the same. And she *and* Molly will be champion barrel racing rodeo cowgirls."

"What if they don't want to barrel race?"

"I think they will. Molly already loves horses and riding on our laps. I've been thinking we ought to get a Shetland for her."

"Oh, Jake, she's too little."

The waitress brought their food and set it on the table. The liver and onions Jake had ordered made Kate queasy. "That doesn't look too good. I'm glad I'm having soup and salad."

"You've cooked liver and onions at the ranch. S'pose you'll be back to normal soon?"

"What's normal? Nothing's the same since we had Molly. Kids have a way of taking over."

"They do, but I wouldn't trade the life we have for anything in the world."

"Me neither."

Their eyes met in mutual love as they began to enjoy their meal.

After a few bites, Kate said, "This is so civilized. No spilt milk or mashed potatoes on the floor."

Jake laughed. "Yep, we gotta be thankful for this while it lasts."

Two nights later, Kate awoke with a contraction. She had been right about the baby coming soon. She waited until the contractions were fifteen minutes apart before she woke Jake. He jumped out of bed in a near panic.

"We're not at the ranch now," Kate said. "You don't have to hurry quite so fast."

He scratched the stubble on his face. "Do I have time to shave?"

"Sure, but it's almost time to go."

Kate's labor lasted a little over four hours that morning of August 4, 1962. Jake paced in the waiting room after Kate was taken to delivery. It wasn't long before a nurse came and told him he could go in to see Kate.

Her raised eyebrows and smug grin confirmed she had won their bet. "You now have a little cowboy," she said with contentment, then added, "but no new hat."

He bent down and kissed Kate, then looked around for the baby.

"The nurse will bring him back in a few minutes," she assured him.

"What'll we name him?" Jake asked. "We haven't settled on a name yet."

"We talked about several, but mostly for girls, I might add."

"How about Matthew? Jesse's son Danny is named after my dad. Maybe we should make this little guy Matthew James, after your dad."

"That would really please my dad, if he were with us. And Grandma and Grandpa, too. They only had one son."

"Maybe we need to get to know this baby a little before we know what his name should be," Jake said.

"No, I like the name Matthew James."

Just then the nurse arrived. "Congratulations to you both. You have a fine little boy here."

Jake held out his arms to take the baby.

"Do you need any help with nursing?" she asked Kate.

"No, I think I can manage, thanks anyway."

After the nurse left, Kate and Jake looked in awe at the new miracle in their lives.

"You're a wonder," he whispered to Kate as she put the baby to her breast. It wasn't long before the baby began to suck.

"How do they know to do that so soon?" he asked. "Of course, newborn calves and foals start right in, too."

Kate held little Matthew's hand and studied the tiny blue eyed, brown haired baby boy as she whispered, "I'm so glad you're here and we can hold you now."

Kate looked at Jake and seeing him moved with emotion that brought tears to his eyes, she caught his hand and squeezed it, conveying her understanding without words.

After three days in the hospital and an appointment set for the circumcision, Kate and Jake took Matthew James McClary home. Maureen was in high spirits when they arrived, and Charlie was delighted to be the grandpa once again. Molly, on the other hand, was skeptical.

"Would you like to hold your baby brother?" Kate asked as she sat on the couch and moved the blanket so Molly could have a good look.

Molly shook her head and moved over to Jake who set a diaper bag where Kate could reach it. He picked her up and said, "Someday, he'll be big enough to play with you. You'll like that, won't you?"

"He's too little anyway," she said stubbornly.

When Kate expressed her concern that Molly didn't seem very happy with her little brother, Maureen said, "She probably thinks Matthew gets a lot of attention. We'll have to go at this gradually . . . let her see she's not left out."

Matthew was not as easy a baby as Molly had been. He proved to be fussy, and neither Kate nor Jake were getting much sleep. Kate worried because Jake was still haying.

"Is it safe for you to be operating machinery? You don't get enough sleep," she asked after a particularly difficult night.

"Oh, I wake up when Matt cries but I go back to sleep while you're nursing or walking with him," he said, trying to reassure her.

Kate said to Marie one morning when the baby was two weeks old, "I don't know what I would have done without you this summer. I can't imagine how I could have cooked for a hay crew after being up half the night with a cranky baby. The days aren't much better either. The doctor said he's fine, just a little colicky." She laughed and said, "There's no such thing as a 'little' colicky."

At last, all the hay was stacked, machinery put away, and they were bidding their summer help goodbye the second week of September. Kate watched from the porch as the last pickup drove down the lane toward the county road. Maureen joined her with glasses of lemonade in her hands. "Let's sit a bit."

"Did Marie and Don work for you and Dad during haying when you were on the ranch?"

"No, Jesse has known them for a long time. I know Don worked for other ranchers during haying and I think Marie cooked for hay crews. When he asked them both to come for haying here, Marie agreed to cook. It gave Mary Anne time with her kids and she likes to work in the garden and yard."

"She is a wonderful cook and I appreciate how she keeps the kitchen clean . . . and washes the separator too."

"Their boy, Brad, is a good worker. I thought Jake's haying season went very well."

"It did, thanks to all our good help."

Jake had taken Molly for a ride on his horse and the baby was asleep so they had some time to visit about how Dan's death and Matthew's birth had changed life for all of them.

"We're glad you were here for Matthew's baptism. Wasn't it something that it rained on Saturday and Father was able to do the baptism last Sunday?"

"I'm sure God arranged it that way," Maureen said with a smile. "I'll stay longer if you need me, but I want to spend some time in Saratoga with Jesse and his family before I go back to Arizona."

"I'll tell Jake. He mentioned that he would take you whenever you're ready to go. We'll miss you. You have been a lot of help with the children."

Over the next few days, Matthew became less colicky and he often fell asleep while he was nursing. Because he was settling down, Kate decided she wouldn't upset him by taking him to Saratoga.

"Saves packing a car load of baby things," Jake joked. "At any rate, I won't be gone long."

Kate held Matt as she and Molly walked to the gate to say good-bye to Jake and Maureen. Kate thanked her again for everything she had done.

"My dear, I'm the one who needs to be saying thanks. All of you make me so happy, even though it's sad to go back without Dan there. He wouldn't want me to be too depressed though."

"Dad always had a cheerful outlook," Jake said. "He told me he knew he'd be leaving you alone, but that you had kids and friends to look after you."

"He and I were blessed in that regard."

Jake kissed Kate and the kids. Before he got into the Buick, she whispered in his ear, "When you get back, we need to go shopping for my new boots."

He tapped her bottom lightly. "You're impossible, you know that."

———•———

By the time Jake got back to the ranch, Charlie had cleaned out the corrals and fixed a gate that needed a new latch. Jake went out to bring a bay gelding and the Appaloosa into the corrals so he could start breaking them. He spent a lot of time working with them and had them pretty well broke before they needed to bring the cattle home from the forest.

Cows started out of the mountains as soon as it began snowing up there. Ten days later, all the cattle were in and it was time to wean and get ready for shipping the yearlings, culls, and a couple of old bulls. Jake made a trip to buy bulls while he could still drive out easily. Two of the new bulls got away one night. The next morning Jake and Charlie mended the fence the bulls had torn down and then mounted their horses to find the bulls before they wandered too far.

Some hours later Kate heard the outside door of the mudroom open, and after a few moments it closed again. When she heard the pickup leave the yard, she would have gotten up to see what was going on but she was in the middle of nursing Matt. By the time both men came in she was in the kitchen starting to fix dinner. Jake went into the living room and sat down with his head in his hands.

Alarmed, Kate asked Charlie, "What's the matter?"

"It's Buck. Jake was running him and he stepped in a badger hole. It broke his leg and Jake had to put him down."

"Oh, no . . ." Kate said. "What about Jake? Was he hurt?"

"He took a bad fall but I think he's okay. He's just sick about Buck."

Kate went into the living room and knelt down before Jake. She put her hands around his. "I'm so sorry. Buck was your favorite."

With tears in his eyes, Jake looked up. "He was such a good horse. Shooting him was the hardest thing I've ever done, but I had to do it."

She put her arms around him and held him close. Molly toddled out from her bedroom and saw her dad all broken up. "Why are you crying, Daddy?"

Jake picked her up. "Buck got hurt and . . . he died."

Molly put her arms around his neck. "You can have my horse, Daddy."

"Thank you, sweetheart. Candy's yours. I'll find another horse to ride, but none of them will be as good as Buck."

It would have been a quiet supper except that Molly chattered away and wanted to give Matthew something to eat.

Charlie shook his head. "Things have sure changed around here."

Jake grunted. "She's never quiet, except when she's sleeping."

———•—•———

"When are we going to town?" Kate asked Jake. "I've made a long list and we also need to take the baby and Molly in for check-ups before winter."

"Try to get an appointment right away." Turning to Charlie he said, "You ought to come along too, Charlie. That doctor you had last summer might want to check you over."

"I don't need a checkup. But I'll go with you. I need a few things and maybe I can keep an eye on the kids while you two do your shopping."

"That'd be great. I was beginning to dread taking both of them."

Sure enough, Charlie had his hands full keeping Molly occupied in the truck while Kate and Jake ran their errands. He was good about giving Matt the attention he needed, too, but grateful when he had a chance to get out and do his own shopping.

"Boy, I'm glad that's done," Jake said when they headed out of town. "I vote we don't stop to eat with these two."

"There are plenty of leftovers for supper back at the Bunkhouse," Kate said.

Charlie readily agreed. "Let's keep going."

The two men did the chores while Kate put everything on the table. She had to feed the baby before she could have her own supper.

As soon as Molly and Matthew were asleep, Kate joined Jake in the living room. He had a blazing fire going and handed Kate a plate of food he'd fixed for her. "Sit down and relax," he said. "I bet Charlie won't want to go along on any more outings with us, unless we leave the kids behind."

"Are you suggesting we hire a babysitter?"

"Doubt if we'd find one within a hundred miles."

Kate finished a bite. "They do wear us out. Whose idea was it to have these kids, anyway?"

"Surely you haven't forgotten how anxious you were to have kids?"

"Children are the greatest joy, and the greatest sorrow," Kate said, her voice strained.

"I know," Jake said softly, knowing she was thinking of Jeremy.

———— • ————

A few days later, Jake hurried into the kitchen from outside. "Well, I've decided on another horse. He doesn't look like Buck so maybe that will help."

"Just so he's not red," Kate said.

"No, in fact, it's that Appaloosa you thought was such a pretty colt. His mother was always gentle and easy to ride. Maybe we can all go for a ride tomorrow."

"I doubt it. You can carry Molly but I'm not sure about taking Matt."

"We'll have those kids riding before you know it."

The thought of putting Molly or Matt on a horse made Kate shudder, but she imagined Jake doing just that.

# Chapter Twenty-Seven

**Snow** was four feet deep by February 1963. Kate was on pins and needles worrying that one of the kids might get sick. She had good reason when Matt developed an ear infection. The otoscope she kept in her doctor's supply case had confirmed it. The pediatrician in Jackson promised to put an antibiotic in the mail for her that day.

"It's here," Jake said the following midday after having skied out to check the mailbox. "Looks like he sent some medication for fever, too." He smiled at Kate and said, "Guess what, the county road has been plowed clear to our gate." He thought a moment and added, "I wonder if that was Don's doing."

Kate was busy preparing dinner. She took the package from Jake while he began setting the table. "I'm so relieved. Of course, I don't know how we'd get to the county road," she added doubtfully. "This medicine came just in the nick of time . . . Matt's temperature is 103°."

She started Matt on the medicine and rocked him until he went to sleep, but he didn't sleep long. After he fussed for a time, she administered the fever medication. By the third day, Kate was fairly sure Matt was over the worst of it. She continued to fret about the fact that they were snowed in without any way to get out should a real emergency occur.

Jake was doing up some supper dishes and lost in his own thoughts when Kate confronted him. "I need you to do something for us," she said.

He wiped a plate and set it on the counter. "Whatever you want."

She stood with her hands on her hips. "You might regret you said that."

"What's up? Did someone plug up the toilet?"

"Remember, you said whatever I want."

By the tone of her voice, Jake knew this was something more pressing.

Kate continued. "We've gotten through Matt being sick this time. Who knows what might happen the next time one of our kids get sick. One way or another we're going to get a snowplow straight away."

Jake couldn't get a word in edgewise if he wanted to.

"You call the dealership and order a plow big enough to keep our road clear. If you don't want to do it, I will."

He put up his hands with palms outward. "Okay, okay. I'll order one. I just hope Don will bring it out. He plows roads all winter so he'll probably do it."

Kate glared at him as if she wasn't sure he'd carry through. "And what you call my money is going to pay for this machine," she added emphatically.

Again, Jake put up a hand to protest.

She went on, "Don't argue about it. We have to be able to get out of here if anyone gets sick or, God forbid, really hurt."

"Kate, I've worried about it, too. Consider it done."

True to his word, Jake called the dealership and told them to order a good sized Caterpillar and to attach a snowplow to it. He left instructions to call as soon as it arrived. A couple of weeks later it was ready. Don and another fellow brought it to the ranch gate on a flatbed. His partner took the truck and trailer back to town and Don began to clear the lane. It took him most of the day to push the packed snow off the road. Don was experienced and did a good job.  He even stayed the night and helped them feed the next day before Jake drove him home. Kate could hardly believe it when Jake arrived home and reported that he had been able to drive the pickup all the way to Don's house outside of Pinedale.

Jake brought in the groceries he'd picked up in town.

"Charlie, can you give me a hand?" Jake asked, motioning him outside.

Kate offered to help but he told her it was a surprise.

A few minutes later the men came into the house carrying a large box. They set it down in the living room and started to take off the cardboard.

"A television set!" Kate said when it was finally uncovered. "Let's put it over there," she said, pointing to a space between the fireplace and the window. "We can move the furniture so we can see it and still stay warm."

After positioning it, Jake went to get the ladder and before evening he had the antenna fastened to the roof.

"I assume you paid for the Cat . . . *and* the television set, with *my* money," Kate said, with lifted brows.

"Yep, you're broke so I guess you'll have to stay here and work for your room and board."

They ate supper early, anticipating an evening watching television. "Go tend the baby and I'll do the dishes, Kate," Charlie said, scooting his chair back from the table.

"Oh, sure," Jake said plaintively, "you two take the easy jobs and I have to do the chores."

Kate set Molly down from her high chair. Molly started for the living room where Matthew was on a blanket on the floor. Kate turned to Jake and said, "Check the spouts on the separator. Remember, you put it together a while ago." She was out of the kitchen when she heard him say, "I know how to put the separator together."

However, a half hour later, she heard Jake yell, "Oh, hell," and she knew he had mixed up the spouts. After he cleaned up the spilled milk and finished separating, he rinsed the bucket and strainer then went to the living room where everyone was anxious to watch their new television set. Jake made a face at Kate before he began working the knobs on the TV. She tried to keep a straight face.

Jake explained that they had three channels, Casper and Riverton in Wyoming and one from Idaho Falls, Idaho. Charlie was surprised. "I sure didn't expect that we could even get television out here, let alone pictures as good as these."

"Petersons said we are in a good spot to get reception from one of the translators."

Jake moved from channel to channel, having a hard time deciding what to settle on. Molly could hardly contain herself.

"Hey, how about that?" Charlie said when he saw that *Gunsmoke* was about to begin.

"Yes, let's watch *Gunsmoke*, Daddy!" Molly shouted.

"All right, all right, settle down. *Gunsmoke* it is."

Kate put Molly and Matt in their pajamas during a commercial and both fell asleep before long. During the next commercial, Jake and Kate put the kids in their beds. The grownups watched the news before they went to bed themselves.

Watching newsmen discuss the world situation one evening, especially the civil rights protests and newspaper strikes, Kate commented, "Sometimes, I wish we didn't know all that happens in the world. There seems to be so much unrest."

———◆———

By the time summer came around again, they'd become accustomed to watching a few favorite shows on the television but no one had wanted to entirely give up their card games, the occasional music session, or dance time. While they enjoyed all these pastimes, Molly and Matt were such a handful that it curtailed much of their entertainment.

Grandma McClary left Phoenix again in May and stayed with Jesse and his family in Saratoga until the first week in July. She planned to stay with Jake's family until September then go south again. Jesse told Jake on the phone he would be bringing their mother to his house on the seventh of July.

Kate and Jake needed to make room for her. Although Charlie offered to move to the bunkhouse, Kate said they would get the full-size bed out of storage in the garage and put it into the kids' room after they moved the kids' beds into Jake and Kate's bedroom.

"Geez, maybe we need a bigger house," Jake said as they were finishing up. "Matt and Molly won't be able to share the same room forever." Kate agreed, but they didn't have time to think about that right now.

Molly was all excited about her grandma's arrival, more so than Matt. Even though Maureen had looked after him right after he was born, he wouldn't remember that, and a stranger in his midst put him off guard.

After he got used to her, he let Maureen dress him and feed him as well as clean up the mess he made when he tried to feed himself. She read to both of the kids and took them for walks, so it wasn't long before Matt decided he liked 'Gamma'.

The McClarys seldom missed Sunday Mass before haying, even though they had to drive almost forty miles to town. During Mass one Sunday Molly tried to talk non-stop and Matt kept slipping out of the pew. It drove Jake nuts.

"Somebody needs to keep these two at home," he burst out on their way home. "I can't believe they can't be quiet for forty-five minutes."

"How are they going to learn how to behave in church if they don't go?" Kate asked. She glanced at Charlie and Maureen in the back seat. "I hope you weren't too embarrassed by their behavior."

"I was tempted to take them out but it wasn't my job," Charlie replied. "Besides, they're just kids. I've seen plenty of kids act up in church before. Once I saw a dad pick up a noisy tot and start out with him. The kid yelled, 'Don't hit me, Dad, don't hit me.'"

Maureen laughed at Charlie's story, which lightened the mood.

"I knew the guy," Charlie continued. "I doubt he ever once hit that kid, but he was terribly embarrassed by his son's shouting."

"Jake, you're payin' for your raisin'," Maureen said. "Taking you and Jesse to church was no picnic either."

"Amen," said Kate.

"She's saying that to make you feel better," Jake said.

Maureen caught the glint in his eye in the rear view mirror. "Enough of this talk. Kids will be kids and church is one of the places where they have to learn to behave."

———•———

Marie and Don had been at the ranch for summer work since the middle of June. They had opted to stay in the bunkhouse. "We'll just make all the boys stay in one room and we'll have the other one," Don told Kate soon after they arrived. Marie took over the kitchen right away.

She had dinner ready when they got home from church and Brad had arrived while they were gone.

A couple of weeks later, Jake and Charlie started mowing hay. The rest of their crew arrived and they all headed for the far field. Chris and Carl were the only hands that had hayed before but the other two boys quickly learned how to rake hay. Carl took over Charlie's mower and Charlie went back to driving the plunger. Chris and Don drove the sweeps and Brad stacked as usual. Marie took dinner to the field until they got closer to the house and everyone appreciated that.

"We're so modern now using these tractors," Jake told Kate and Marie that first evening. "Only the sweeps still have teams. Haying should be easier but I miss those horses."

Charlie was bringing in firewood when he heard Jake's sentiment. "Me too."

Marie helped Charlie with his load.

"If we could only convince Kate that she needs an electric or gas cook stove, we'd be able to quit chopping all this wood," Charlie continued with his usual banter.

"Sorry you have to chop all that wood but I don't mind cooking on this stove," Marie said. "I'm not all that happy with the electric stove I have at home, so don't go modern on my account."

"You guys are troopers," Jake said. "I don't know what we'd do without you and Don. We surely couldn't get through haying season."

"Well, we're getting on, you know. One of these days we might have to give it up. But not yet," she added emphatically.

"Good," Jake said. He patted her on the shoulder.

When Matt's first birthday came around in August, Marie prepared dinner but Kate made a birthday cake. Matt ate everything with his hands, so the cake was all over his high chair and the floor before he was done. Maureen took the kids to the bathroom to wash their hands and faces while Kate patiently cleared the mess in the kitchen.

Jake took the broom from Kate and began sweeping the floor. "I'm glad we're done with this birthday," he said. "At least the kids had fun, even though I think Molly was feeling left out. Maybe we should have had a package wrapped for her."

"No, she had her birthday presents and they need to learn that they each have a special day to celebrate."

"You're right. I guess we'll have to get used to having birthday parties. Maybe the next one won't be so messy." He put the broom away. "Although I don't think we can count on it."

On the last day of haying, Brad told everyone he probably would not be haying the following year. "I'll be graduating the last week of May. I'm hoping I can partner up with some vet." They all raised their water glasses and wished him success.

"I don't know how we'll manage to get a stack of hay built," Jake spoke. "You've done it for so long. Charlie and I are too old to get up that high."

"How about you, Chris?" Jake asked. "Think you could build a stack?"

"Not as good as Brad, but I'd like to give it a try," he said earnestly. "I'll need to earn what money I can for college."

"That's great. We'll count on you then," Jake said.

After the machinery was put away for the winter, Jake thanked his hay crew and gave them their paychecks. Even Marie and Don were packed up and ready to go after all the goodbyes and good luck wishes were said.

When the last pickup disappeared from view, Kate got a wistful look. "I used to look forward to the peace and quiet when everyone left. Now there's no time to think. Those two kids of yours keep me . . . and Mom busy."

Jake said thoughtfully, "Let's think about what we can do for Brad when he becomes a veterinarian. He's worked hard and he'll be a good animal doctor."

"You're right. We'll have to think of something."

The kids were playing in the yard and Jake said he was going to saddle up and turn the work horses into another pasture.

"By the way," Kate said, "Molly pesters me every day to let her ride Candy. Do you have time to take her?"

"Not right now but I'll let her ride to the mail box with me this afternoon. She'll be riding that pony all over the place before you know it."

"Not bareback, Jake. And I mean it."

"Yes, Ma'am." He saluted her and went out the door.

# Chapter Twenty-Eight

**Kate's supper** of stroganoff and green salad didn't go over well with the kids. She served it a few nights after haying season, when things were back to status quo. Maureen would have liked to prepare something her grandchildren favored eating, but she knew enough to not speak up on that matter. Meddling in family affairs and the raising of children wasn't something the McClarys engaged in.

Being astute, Kate could see that Mother McClary was feeling sorry for the kids. She tried to ease the situation with making small talk, but Jake wasn't in the mood. "Kids ought to learn to eat whatever everyone else is eating," he said. "Mom would have made Jesse and me eat whatever was on the table."

Maureen smiled at Jake. "I guess I would have, but you two have to discipline your children in your own way. Just be sure you agree on how to do that."

Jake fell silent.

"Did you hear that, Jake?" Kate asked.

"Yes, I heard it."

"I think we agree on most things," Kate said, looking at Jake to agree with her.

"Kate doesn't always do what I tell her to do," Jake teased, easing the tension in the room. "But I have ways to persuade her to my way of thinking."

"Oh? Is that so?" Kate replied, before giving Maureen a knowing look. "I just hope our kids turn out as fine as yours did."

"I'm sure they will, dear."

"In the meantime," Kate said pointedly to Jake, "*your* kids need to be cleaned up and put into pajamas."

"Yes, Ma'am. Right away, Ma'am." He got up and put a hand on his mother's shoulder. "Of course, when they are in bed asleep, they'll be *her* kids."

Maureen nodded her head and joked. "I can see I don't need to worry about you two anymore."

After that was sorted out, the dishes were done, and the kids tucked in for the night, Maureen said, "I'd like to spend a few days with Jesse and Mary Anne before heading back to Arizona. Maybe you'd all like to come to Saratoga with me."

"We haven't seen their family for quite a while," Kate said. "They've been asking us to bring the kids."

"What do you think, Jake?" Maureen asked.

"Why not. A change of scenery could do us good," he replied.

Rough roads had taken a toll on Kate's old Buick. Jake said they needed a new car and would trade it in when they got to Rock Springs. Kate was excited at the prospect and suggested they trade for a station wagon so it could carry more things.

Jake's wry comment brought smiles from everyone. "Oh, yeah, that's what we need—something that will carry more things."

By the time Kate had enough kid stuff and their own suitcase packed into the Buick, Jake wondered if everyone could fit in. He moved things tighter and got Maureen's bags in. Charlie had helped and joked, "Good thing I'm not going. I wouldn't like hanging on to the top." They bid him goodbye and set off with Maureen next to Jake and Kate in the back seat with the kids.

They looked at several cars before they settled on Kate's choice —a shiny dark blue Chevy station wagon. Kate got a now eager Molly to help with the kids' bags while Maureen looked after Matthew.

"This car will be full, too," Jake grumbled. "Just remember, we can't buy anything on this trip." No one seemed to take him seriously.

"I noticed that a lot of the leaves have turned already," Maureen said wistfully after they had gone a few miles. "Summer is such a busy time and it goes so fast."

"That is so true," Kate responded. "I do like the fall colors but they don't last long and before we know it, it's winter again." She tucked a blanket around Matt who had fallen asleep on her lap. "My favorite time of the year is when things start to turn green in the spring."

Jake smiled at his mother. "As for me, I like the changing seasons. Makes life interesting."

Molly fell asleep and the grownups enjoyed uninterrupted conversation the rest of the way.

Their older cousins entertained Molly and Matt while the women made meals and visited. Jake and Jesse talked about their hay crops and cattle prices. Jesse told Jake he had already contracted his calves. When Jake learned how much Jesse got, he offered his opinion that it might be better to wait since the price had gone up in the past week. "Don't wait too long, Jake. Prices can go down, too, you know," Jesse responded.

Two days passed quickly before Jake said it was time to start home and once again, everything was loaded into the car. This time Jake lowered the seat back and made room for the kids to lie down.

"I wonder how much longer Mom is going to be able to make these trips," Jake pondered on their way home. "She's seventy-eight and seems in good health, but it must be tough for her with Dad gone. He was older and probably wouldn't have gone to Arizona in the first place except for his failing health."

"There are several other widows who are good friends. She said they spend a lot of time together, playing bridge and going to plays and musicals. Your mom isn't the type to indulge in self-pity," Kate said thoughtfully.

"You're right; she makes the best of things."

"I know." She looked at Molly and Matt. Molly was looking at pictures in one of the many books Abby had given her. Matt had fallen asleep on the flat surface with one arm draped over Molly's lap.

"Sure is quiet, for a change," Jake said.

———•———

Molly had been riding a small saddle that Jesse's kids had given her. Jake suggested that they use it for Matt when he got a little older and they should get a new one for Molly. Kate could see where this was leading and insisted that they still needed to take Matt on with one of them. "I guess Molly does okay on Candy but you know, with a new saddle she is going to want to ride every day."

One day a few weeks later, Kate and Jake were in the barn brushing the horses. Kate told Jake he was right. "Molly's a good little rider."

"You sound surprised."

"No, I just didn't expect her to catch on so quickly."

Jake checked on Matt who was playing with a kitten near the manger, then glanced out the barn door to watch Molly riding Candy around the corral. "I think Candy has a loose shoe. I'll have to check that right away."

"Don't say a word about fall roundup. I don't want Molly fussing because she can't go with you."

"She's too young for that, I know. But I wish you could go along."

"One of these days we'll all go."

They finished with the horses and Jake called Molly over so he could inspect the loose shoe. "I'll have to replace this shoe. You and Matt go with Mom to the house now." When he finished with Candy, he went to the house and asked where the kids were. Kate said, "Come see." They were playing tag in the backyard. Matt kept falling down and when Molly tagged him, he shrieked at her. She wasn't the type to let him win for his own sake.

Kate took Jake by the hand. "Follow me, I want to show you something." She led Jake out the door to the front yard. "I don't think you've noticed this all summer."

"What?" Jake asked, feigning unaware.

"See." Kate pointed at her sagebrush.

"Has it grown that much?" He broke off a twig of the healthy two-foot-high sagebrush and sniffed its distinctive odor.

"Isn't it something?" Kate sniffed a sprig too. "Maybe we could plant a couple more along that fence."

"Maybe, when I get time. Besides, who is this 'we'?"

"I realize it's a chore but I love sagebrush and it's all out there." She waved her arms toward the desert land beyond the meadows.

"I wonder if any other rancher has ever planted sagebrush," Jake said in his inimitable wry manner.

"You're not like most other ranchers."

"You're right. Most ranchers don't obey their wives like I do, much less plant sagebrush in their front yards." He kissed her on the nose and called for the kids to come in.

— • —

Jake's nightly ritual was to turn on the TV after the kids were in bed, sit in his recliner, and watch the westerns they had access to. Missing an episode of *Gunsmoke* could make him cranky to the point where Kate wondered how he'd survived on the ranch all these years without a television. Neither of them was prepared for what they were about to witness when Jake turned on the set the evening of November 22, 1963.

"Kate, come quick," he yelled.

As soon as she comprehended the tragic news, spontaneous tears rolled down her cheeks. She stood zombie-like until Jake motioned her to sit down.

"I'll go get Charlie," he said.

Charlie sat down on the edge of a chair with eyes glued to the unfolding story. "Why would anyone do such a thing?" he asked, shaking his head sadly.

Like everyone else in the country, a shocked Jake, Kate, and Charlie watched the replay of President Kennedy's assassination and the events that occurred after his death.

When Jake brought in the mail the following Tuesday, he mentioned to Kate that the papers and magazines were covering every detail. "I guess this was a good time to have the radio and television. Even so, it's hard to believe such a thing really happened."

———•———

One evening after Molly and Matt were tucked in, Kate and Jake settled in front of the fireplace.

"I think it's time the kids have separate rooms," Jake said.

"We could put them in the bunkhouse," Kate responded.

"This *is* the Bunkhouse."

"I know. I was teasing."

"If the ranch bunkhouse was attached to this house we wouldn't have to build on more rooms."

"Build more rooms?" she asked. "Are you thinking of doing that?"

"It's exactly what I'm thinking. We managed to have room for Mother this year, but I'm not itchin' to sleep in the same room with those two again."

"Is it that bad?"

"No, but I like to have you to myself," he said.

"Where would we put more rooms?"

"On the west side. Our room is big. We could make a narrow hall along the inside wall and still have plenty of room. The bedrooms would be out the west end."

Kate listened intently.

"We might have to take out the window of the den on that side but there's still one on the south wall. I'll talk to a guy who builds log houses and see if he can start on it in the spring."

"It's a great idea, Jake, but can we . . ."

"Sure, we can afford it."

They made a trip to Rock Springs with the kids for winter supplies even though they expected to be able to drive out when they needed to. Jake had commented that, yes, they had a Cat but not much time for plowing snow."

On the way home, Kate offered to drive. Jake took her up on it. He slept most of the way while Kate drove. At a turn in the route they always took, a herd of cows had ambled into the middle of the road. Jake awoke with a start when she slammed on the brakes and lay on the horn.

"That was a close call," Kate said. "It's a good thing I'm a good driver."

Jake grunted and fell back asleep.

When they arrived home, Charlie was waiting to help unload.

"I'm glad to see you," Jake said. "Look at how much stuff we've got. That's what happens when you take a woman and two kids to town."

"Guess you didn't know what you were getting into," Kate said cheerfully.

Charlie quietly carried in some grocery bags and set them on the counter in the kitchen. "I'll help unpack these and let you know if there's anything too extravagant," Charlie joked to Jake. He pulled out one of several packages of Nestle's chocolate chip cookies. "I guess here's a culprit."

Kate said, "You can open the bag and have some, but I know you like my chocolate chip cookies."

"I do. You just don't seem to make many these days."

Kate shook her head, "Either I'm not very organized or I don't have time to do all I used to do."

Jake took a couple of the cookies. "Well, with Christmas coming soon, I guess we ought to keep some of these," Jake said. "Otherwise, what will Santa get with his milk."

They'd been telling Molly and Matt that Christmas was near and they needed to be good so Santa Claus would come. Molly kept a close watch on her brother and wasn't shy about speaking up when she thought he was being naughty.

Once when she scolded him Charlie said, "He doesn't pay much attention, does he?" Matt went on running a toy truck over the coffee table and making zoom zoom noises as if he hadn't heard his sister.

"It's clear as ice that Molly takes after her mother," said Jake. "Bossy."

"That must mean Matt takes after you," Kate said. "He ignores her."

Charlie looked at the two of them. "This isn't going to be some kind of contest is it?"

"Have you ever known that to be the case around here?" Kate asked, looking intently at Jake and about to burst into laughter.

When Jake switched on the Christmas lights that year, Molly's and Matt's eyes lit up as brightly as the bulbs on the tree. They'd never had tree lights before and Charlie wondered what kind of precedent they were setting. Kate told him it was a sign of the times. "We just aren't used to having lights on our tree but we have kids now."

They talked about going to the Boulder Community Hall for New Year's Eve but in the end, they decided taking two kids out in the cold wasn't a good idea.

"My folks took us to community dances when we were kids. We played with all the other kids and we all ended up wrapped in coats and asleep on the floor near the potbellied stove," Jake said. "Somehow, that doesn't seem like such fun anymore. Besides," he added, "I haven't been to one in so long I don't know if folks even take their kids with them anymore."

So they celebrated New Year's Eve in their usual way. They managed to have Molly and Matt in bed asleep at their regular bedtime.

"I'm surprised that Molly didn't ask me why I'm wearing a dress," Kate said. "If I'd told her I was going to the Bunkhouse Ball, she sure wouldn't have let anyone put her to bed."

Jake and Kate jitterbugged; they all did *Put Your Little Foot* a couple of times then saved the best for the last—their favorite waltzes.

Kate set out peach cobbler with cream. They sat at the dining room table and enjoyed what had become their traditional New Year's Eve treat.

Charlie asked Kate for one more waltz. "Then, I'm off to bed and you two can dance all night if you want to."

Kate and Jake danced another waltz before they decided they needed to get to bed. "That Molly gets up early and she wants everyone else up, too," Jake said as he closed up the Victrola.

———•———

Once in a while Kate bundled the kids up so they could all ride along on the sled to go feed the cattle. Most of the time it was too cold to venture out, but being cooped up in the house with two kids made her long for getting outside. She told Jake she loved them dearly but they drove her to distraction.

"How about you staying with the kids today and I'll help Charlie feed," she said to Jake one morning.

"I'd love to but I don't want you to have to work so hard."

"You'd love to," she repeated wryly. "You're not very convincing."

He went out to help Charlie hitch the teams. Kate stood at the Dutch door with a cup of coffee in her hand like most mornings, wistfully watching the ritual.

Spring finally arrived and with it an invitation to Brad's graduation. "We're going to that," Jake said decisively. "I talked to Chris and he'll come stay at the ranch while we're gone. Marie and Don will come after Brad graduates."

That night, lying in bed, Jake again brought up the subject of what they could do for Brad.

"I'll tell you what I want to do," Kate said. "We haven't used much of the money I had when I came here, and there's plenty to get our own kids through college. I want to help Brad set up a vet practice here in the county."

"That's a big order, Kate. Are you sure?"

"Yes, I am. Brad has been a godsend to us over the years and he doesn't have money to have his own practice. His parents have worked so hard here and we owe all of them our gratitude. I'm just glad we have the money to do this."

"He might not accept it, you know."

"I know, but we have to try. I'm sure he'll want to pay us back, and we'll make it easy for him if he insists. He's been thinking of getting married to Emily and maybe this will help make that possible."

"You're right. Brad's such a responsible young man, he wouldn't want to start a marriage in debt or working for the wages another vet might pay him."

"I'm glad you agree," Kate said, snuggling close to Jake.

"I've never known anyone like you . . . obviously I never did or I would have married her." He gave Kate a squeeze. "Since there's money to do it, I'm with you."

"I half expected you to think it was too much."

"Maybe this proves I didn't marry you for your money, huh?"

"I don't know. We're not through living yet," she teased.

# Chapter Twenty-Nine

**In between** the usual spring work, Jake and Charlie built a new loading chute. From the chute they put in a pole fence along the driveway of the ranch. Another pole fence from the chute made an eight-foot-wide corridor leading to an opening in the corral. Kate was curious as to why the men had done this, making extra work for themselves.

"It'll be easier to load cattle onto trucks for shipping in the fall," Jake explained. "The loading chute over at the Orland Place needs too much work and the road up to it is scattered with boulders. The trucks can back up to this one a lot easier."

"I like it. Molly can ride Candy in the corral and up and down that walkway and I'll be able keep an eye on her from the house."

Once Molly figured that out, one of the grownups had to catch and saddle her pony nearly every day so she could ride. Kate tried to limit Molly's ride to when Matt was asleep, but it didn't always work out that way, and she often had to take him out to the corral to watch. Sometimes she would catch Misty so she could take Matt for a ride, too.

Jake hired George Mallory, a local contractor, to do the addition to the house. George came the last week in May, and with his crew of three they had two bedrooms and a bath going up in record time. When Jake told George they would be gone to Fort Collins for a few days he asked them to stay on the job. Chris arrived to do the chores on the ranch while the McClarys and Charlie went to Brad's graduation.

Attending the graduation and having a couple of days to visit his brother, Will, gave Charlie a much needed break. Will and his wife, Alice, lived on a ranch about fifteen miles west of Fort Collins.

Jake, Kate, and the kids planned on doing some sightseeing while Charlie spent time with his brother and sister-in-law.

***

Everyone cheered when Brad received his degree, making him a Doctor of Veterinary Science. No one was more proud than Jake and Kate. They invited Brad's family to dinner at a restaurant that evening to celebrate. Jake had already made the arrangements.

On the way over, Kate tapped Jake on the arm. "That's the first time you ever invited people to 'dinner' when it's in the evening. What happened to 'supper'?"

"Just trying to impress my city wife."

"I'm not a city gal anymore, in case you hadn't noticed."

"You certainly aren't."

Molly and Matt had fallen asleep in the back seat next to Charlie and were disgruntled when Jake woke them up to go into the restaurant. "I want you kids to behave now," he told them, shooting Kate an imploring glance.

The prime rib meal was delicious and gratefully received by all. Aside from getting out of their chairs a few times, the kids were on good behavior. They were most attentive when it came time for Brad to open his graduation gifts. Brad let them open the wrapped packages, careful to collect each card with each package. There was money in several cards so he set them aside. When he finished, he thanked everyone and sat down.

"You didn't receive a gift from us because we couldn't wrap it." Jake said, standing up and pulling Kate to his side.

Everyone was all ears hearing Jake's announcement.

"You, Marie, and Don have been the best help we could imagine on the ranch. We want to thank you for that. And no one stacks hay like you do."

That brought forth a few guffaws and a round of applause. Charlie, who was sitting on one side of Brad, gave him a hearty clap on the back.

Jake continued. "Kate and I want to set you up in a veterinary practice in Sublette County, if that's where you'd like it to be."

Brad's parents gasped with surprise. Emily, who was seated on the other side of Brad, took his hand. He was so stunned he hardly knew what to say. "Yes, I do want to stay in the county. What you're offering is a lot and I can't thank you enough. I'll do my best to live up to everyone's expectations of me." He looked around the table.

"You'll make a fine veterinarian," Kate said. "We know you work hard and will make a lot of animals well."

That brought more applause. Brad thanked her and then he whispered in Emily's ear. They both got up from their seats. "Emily and I have known for a long time that we wanted to be married," he began. "I wasn't sure how I'd support her. Now you've made that possible, and we want you all to know that we are now officially engaged."

Molly ran over to hug Brad while one and all converged on the young couple to congratulate them. Marie and Don tearfully thanked their dear friends, Jake and Kate, for the opportunity they had afforded their son.

Back at the motel, with the kids finally asleep, Jake suggested they drive down to Estes Park the next day after they took Charlie out to his brother's house. "I've never been there but I guess it's something to see."

"The mountains are beautiful. My dad took me there years ago and we had a great time skiing."

The next morning, they left Charlie off and since no one was home at the time, Jake and Kate set out to see the mountains around Estes Park. The kids didn't enjoy the sightseeing as much as Jake and Kate, but they were excited as could be the next day when Jake took them to Denver to go to a zoo.

After an exhausting day trying to keep up with kids that were alternately thrilled with some animals and wary of others, Jake told Kate, "I'll be glad when it's time to pick up Charlie and start for home. Sightseeing isn't all it's cracked up to be, especially with these two rowdy kids who keep us running after them."

"I'm with you," Kate said. "It'll feel good to be back in our own environment."

The next day, they hardly were out of the car at Will's place before he stepped up to greet Kate. "We've heard a lot about you. Charlie calls you his daughter and I can tell he thinks the world of you and your family."

"The feeling is mutual," Kate replied graciously. "He's so good with the kids and he looks after all of us."

"It's good to see you again, Jake, it's been several years," Alice said. She turned to Kate. "I've got a fried chicken dinner ready. Hope you're all hungry."

"We do love fried chicken. But you shouldn't have gone to a lot of trouble."

"Are you kidding, we love the company."

Kate spooned gravy over Matt's potatoes. She glanced at Will and Charlie sitting next to each other. "I sure can see the resemblance between you two. You're not twins, are you?"

Will's response was amusing. "No, but I guess we do look a lot alike. As kids, some folks had trouble telling us apart. When we got in trouble, we'd always blame it on the other one, but that didn't fly with our mom and dad."

"But basically we got along pretty good," Charlie said. "Kinda like your two kids, get along okay and even look a lot alike." He pinched Molly's cheek.

"Grandpa," she said. "Matt and I don't look alike. He's a boy and I'm a girl."

"Oh, yeah, you're right," Charlie agreed.

While Kate helped Alice with the dishes, Will took Jake and Charlie out to the barn to show Jake a horse that had a wire cut. "Charlie says you're as near a vet as any rancher he knows. What do you think?"

"I think Charlie fed you a line."

"No, I didn't. I tell Jake he's a good vet," Charlie said. "That way, he'll do most of the doctoring."

Jake inspected the cut on the horse. "It looks like that Blue Vit-rol is doing the job. Seems to be healing pretty good."

Kate urged Will and Alice to come up to their ranch sometime. Jake echoed his wife's invitation while corralling the kids into the station wagon. "Settle down, we have a long way to go," he told Molly and Matt.

Charlie and Will assured each other they would talk once in a while. "Now that you've got a phone," Will said, "there's no excuse not to keep in touch. Neither one of us is very good about writing letters. Martha was good to write. We all miss that dear lady." The two men met with a bear hug and Charlie kissed Alice on the cheek. Jake and Kate thanked them for the great meal and urged Molly to thank them too. Matt's thank you was more of a grunt.

Both kids fell asleep in the back of the station wagon so the grownups were able to enjoy the drive over the mountain to Walden and on to Steamboat Springs.

"I can sure see why everyone likes to ski here around Steamboat Springs," Kate said, admiring the ski runs up and down the mountains.

"And these lush meadows look like these ranches will have lots of hay this year," Jake said.

Charlie didn't comment so Kate glanced back to see that he was dozing, with both Molly and Matt asleep on his lap.

At Craig they turned north into Wyoming then followed the freeway to Rock Springs.

The kids were awake and clamoring for something to eat before they reached Rock Springs. Jake stopped so everyone could eat, and then bought gas before they set out on the last eighty-five miles to the ranch.

It was midnight before they arrived home. They took in sleeping kids, leaving everything else in the car until morning.

A tour in the morning showed Jake that the addition to the house was looking good. The carpenters came about nine o'clock and set right to work. Two men shingled the roof while George and another fellow installed windows.

"I brought out the doors, but that will have to wait until to-morrow," George said.

"Thanks. By the way, do you do cabinets, too?"

"We can. What do you have in mind?"

"Look over our kitchen. We don't need new cabinets, but we need to take one out so we have room to put in a gas range. I'd take out the old Majestic but it might cause a divorce."

George laughed. "I know what you mean."

"Okay, we'll talk more about it in the morning."

Jake knew he'd better let Kate know what was up so after the kids were in bed he took her into the kitchen. "George is coming back tomorrow and we need to decide where we can put a gas cook stove."

Kate looked at him in disbelief.

"I know you don't want a new stove. You can use this one too but I'm sure you'd like a range if you had one. I think we ought to have a gas stove because the electricity goes off now and then."

"But . . ."

"No buts. I told George we wouldn't take this stove out."

"I like cooking on this old stove, but I guess we have to get a new one."

A couple of weeks later, Kate was grumbling about how hard it was to regulate the burners when Charlie stepped forward. "The bread sure comes out looking good, doesn't it?"

"All right, you and Jake win—this time."

"It's all in the name of progress," Jake spoke up. "I'm surprised a city girl like you doesn't realize it."

"What do I have to do to convince you that I'm not a city girl anymore?"

"I could name a few things, but not in front of Charlie."

"You're incorrigible, you know that?"

"I'm going to bed," Charlie said. "I'll leave you two to your arguing or whatever it is you two lovebirds have in mind."

Early in June of 1965, Marie called Jake to let him know that Don wasn't feeling well and she didn't see how they'd be able to come for haying season. Brad was working with a veterinarian as an intern until he could work out the details of setting up his own business, so he wasn't available to help them out.

"It's okay, Marie," Jake said. "We've come to rely on you two but we want Don to feel good again. We'll manage," he said light-heartedly. "We'll check on you as often as we can."

Now that the addition to the Bunkhouse was completed, Jake and Kate made time before haying to go to Rock Springs for beds and dressers. It took at least a week to get Matt to stay put in his room. He was so used to sharing a room with Molly.

Not too long afterwards, news of Don's heart attack alarmed them. It was clear they couldn't rely on Marie and Don to come anymore.

Jake had bought a swather earlier in the summer so he could cut the hay and leave it in windrows. Robbie came to rake at the suggestion of Chris, who had become expert at building stacks. Robbie learned fast and proved to be a good hand on the scatter rake. Jake managed to hire two fellows who came to the county looking for work. Both had worked on a ranch before so Jake put them on the sweeps. The new equipment and good help got them through haying with no major problems.

Kate missed Marie but managed to cook for the hay crew in spite of two busy kids underfoot. Sometimes she restricted them to the yard, and after a spanking when they wandered out, they obeyed. Chris had seen how Brad helped out with milking or doing dishes and stepped right in for whatever needed to be done.

It was great news to learn that Don seemed to be making a good recovery.

———•———

Winter arrived and they all caught colds at one time or another. Kate used her nursing skills to ease discomforts from coughing, stuffy noses, and sore throats. She was rubbing Mentholatum on the kids' chests one evening and suggested that the men ought to use some too.

"A hot toddy will do the trick for me," Charlie said, surprising her because she'd never known him to take a drink of whiskey. "You need one too, Jake?"

"Sure." Then he winked at Kate, "I wouldn't mind having Kate rub *my* chest, though."

"Go on, you two. I have all I can do to get these kids into bed and just hope this hot tea with honey and lemon stops their coughs."

By Christmas everyone was well and excitement ran high in the household as they celebrated the holidays. The new games and toys, along with some approved TV cartoons, kept Molly and Matt entertained when it was too cold or stormy to take them out with the men to the feedground.

When the weather began to warm up, Kate told Jake she would be glad when the kids could play outside. "And," she added, "I've seen enough Mickey Mouse and Tom and Jerry cartoons to last me a long time. Television does keep them occupied while I'm busy though."

———•———

Spring in 1966 brought buckets of rain and the inevitable mud, which kept the kids inside. Kate tried to keep them occupied as best she could with puzzles, games, and reading stories to them, but she had her hands full most of the time with cooking and doing laundry. Maureen had sent word she didn't want to make the long trip this year. She assured them she wasn't sick, just slowing down.

———•———

After a two-day rain, the road from their house to the county road was pure mud. One cloudy morning at breakfast they were discussing how the rain showed no signs of letting up. "It makes for some pretty sloppy corrals," Charlie remarked.

"We can sit here all day and talk about the weather, but there's nothing we can do about it," Kate said. "Let's talk about Molly and her schooling. Don't forget she starts this fall and I'm not teaching either of these kids at home."

"Why not?" Jake asked. "Just out of curiosity."

"First of all, I'm not a teacher. And let's not forget, I've played Scrabble with you two and you can't spell worth a darn."

Jake covered her mouth to stop her from saying more. "Okay, we don't want to be teachers, either. Besides, we don't have the time."

Kate twisted away from his hand and went on to make her point, as if she hadn't heard Jake. "Plus I always have to keep score so I don't trust you with arithmetic. Not to mention, neither one of you has been far enough off the ranch to know much about geography."

Finally Charlie prevailed with his voice of reason. "I'm sure the school bus will come to the gate. The Petersons have had one for a long time. A few more miles won't make much difference."

"Let's hope so," Kate said.

"Have you talked to the superintendent yet?" Charlie asked.

"Yes," Jake replied. "It's all set for Molly to go to Boulder School this fall."

Kate looked surprised. "When did you arrange that?"

"The day before yesterday when I went to town. Guess I forgot to tell you."

"You must have, but I'm glad that's been taken care of. Jackie Peterson said they go to Boulder for eight grades. It seems like a long way to ride a bus."

"It's about twenty-three miles," Jake said. "The kids will get used to it. I hope you can."

"I've gotten used to a lot of new things these last few years. One more thing won't bother me at all."

Her pretense at being stern set the men laughing at her, and Molly wondering what they were talking about.

———•———

Since they still used horses for the sweeps, Jake and Charlie went out to bring them in off the desert before haying time. The ground had dried some so Kate went out to pull the weeds in her bed of petunias. Matt was nearby digging in the dirt with his toy shovel and Molly was riding Candy in the corral. Unexpectedly Kate heard the click of the gate latch and Molly yelling, "Momma, Matt got out of the gate." She stood up, frozen with terror. Matt was headed for the corral across the road. With a quick glance Kate saw the horses galloping up the lane headed for the open gate to the barnyard.

"Matt, come back," Kate screamed, running like the devil after him. Seconds before the horses would have trampled him Kate scooped Matt up and slammed both of them into the pole fence along the road. The horses ran past, kicking up dust. The sound of their hooves was deafening. Jake jumped off his still moving horse and caught Kate before she slumped to the ground.

"Are you all right? What happened?"

"Matt . . . got out of the gate . . . was running across the road," she gasped.

"I saw you running but I never saw Matt."

Kate shook her head and started to cry. "I caught him just in time, but he could have been killed."

Charlie shut the gate on the horses and ran back along the fence to where Jake was holding Kate and Matt. Expecting the worst, he knelt down where he could see them. "Oh, Lord, Kate, I thought one or both of you had been run over. Are you okay?"

She nodded through her tears. When she was able to stop crying, Jake helped her up. Molly had climbed off her horse and was watching in horror from top of the fence. Jake helped her down, then picked up Matt and they all started for the house while Charlie led their saddle horses toward the barn.

That night, after they were settled in bed, Jake held Kate in his arms. She was still visibly shaken. Neither of them spoke about how close they had come to losing their little boy.

<hr>

Fortunately, Jake's crew from last year came back to hay again. Things went smoothly if more slowly, and Jake missed his old crew.

Chris had turned out to be a good hand and helpful around the house. He usually did the milking but was always quiet and went to the bunkhouse soon after supper.

Come September, Jake told Kate how long it had taken to get the hay up that year and he'd have to think about getting a baler sometime soon. "Although, Scott Williams told me he has one and spends a lot of time cleaning it out or repairing something. I hope they have been improved since he bought his."

On her forty-first birthday, Kate confided to Jake that she didn't mind cooking for the branding crew, but she would be glad when she could work in the field again.

"You will, one of these days. Look how fast those two kids are growing."

They watched as Matt rode his stick horse around the coffee table in the living room. "It looks to me like working in the field is years away."

By now, six-year-old Molly was a regular tomboy. She rode with the men at every opportunity and sometimes Kate would go along, holding Matt on her lap. Molly kept reminding Charlie that she'd be going to school soon and he'd have to gather the eggs by himself, at least during the weekdays. He always replied how much he'd miss her. Secretly, all the adults were anticipating a little more peace and quiet when Molly went off to school.

 **Chapter Thirty**

**One day, Jake and Kate** took the kids on horseback down to collect the mail. As usual, Jake carried Matt on the front of his saddle as Molly trotted off on Candy, ahead of the others. It amused her parents that she'd trot ahead and then come back and start all over again.

"I hear the Petersons have a new stock truck," Kate commented. "And they use it to take their horses to where they want to work cattle. It might be convenient, but that sure puts a new light on the old ranching ways."

"I know what you mean. We don't have as far to go with our cows to the mountain and back, so I don't see any need for a new truck to do that." He reached up and adjusted Matt's hat.

About that time, Molly came trotting back to them. "Daddy, I just saw a squirrel."

"A squirrel? I don't think we have squirrels around here. How big was it?"

She held her fingers apart and Jake was surprised that she quite accurately marked the length of a gopher. "I think you saw a gopher. Did it run across the road?"

"Yes, and there was another one, too, down the road. Can we catch one?"

"No, that's not a good idea. A gopher would bite you even if you managed to catch one."

Molly trotted back to see if she could see another gopher.

Jake pointed to Matt, then Molly. "This cowboy and that cowgirl are going to need a way to take their horses to rodeo someday. That old stock truck that Jesse and I used when we roped at a rodeo wasn't much good when we used it and it sure won't do for this young cowboy to take his horse to the rodeo."

"That seems a long way off, but the way they're growing, it won't be all that long, I guess. If he even wants to rope," she added.

"He tries to rope now. It's funny to watch him, but he'll get the hang of it."

"I suspect you're going to be taking your cowgirl to a rodeo to barrel race one of these days."

"I'd like to."

"Something worries me, Jake."

"About barrel racing?"

"No, about our kids being so isolated that the only time they get to play with other kids their age is when we stay for coffee and donuts after Mass. I'm wondering how they'll do in school."

"Molly seems to do okay. The Madison girl is about her age and they have fun together after Mass."

"Yes, I talked to Christine Madison after Mass last Sunday and the two girls will be in school together and in the same grade. They live this side of Boulder. Maybe we could have them over for supper sometime soon. I think she said her oldest girl is in third grade and they have a boy a little younger than Matt."

"Sounds good to me. It would help Molly to have a friend in the same grade and riding the same school bus."

The Madisons accepted an invitation from Kate to come for supper the following Saturday evening. Afterwards, Kate wished she'd thought of having them over a lot sooner. The McClarys and Madisons played pinochle while the kids played with toys. And they managed to gather once more at the Madison Ranch before September. By then Molly and Carol Ann Madison were excited about beginning school.

One evening Kate was crocheting and Jake was reading a magazine when Kate brought up the fact that they didn't have many friends, other than their neighbors. "We've met some people at church but we never see them anywhere else. Do you think people might think we're anti-social?"

"Maybe they do. I don't really know. I've never been an active member of the cattlemen's organization, but I know a lot of ranchers in the county. I guess you could go to a homemaker's club if you want to. I think my mother went to one sometimes."

"I am perfectly content to stay at home unless we need something in town. I enjoy the county's traditional events that we've gone to and I have visited with a few people who were there, too. I just realized that getting together with the Madisons is pleasant and the kids do have fun."

Jake yawned. "I suspect we'll get enough socializing when the kids get in school. As I remember, sports and school activities kept my folks plenty busy."

"I didn't do any sports and wasn't asked to be in any plays so my folks didn't go to many things at school," Kate said wistfully.

———•◆•———

"Why can't I wear my boots?" Molly whined.

"Because you want to dress up for school. Those boots don't go with this nice skirt and pretty blouse," Kate said. She made sure Molly tied her shoes securely. "You need to hurry. We don't want to be late for your first day of school."

Kate drove Molly to Boulder and met her teacher, but Molly was emphatic that she could ride the bus home. While she watched some of the other girls arrive, Kate made one observation—most of the girls wore pants. *That makes sense*, she thought, surmising that most of them rode several miles to school on the bus and would surely be exposed to some real cold weather before the winter was over.

Kate got home just before time to fix their dinner. She sat down to eat and said grace, then said to the men, "I thought Molly would be scared or at least not want me to leave her but she was happy as a lark going off to school for the first time. I was the one feeling sad."

"Wait till Matt leaves. Neither of the kids have been away from us for very long at a time, so I expect seeing him go off will make you cry."

"You sure have a way of putting things," Kate said, knowing he was right.

Both she and Jake had longed for another child but apparently it wasn't meant to be. They often commented on how blessed they were to have Molly and Matt.

Jake thought about his mom and how the kids had missed her that year. "I wish we could get down to spend a few days with Mom before winter sets in," he said. "But we've got a lot to do this fall, and Molly will be in school. If there's not too much snow and Chris can come help Charlie, we'll try to go for Thanksgiving."

That seemed to satisfy Kate who had mentioned that the kids often talked about their grandmother. Of course, they didn't even know her mother. She had exchanged a few letters with her mother after Lillian wrote to thank them for their hospitality and the money Jake had given them. Kate enclosed pictures of the children in two of her letters. Lillian seemed to be glad to have them and commented on how much Molly and Matt had grown.

———•———

Molly came home from her first day at school and chattered on about her teacher and her new friends. "Recess is fun. I like the slide best but Carol Ann likes to swing. She always wants me to push her higher."

Kate suggested that she eat her supper first, and then tell them about school.

Molly took a few bites and started up again, "There's a boy in school who sits behind me. He said I don't write my name right. I told him it was none of his business, then he said his mom has a cat named Molly and he likes the cat better than me."

The grownups exchanged glances now and then, sure that the others were just as amused. Matt insisted on telling them that he had roped the black cat that afternoon. "He scratched me, see." He showed them a tiny red mark on the back of his hand.

When things quieted down for a few moments, Charlie asked, "Can you two remember that first winter after Kate came? Things aren't the same anymore."

"Kinda hard to believe how much has changed," Jake said. "It used to be so peaceful and quiet."

"Maybe quiet, but not too peaceful at first as I remember," Kate said.

"Matt, clean up your plate," Jake demanded.

"I don't like beans."

"I know you don't, but you need to learn to eat beans."

—•—

It was a chore keeping Matt occupied when the weather was foul. She looked forward to when they would start feeding the cattle so she and Matt could go along sometimes. Occasionally, she drove out to the sagebrush flat and helped him look for horny toads and sage chickens.

One morning, Jake spied Matt trying to rope the milk cow's calf. He ignored it when the calf ran to the other side of the corral and Matt seemed to give up, but that afternoon he called Kate to the window when he saw Matt chasing the calf again.

"If he ever gets the rope around that calf's neck, he'll be dragged all over the corral. He's liable to get run over, too."

"He has to stay out of that corral," Kate said.

Jake went out the door and a few minutes later, he carried a squirming Matt into the house and sat him down on a chair. "I'm not going to tell you again. That calf is liable to kick you or at least knock you down. If I catch you in that corral again, you're going to get a good spanking."

Matt puckered up his brow and stuck out his lower lip while glaring at his dad.

"Sit there until you quit sulking," Jake told him. Matt didn't even know what the word sulking meant, but Kate figured that he knew he had better mind his dad.

He sat fidgeting for about twenty minutes. "Can I get up now?" he asked his mom.

"Yes, but you stay out of that corral."

"Okay."

They didn't catch Matt going to the corral anymore, but he tried roping everything from the cats to the fence posts. He even took a crack at roping Molly when she came home from school one day. She grabbed the rope and wrapped it around his legs. She left him there tied up and screaming until he got loose.

—•—

The fall weather was mild, so gathering and shipping went well. Everyone looked forward to traveling to Phoenix to have Thanksgiving at Maureen's. Charlie begged off going and assured them that he would take care of everything at home.

"Thanksgiving won't be the same with you folks gone," he said.

"You'll probably be glad to have some time for yourself," Kate said. "These kids don't give you much peace."

The two-day trip went well except when the kids got to squabbling, then Jake would threaten to stop the car and give them both a good swat. That usually quieted them down until one or the other wanted something the other one had. Once in a while they would both fall asleep at the same time. Jake and Kate welcomed the quiet time. They reached Maureen's apartment late on the second day.

A stranger in a nurse's outfit met them at the door of Maureen's apartment in the retirement community, alarming Jake and Kate.

"What's wrong?" Kate asked anxiously.

"She had a TIA yesterday and we're just keeping an eye on her."

"I'm her son and this is my wife," Jake said.

"Yes, she told me you were coming. My name is Edith."

Maureen came from her sitting room and greeted them with hugs and kisses. She turned to Edith. "I'm fine. I appreciate you checking on me."

After Edith left, Maureen explained that the retirement compound kept a nurse employed to help anyone who needed assistance.

Molly and Matt were bewildered by what was going on. Matt hung on to Kate's pant leg while Molly looked around wide-eyed.

"What does your doctor say about yesterday's mini-stroke?" Jake asked.

"We just got back from the doctor's appointment and he gave me a list of do's and don'ts to prevent another attack." She picked up a paper from the table and handed it to Kate. "I intend to follow it to the letter. I don't want another of those, although he said I had a mild attack and to consider it a warning."

Kate looked over the paper. "We're glad you're okay. Have you had anything like this before?"

"Oh, no. The doctor said a bit of plaque broke loose and traveled to my brain. He did some tests for cholesterol or something."

Given Maureen's scare, Kate insisted on cooking their Thanksgiving dinner and doing the clean up. Molly helped out by setting the table. After dinner she stood on a chair to dry the dishes. Later, Kate took Matt and Molly to a nearby park so Jake and his mother could have a good visit. When they returned, Jake and his mom were watching a football game. The volume on the TV was low.

During halftime, Maureen said, "I'm going to tell you something and I want you to do as I say."

Her decisiveness got their attention.

"I want to get an apartment in Pinedale."

Jake looked downright surprised.

"The weather won't be as good as it is here, but I think it's time to move closer to my family."

"We'd like that, Mom," Jake said.

"I'm not sure what they have in Saratoga, but I think I'd rather settle in Pinedale. I hope I can find an apartment."

"You can live with us, you know that," Kate said.

"Yes, dear, I know that. But you have your busy lives and I like my quiet life. I just want to be closer to home."

The game had started up again and gotten Jake's attention.

"One more thing," she said, drawing Jake away from the game. "I want to go with you now."

"Well, I think we can arrange that," Jake said. "It won't hurt for Molly to miss a couple of days of school."

It took Jake and Kate until Monday to help pack her things and take the items to Goodwill that she wouldn't need in Pinedale. The director of the retirement compound said they had a waiting list and she could arrange for another senior to rent the apartment. Accomplishing all these things was no small feat over a long holiday weekend.

They set off with Maureen next to Jake in the front and Kate in the back seat with the kids. The trip took two days, with only necessary stops. By the time they got to the ranch, Maureen had heard a lot about the horses her grandchildren rode and almost everything Molly was learning in school. Matt told her several times that a cat at the barn has some baby kittens.

When they arrived at the Bunkhouse, Maureen was surprised to see Jesse and his family waiting to greet them. Jake had called to let them know Maureen was coming home with them. Maureen reached out to Charlie who bent to put his cheek next to hers as they greeted each other.

Two months later, in spite of snow and feeding the cattle, Jake and Kate moved Maureen into her apartment. It was a bonus, she said, to find Dorothy Warren and Peg Larson living in the same apartment building. The women had known each other for many years.

 # Chapter Thirty-One

**In Wyoming,** everyone welcomed an Indian summer. So in the fall of 1967, with the clear blue sky and days that were deceptively warm for wading in the shallows of the creek, Kate found herself giving in to Matt and Molly's begging to wade and look for fish. In spite of not finding any fish and coming out of the water almost blue, they braved the icy stream. *At least,* Kate thought to herself, *I only have to do this on weekends since Molly goes to school.* She was glad when the kids decided they'd had enough. The kids wanted to go along when Jake or Charlie went riding, but Jake was emphatic that they couldn't watch kids and gather cattle, too.

One morning, after they had shipped the yearlings, Jake sat down with a cup of coffee to read the stock market reports.

Kate was bustling about the kitchen when the phone rang. The voice on the other end introduced himself to Kate as Arthur Borden, her mother's lawyer. Kate stiffened.

"I haven't spoken with my mother for some time. What is it that she wants?" Kate asked.

"I'm sorry to tell you that your mother passed away yesterday."

"Oh dear, what happened?"

"She fell on the sidewalk outside of a restaurant, hit her head, and never regained consciousness."

Jake was sitting at the table and saw the color drain from Kate's face. She looked like she was about to faint. He walked over and put his arm around her waist so that she leaned against him.

"I appreciate you letting me know," Kate said softly. "Was her husband with her?"

"I guess you haven't heard," Borden said. "He died of a heart attack about four or five months ago."

Kate held her composure. "What about the burial?"

"She had a will and some instructions that she left with me when her husband died. It was her wish to be buried next to him at the cemetery here in Reno." Borden cleared his throat. "Naturally, I want to make the arrangements in accord with your wishes."

"I appreciate that, but I don't see any way that we can get away from here right now. Go ahead and do what needs to be done." Kate clasped Jake's hand. "Thank you for calling and letting me know."

"Before you hang up, I understand you were estranged from your mother, but there's something else," he continued. "She had quite a lot of jewelry and it was her wish that I deliver it to you personally. The house and car went to Grayson's son. I would like to come to Wyoming to give the jewelry to you."

"You had better come right away or wait until spring. Our weather's not very predictable."

"Just give me directions and I'll be there."

"My husband can tell you better than I can." She handed the phone to Jake.

After they hung up, Kate said with a voice that wasn't quite steady, "It's odd to hear from a stranger that your mother's husband died months ago and your mother just died."

Jake pulled her close. "I'm sorry about your mother. I wish you'd had a better relationship with her."

"Truthfully, I don't even know how to take this news. It saddens me but I think the loss happened so long ago that I can't feel much of anything right now. I've never felt that we knew each other as adults."

"A loss is a loss, Kate, and you might well grieve."

Kate's mind was elsewhere. "Why do you suppose this lawyer would travel all the way from Reno to bring me my mother's jewelry?"

"I don't know, except your mother wore some pretty expensive jewelry when she was here. There were rings on at least four of her fingers and I'd guess that her earrings had real diamonds in them."

"It doesn't add up somehow." She busied herself with making loaves out of rising dough. "Maybe my mother thought she ought to make her daughter more fashionable."

"Would you like to go for a horseback ride? I'll take Matt on with me and you can have a little time to think about your mother's passing. We could wait till Molly gets home and we could all go."

"I'm okay. I want to finish the bread. Let's take the kids for a ride after school so Molly can go too."

———•———

Mr. Borden drove into the ranch the following Saturday. Kate and Jake greeted him warmly and asked him to stay for dinner.

When they'd finished eating, Borden thanked them for a wonderful meal and suggested they take care of business so he could start home soon. "It really is a long way out here," he said with a smile.

Molly and Matt were curious as to the business at hand and asked if they could stay around. Jake told them it was grown-up time and, besides, Molly needed to do her homework. Charlie offered to take them off to their rooms.

Mr. Borden set a large leather jewelry chest on the dining room table. Astonished by the elegance of the box itself, Kate watched as he unlocked the chest, lifted the lid, and pulled down the front panel. He rolled down velvet ring bars with over a dozen rings set with precious stones, opened necklace and pin drawers, and pulled out a jewelry travel case so she could see the entire contents of the chest. He handed Kate a list of all that it contained. "This is the list your mother left with her will. Please be sure that everything is there, then if you would, please sign this release."

Overwhelmed by the rich display, Kate asked Jake to help inventory the many pieces of fine jewelry. When they finished and every item was accounted for, she signed the paper.

Then Borden handed Jake another piece of paper. "I was instructed that at her death, I was to give you this envelope. Please sign this release to show that I've given it to you."

Jake signed then handed the document back to the lawyer.

Mr. Borden was eager to get going. "When the estate is settled, the money that's left will be divided between Grayson's son and you, Mrs. McClary, so I'll be in touch when the time comes."

Jake walked Mr. Borden to his car. They shook hands and Jake thanked him for driving all that way to deliver the jewels. He sauntered back to the house thinking about all that had transpired.

"Can you believe what just happened?" Kate asked as he walked through the door. "Maybe you were right. When old age was getting near, Mother must have had a change of heart and thought of us." She looked at the envelope Jake had left on the table. "What do you suppose she had to say to you?"

They sat down. Jake opened the envelope and let out a loud whistle. He read the brief note to Kate. *Thank you for your generosity. Lillian will see to it that you get this cheque.* It was signed Grayson Crawford, Esq. The check was made out to Jake for twenty-five thousand dollars from the estate of Grayson Crawford.

"I believe that title indicates that he was a lawyer," Jake said. He thought about it a minute. "Maybe he was retired by the time we met him."

"Will wonders never cease," Kate said in disbelief. She sighed and said, "I feel rotten." She held her head in her hands. "I should have been more forgiving. Here she left me things that meant a lot to her and I don't even know how to feel about that . . . or even about her death."

"I feel rotten, too. I gave them money grudgingly. I wasn't even gracious about it. But, I'm also glad to be witness to this kind of integrity."

"He must have hit a jackpot," Kate said.

"You're probably right," Jake said with a smile. "Of course, maybe he had stocks or property. He didn't deny being a gambler but that would hardly accumulate enough for their style of living." He put his hand on Kate's arm and said, "Let's give them the benefit of the doubt."

"You're right. To be truthful, I want to feel better about my mother," she said thoughtfully.

Kate looked at the assortment of expensive jewelry still on the table. "I doubt I'll ever wear many of these jewels, but we'll give them to the kids someday."

"And we'll give the kids this money when it's the right time."

"Do you think Molly will be interested in this kind of jewelry when she grows up?" Kate asked.

"I don't know. Maybe. She's got pretty expensive tastes already, which I think she gets from you," Jake teased. "Remember, the saddle she picked out cost us a pretty penny."

# Chapter Thirty-Two

**Over time,** Jake and Kate got involved with what went on socially in the county. Most ranch wives shopped at the local grocery store on Thursday, the store's sale day. Kate got into the habit of going to town to shop on Thursday and became acquainted with other women. She was invited to join Cowbelles, the women's organization affiliated with the Green River Valley Cattlemen's Association. After attending a yearly business meeting, Jake was appointed to a committee and became active in the association. Kate was slower to become involved but eventually looked forward to meeting with women whose ranch lives were much like hers.

When Molly turned ten, she wanted to become a 4-H member. "I want to have a horse project," she insisted when Kate tried to interest her in sewing or cooking. Unfortunately, Molly was more interested in working with her horse than keeping records, so it was a constant battle to get her to do her record book. She and Gray, the horse Jake broke for her in time for 4-H, performed well at the county fair, and a purple ribbon hung over the post of her bed.

Since they were seldom involved with activities away from the ranch early in their marriage, Jake and Kate began to feel the strain of keeping up with everything. They were hardly ready to take on more when Matt had his tenth birthday and told them he wanted to have a 4-H steer project. "You get money for steers," he said.

With some misgivings about his motivations, Jake helped Matt pick out a good-looking steer, and with the help of his 4-H leader, Matt worked out his feeding and grooming schedule. His diligence at working with his steer paid off because his was the Reserve Champion in the class and Matt garnered a Grand Champion ribbon for showmanship. Jake confided in Kate that he was afraid that Matt's heart would be broken when the time came to let his beloved steer go off to be slaughtered. Matt got a good price for his steer but letting him go was pretty tough on the kid.

After the 4-H leader said it was time to turn in their record books, Kate said to Jake, "I hope Molly's will be as accurate as Matt's. He keeps a good record of everything. Molly can't be bothered."

Kate took the record books to their 4-H leader and came home with information about Achievement Day. They attended with all the other parents, leaders, 4-Hers, and Extension Agents and watched as each one received recognition for their projects. They were almost home that evening when Kate commented, "That was a good way to end the year. Are you kids going to take 4-H again in the fall?"

"I'm going to take two projects. Gray and I are going to be Grand Champions next year," Molly announced confidently. "And I'm going to have a steer next year, too. Since I don't sell my horse, I don't make any money."

"Oh, Lord," Jake moaned. "I wondered when she would catch on to that," he said in a low voice to Kate as the kids were getting out of the car.

———————

There were school events to attend and an occasional dance at the community hall. Charlie usually stayed home, claiming that his rheumatism made it hard to dance. But he would dance a waltz with Kate at home most anytime Jake put on a record.

In second grade, Molly had come home from school with chicken pox and passed it on to Matt. When Molly came down with the mumps a couple of years later, Kate worried about the rest of them getting mumps. Charlie and Jake assured her that they'd had mumps as kids, and since she remembered her bout with the disease, she surmised Matt would be the only one. And she was right.

"I hope they don't get the measles and we're done with childhood diseases," Kate told Jake one night.

"Doesn't everybody get the measles?" Jake asked.

"Not very often anymore. Everyone receives the immunizations as an infant."

Molly and Matt's years attending school in Boulder went by quickly and Kate dreaded the day they would have to ride the extra twelve miles to school in Pinedale. The kids never did complain about the long bus ride but when Molly was about to enter her sophomore year, she'd wanted to play basketball but complained that she couldn't because she had to ride home on the bus right after school let out.

Kate felt bad that Molly wasn't able to take part in the extra-curricular activities, however, neither she nor Jake could see making a trip to town every night to bring her home. And there would be the games, too.

"There is one thing we could do," Jake said. "You and the kids could move into town for the school year. Mom did that for Jesse and me the two years we were in high school in Pinedale."

"Oh dear, is that the only thing we can do? I don't want to leave the ranch and you and Charlie. I'd be bored to death in town."

Jake thought about it for a few minutes. "There must be other parents around here whose kids are in sports. I suppose we could car pool with them." He rubbed his chin and added, "I would hate to ask any of them to come clear out here to bring our kids home, though. Matt is already talking about playing football. He will be in high school next year and naturally, he wants to play sports like the other kids."

So that settled it. Kate, Molly, and Matt moved into an apartment in Pinedale in time for Molly to play basketball that winter. Games and bad weather determined when they could spend a weekend at the ranch. They always returned to town with milk, cream, eggs, and the butter Charlie or Jake had churned for them.

As Jake had predicted, Matt signed up for football at the first opportunity, although he wasn't getting to play that first year. His sophomore year was a different story. He handed his dad a schedule the first time Jake came to town.

"I'll try to make most of them," Jake assured him. He couldn't always manage to make their games but he was there for as many of Matt's football games and Molly's basketball games as he could that winter.

Kate kept Jake apprised of the kids' grades and social activities by phone. During one call, Jake said, "Matt sure loves football. I know he'll want to be in the high school rodeo club, too. I hope we're up to all the running around and can keep the ranch work done."

"Molly manages to take part in basketball and the rodeo activities," Kate responded. "That means a lot of trips around the state for us."

"They're going to be out of school before we know it," Jake said flatly.

By the time Molly graduated from high school, Jake and Kate had attended a great many sports events and rodeos. They determined that they would keep going until the last rodeo Matt could participate in as a high school student.

As a family, they had been to a lot of 4-H meetings and county fairs. Matt and Molly had been to the Wyoming State Fair several times with their animals and they both had bulletin boards full of ribbons and shelves full of trophies.

The summer after Molly's graduation, they struggled to get the hay up because of constant rains. They lost two bulls who were hit by lightning, and cattle prices were the lowest they'd ever had. They managed to get Molly and her belongings to Laramie so she could start college at the University of Wyoming before bad weather started the worst winter they had known on the ranch.

Kate and Matt moved into town for his senior year. Kate developed a bronchial infection that required several visits to the doctor. Jake and Charlie were snowed in and they hadn't had time to try plowing the road.

"Christmas break starts Thursday. Molly will be here Friday. Can't we come home?" Kate asked plaintively.

Jake got the Caterpillar started and plowed some each afternoon, hoping he could clear the lane.

When Kate telephoned again, Jake said, "Call me when you head for the ranch and I'll meet you at the gate. I think we'll have to meet you with the team and sled but at least we'll have you home for a few days." Jake passed on this information to Charlie, who grinned and said, "That's great."

When it finally came time for Matt to graduate, Kate could hardly wait for the day when she could stay home.

Matt's high school graduation ceremony was quite an event, particularly poignant because Matt was valedictorian for his class.

As they were on their way home from graduation, Jake said, "I'm glad Molly likes the University of Wyoming. Matt received several scholarships to go there, too, but it sure is hard to let them grow away from us."

"At least they're home for the summer. As for me, spending the winters in Pinedale was okay while the kids had to go to school, but I'm happy to be back home for good," Kate said cheerfully.

"I'm just hoping Molly and Matt will continue to help with haying. I don't know how we'd manage without them." They were quiet most of the way home until Kate said, "Have you noticed how often Molly mentions Dave Fitzpatrick? Sounds pretty serious to me."

"I've noticed. When do you suppose we get to meet this wonder boy?"

"I think you'd better call him a man. He sounds very mature and responsible. Of course, Molly wants us to think that."

"I've noticed that, too."

— · —

The summer of 1980 provided a good hay crop and haying was over for another year just in time for Matt and Molly to leave for college. The young people were as eager to go as their parents were reluctant to see them go. Jake and Kate stood arm in arm at the gate and watched forlornly as Molly's Ford pickup and Matt's new Ford pickup, pulling a horse trailer, drove down the lane.

Kate turned around and buried her face in Jake's shoulder, soaking the front of his shirt with her tears. "We've always known this day would come. At least they'll be in Laramie together," she sobbed.

Jake pulled a handkerchief from his back pocket and dried Kate's eyes.

She continued, "Matt is so excited about joining the rodeo club at UW that he never once mentioned anything about studying."

"He'll find out about that soon enough," Jake said.

"He was a good student in high school. We'll have to trust that he takes his studies seriously. He says he wants to teach agriculture in a high school. I know he can do it, but I can't help wishing that both of the kids will come back to the ranch someday."

Jake thought about Kate's sentiment. "Molly's been taking home economics, right? Can you imagine her staying inside long enough to teach anyone anything?" They both laughed. "I bet she'll end up back here and the only home economics she uses will be for the meals she has to fix or, heaven forbid, taking time to sew a button on a shirt."

Kate was so amused she could hardly respond. Finally, she said, "I'm not betting on her teaching home economics, that's for sure."

They started slowly back to the house. Willie, their border collie, met them at the porch and Jake stopped to scratch his ears. "Well, Willie, it's just us now. No more romping after a ball. Guess you'll have to chase the cats."

"He'd better not." When their cat Jerry died of old age, Kate had never tried to tame any of the barn cats, but she liked them around the place. Willie was of a line of border collies they'd had since her loyal Buster had gone to dog heaven. Willie had proven to be a good working cow dog, but he was playful, too.

———•———

Kate watched Charlie limp toward the barn. He had told her that his rheumatism, as he called it, was getting worse. "But all old folks get rheumatism," he said. She had tried to get him to see a doctor, but he refused. Jake sometimes wanted to help him get up on the sled to go feed, but Charlie always managed alone. Most of the time Kate went along to help feed the cattle.

Molly arrived home from college in time to celebrate Charlie's seventieth birthday in June of 1981. It was the summer between her junior and senior years. She was going with Charlie from the house to the chicken coop when he asked, "Remember when you told me you would be going to school soon so I'd have to gather the eggs by myself?"

Molly shook her head. "I don't remember. Did I really say that?"

"Yes, that's what you said. But you helped on the weekends. And sometimes you'd go with me when I milked the cow."

Amused, Molly said, "I wonder how long Dad is going to keep milking a cow. I don't think many people still milk a cow."

"Well," Charlie opined, "I don't know but we all want our milk and cream. I can't imagine your mom buying that oleo or whatever you call it. Of course, your dad had to go clear into Nebraska last year to bring home our last Mrs. Cowley and her calf. That calf is going to be a good milk cow, so we'll be in business for a while, anyway."

Charlie changed the subject. "Are you going to barrel race this summer?"

"You bet. In fact, I was hoping you'd go to Big Piney on the fourth. I've entered there and at Pinedale the next week. I haven't signed up for any more right away. I need to help out here."

"I'll be there. What about Matt?"

"He entered the calf roping at both of those rodeos. Plus he wants to go to Jackson and some other rodeos, too."

"Your folks are good about getting to all these events. Sometimes they come home pretty tired."

"I know, but it's always good to have them watching. Did you know I won a buckle at the college rodeo in Laramie?"

"Sure, that's the first thing Katie told me when they got home."

Charlie winked at Molly. "Tell me about that young man you seem so fond of."

"Oh, Grandpa."

"All right, you don't have to tell me."

She didn't hesitate for long. "I got to know Dave when I joined the college rodeo team soon after I started UW. He grew up on a ranch near Lusk and was in 4-H, too. I met him at state fair when we were both seniors in high school. His parents moved to Idaho after he graduated and he went with them.

"Idaho, huh?"

He didn't like it there much and came back to Laramie and registered in the College of Agriculture. We started dating when we were sophomores."

"I'd like to meet that young man."

"You will this fall. I asked Mom if Dave could come for Thanksgiving. They want to meet him, too. He and Matt both rope and they're good friends."

"Well, we'd better get these eggs put away," Charlie said as they approached the house. "It's good to have you home, honey."

"I'm glad to be home. I had a chance to work on a dude ranch this summer but I'd rather be here. Wrangling horses for dudes might be alright, but they wanted me to clean cabins. Ugh."

Charlie chuckled and opened the door to the mudroom.

———•———

Jake was paying the June telephone bill when Kate walked into the den. She looked over his shoulder. "What are all these calls to Lusk, Wyoming?" he asked. "I never call anyone there."

"No, but your daughter does. Dave has a job on a ranch near Lusk this summer. I'm surprised you haven't noticed how often she's on the phone."

"They must have a lot to talk about. What do you think she will say when I present her with a bill?"

"She'll say, 'Take it out of my wages,' if I know her. Of course, you don't pay her any wages."

"No, I just pay for her to go to college." He quickly amended his statement. "I mean, *we* pay for her college."

Kate patted his shoulder and went back to the kitchen to sweep the floor.

It was no surprise to anyone that Dave was with Molly and Matt when they came home for Thanksgiving.

Molly introduced Dave to her parents and Charlie, all the while trying to gauge the mutual reactions. She needn't have worried. As Jake told Kate later that night, "He reminds me of Brad."

Kate agreed and added, "Yes, she found a wonderful young man. I hope Matt will be as fortunate with a girlfriend."

He tweaked her cheek and said, "I don't think he'll be asking for your help, but we'll wait and see."

By the time the kids left for Laramie, Jake and Kate were well acquainted with Dave. He had helped out with feeding the cattle, even said he and Molly could do the dishes so Kate could sit down and rest after preparing such a wonderful Thanksgiving dinner. When Charlie suggested that they should all sing while Kate played the piano and Jake strummed his guitar, Dave said, "I'm not sure you want to hear me sing." Everyone assured him that he sang very well, even though he didn't know some of their songs. Next, the Victrola was wound and everyone danced with Kate and Molly. Molly and Matt jitterbugged along with Jake and Kate. Then Jake put on the *Tennessee Waltz* and Kate walked over to Charlie and asked, "May I have this dance?" Molly insisted that Dave give it a try although he protested that he didn't know how to waltz.

"Thank you for a fun evening," Dave told all of them after Jake said they'd better get some sleep. Charlie was first to bid everyone goodnight but he had stayed to the end.

They all enjoyed being together for the next few days. Kate was her melancholy self as the kids pulled away from the ranch to return to the university.

Even though the kids participated in college rodeos, Jake and Kate weren't able to attend many of the events because of the hard winter. The highways were often closed, so some of the events were called off because of the weather and road conditions. Matt and Molly had been able to get home for Christmas even though the trip back to Laramie was a hazardous drive. Kate anxiously awaited the phone call from Molly.

"We made it but there were a lot of cars off the road. We saw two wrecks," Molly reported.

"Thank goodness you got there all right. Promise you won't try to come home until the weather is good."

They didn't see them again until Molly's graduation. Molly had asked Dave's parents to a picnic after the ceremony, where she introduced them to her folks. Once they had eaten, Dave approached Jake and asked if he could speak with him privately.

It disconcerted Dave a bit to see Jake take Kate by the hand to bring her along as they walked down a path in the park. Dave wasted no time in getting to the point. "I'd like your consent to let me marry your daughter."

Jake and Kate had seen this coming and highly approved of the young man who seemed very much in love with their daughter. Kate gave Dave a hug and Jake shook his hand. "Take good care of her," was all he said.

Later, Kate pulled Jake aside. "Molly didn't even try to get a job. She planned all along to come back to the ranch."

"It seems so. Now that she and Dave want to be married the first of September and he's willing to live on the McClary Ranch, that should be the answer to your prayers."

"You're right, it is. Dave has a ranch job near Lusk again for the season."

"I wonder if we'll get any work out of her this summer," Jake said.

"Maybe, if we can keep her home. But be prepared for the phone bill to go up again for the next three months."

Dave spent a weekend at the ranch right away so he and Molly could meet with the priest in Pinedale to make arrangements for the wedding and do some of the pre-marital counseling required by the Church.

He met Molly and Kate in Casper when they went to buy her wedding dress and the engaged couple managed to spend the Fourth of July together at the Lander rodeo.

"My boss said I probably won't get to come back until after hay-ing," Dave said after he'd come to see Molly the last of July so they could meet the priest again.

"That's good," Jake joked. "When you're here, Molly doesn't get much work done."

"Oh, Dad," Molly said, wrinkling her nose at him.

# Chapter Thirty-Three

**Besides** planning a wedding, there was another reason it was a busy summer. Jake and Kate set out to fix up the old homestead cabin. They had told Molly and Dave that they could have the big house.

At first Molly protested. "I think Dave and I should move into the cabin. You and Mom can stay in the Bunkhouse."

"Your mother has wanted to make the cabin livable for her and me for so long, I'm not going to argue about it," Jake said.

"Well, if you're sure that's what you want."

"There is one thing," Jake said. "Charlie has always lived there with us . . ."

"And we want him to always live there with us," Molly said without missing a beat and looking at Dave to gauge his reaction.

"Absolutely, I want him to stay there, too," Dave said.

Molly offered, "I want to help remodel the old cabin. I can make the curtains, if you want me to."

"Thank goodness," Jake exclaimed, teasing her. "Kate, I think we're going to get some return on our money—all that home ec paid off." Even Molly joined in their laughter.

"I can cook, too. I might even invite you up for supper sometime," she said to her dad, returning his teasing.

The cabin had two twelve-foot by sixteen-foot rooms. Jake hired carpenters to come and divide one room into a bedroom and bathroom. "And, this big room will be a combined kitchen and living room," Kate said to Jake. "The Majestic stove can go right there where there is already a stovepipe hole," she told him, pointing to the corner of the ceiling.

"I should have known," he said, slowly nodding his head at her. "I was hoping for a fireplace."

Kate clapped her hands together. "That's a good idea. A small fireplace in that corner over there would be perfect."

"I give in on the Majestic but I think we need a small gas stove too."

"Suits me." Kate responded.

"I hope we have room to eat in here," he joked. "Leave us some room to watch TV. You know you shouldn't sit too close to the screen."

"You can decide—two recliners or the loveseat that's in the living room up at the house."

Jake was quick to say, "The recliners." He thought a moment and said, "What about a refrigerator . . . and a washer and dryer? Maybe we'd better build a house."

"No way. We'll make the bathroom a little bigger and put the washer and dryer in there. And a fridge can go in here, okay?"

They walked back to the Bunkhouse with Kate excited and Jake resigned about their project.

—•—

Plumbers and electricians had been coming and going for over a month. Although Jake had hired the carpenters to construct the bedroom and bathroom, it was Kate who instructed them on how it should be done.

"I do hope you'll put in the kitchen cabinets," she said. "You've done a beautiful job with cabinets in the bathroom. They look great with the log walls."

One of the first things Kate had told Jake was how the logs inside the cabin needed to be cleaned, and she preferred not to install wallboard or anything else on top of them.

He was in agreement since he liked the logs and roof beams. The roof wasn't in bad shape but Jake had it re-shingled. Next, they needed to chink the logs on the outside.

The carpenters were done by the time Jake and Kate finished chinking the logs themselves. They cleaned up around the cabin and made a trip to the dump with the trash.

"It really looks nice, doesn't it?" Kate asked. "Since you'll be haying and I'll be doing the cooking, let's move in after haying."

"I'm glad we finally got the baler. I still want to do the swathing but Molly can run the baler and Matt can pick up the bales. You know, it's easier nowadays but I still miss using horses to put up the hay."

"I'm just glad we still have our saddle horses and can help with the cattle," Kate said thoughtfully.

———•———

They were eating supper a few days before the wedding when Kate remarked, "I was surprised when Molly and Dave said they wanted to have a quiet wedding with one bridesmaid and a best man."

"I think it was sweet of Molly to ask Abby to be her bridesmaid. Abby was thrilled and it certainly pleased Jesse and Mary Anne." Jake looked concerned when he added, "I hope Mom doesn't get too tired with all the excitement."

"For ninety-one years old, your mom is in pretty good shape, I'd say," Kate responded.

"I know, but she is getting frail."

Charlie looked up from eating his meatloaf. "I forgot to thank you for taking me to town the other day, Jake. Seems kinda foolish to buy a fancy suit. I'm not apt to wear it out."

They laughed with him. "Don't worry, you still have at least one more wedding to go to," Jake said with a grin.

The big day was on a warm Saturday. Fall flowers were all arranged, and the music began. No one could have been more proud than Jake as he escorted his beautiful daughter down the aisle. He kissed her, handed her to Dave, and then sat down next to Kate who was wiping away tears of happiness. Maureen, who was sitting beside Kate, reached for her hand and gave it a squeeze.

The Mass was never more meaningful than it was that day for the McClary family. Jake put his arm around Kate's shoulders, and as Molly and Dave recited their vows, his arm tightened.

Abby, on the arm of Dave's brother, followed Mr. and Mrs. Dave Fitzgerald to the front door and onto the sidewalk where they received family and friends wishing them a happy life together. Kate and Dave's mother had prepared a light meal of shish kebobs and several salads along with the wedding cake, which Kate had made herself. They had talked about having chicken salad for the main dish, but Jake said, "We're trying to make a living raising beef and you want to serve chicken!"

Jake and Kate agreed to take the gifts home after Molly and Dave opened them and thanked everyone. When the happy couple left, everyone pitched in to clean the parish hall before Dave's parents and other guests started for their homes.

Charlie rode home with Matt so Kate and Jake had some time alone.

"It sure made me think of our wedding. Simple but beautiful," Kate said contentedly.

"There are two big differences between theirs and ours."

"What?"

"I'm sure they're not going skinny dippin'." Kate laughed at him. "And, they're going to Nashville on their honeymoon."

"You're right, Jake. How could I forget?" She nudged him and said, "That reminds me of something."

"Oh?"

"I suppose you've forgotten that I said you could take me on a cruise sometime since we didn't really go on a honeymoon."

"I haven't forgotten. I hoped you had." She knew he was teasing but she also knew going on a cruise wasn't something he'd always wanted to do.

Kate drew in a long breath and let it out slowly. "Actually, I'm too tired to think about something like that right now."

"Besides, we have to be sure these two kids can take care of the place before we go on a trip like a cruise. And, by the way, about the only cruise I'm interested in is to Alaska."

"I guessed that already," she said sleepily.

A couple of days later, Matt went with Jake and Kate to Rock Springs to bring home furniture that they wanted for the cabin. He helped them move into the cabin and then declared that he planned to spend next summer in the ranchhand bunkhouse and let Molly and Dave have the big house to themselves.

Jake chortled. "I guess he doesn't think it's primitive."

It didn't escape Kate that he had used the expression that both Kate's mother and Jake's old girl friend, Laurie, had used to describe life on the ranch.

Molly and Dave returned from their honeymoon ecstatic over all they'd seen in Nashville. She gushed, "You and Mom need to go there sometime. It's just the kind of thing you'd enjoy."

"We'll see," was all Jake had to say.

———•———

Matt had gone back to college before snow in the mountains made the old cows want to come home. Molly called Brad to ask if he and Emily wanted to help bring the cows down. Brad said he could spare two days but being a veterinarian was keeping him busy.

"I'm glad you could come, too," Molly told Emily after Brad had driven into the yard with a horse trailer and unloaded their horses.

"Wouldn't miss it," Emily said with genuine excitement.

Jake greeted the young couple and told Brad, "We had horses you could ride. The last two horses I broke turned out to be great cow ponies, so Kate named them Bonnie and Clyde and we usually ride them. We still have several others."

"I knew you'd have some but Emily and I really like these two, and they need to be ridden more than we have time to ride."

Charlie was glad to stay home. "Someone has to do the work around here," he joked at the breakfast table before all the others saddled up and started for the mountain.

Kate and Jake followed along behind the others. Jake nodded toward the riders ahead. "These young people have fun together.

I suppose they would have preferred bringing their horses up in trailers, but I want them to carry on our old ways."

"Oh, I don't know. They all love to ride and have good horses. I'm sure they will be tired by night but that doesn't hurt 'em, either. Of course, they said they could gather the cattle faster if you took the horses up in the trailer and didn't have to ride all the way back each night."

"I know. They can do what they want when they're in charge."

Kate laughed. "That'll be the day."

# CHAPTER THIRTY-FOUR

**Jake and Kate followed Matt** on the college rodeo circuit whenever they could. It was harder after Maureen began to fail. The doctor urged them to put her in the nursing home and Maureen declared she wanted that too. Keeping up her apartment was just too much, she told Jake. But that wasn't all; she was forgetting to take her medicine and even had a hard time knowing who was talking to her. Jake and Kate went to see her at least twice a week, sometimes together and sometimes only one could go.

Rodeos kept Matt away from the ranch a lot but he tried to be there to help with haying. In 1984, just before he graduated from the University of Wyoming he told his mother on the phone, "I have a job teaching Ag at the high school in Lander. Isn't that great?"

"I'm so happy for you. Do you want to talk to your dad?"

"Sure. I hope you and Dad don't mind that I'm not coming back to the ranch. You all seem to be doing okay, and we decided a long time ago that our outfit isn't big enough to support two or three families."

Kate smiled knowingly. She had suspected for some time that he was quite serious about his girlfriend, Elaine, but she had two more years at the university and they hadn't made any announcement.

"Yes, and you've trained to be a teacher so I know you'll be good at it. I'll put your dad on."

Jake listened then said, "Good for you. Just be sure you teach kids to work hard just like we've tried to do with you and Molly."

"Thanks, Dad. I'm anxious to see everyone at graduation next week. Elaine is going to help me set up a picnic for all of us after the ceremony. The same place as Molly's was."

Before Jake could respond, Matt said, "I sure hope Grandma can be here. Is there any chance of that?"

"No, son, she's pretty much bedridden now, and getting weaker. Her mind comes and goes. Sometimes, she doesn't know us."

"She didn't know me the last time I was home. I hate that."

"We all do, but she's ninety-five and I guess we can't expect anything different."

"I'll miss her," Matt said sadly. "I'll be glad to see you and Mom. I hope Charlie is coming. Molly and Dave said they'll be here."

"I think Charlie plans to go with us. He hasn't said he wouldn't go. But we'll be there."

Later, Jake told Kate, "Matt said he enjoyed roping at all the rodeos but he has no intention of becoming a professional. He thinks he'll be here for branding, and I hope so 'cause he's the best calf roper we have."

"As good as you?" Kate asked.

"I can still rope but my bones ache at the end of a branding day with that much roping."

"I'm proud of our kids, Jake. They're both college graduates and they are good workers on the ranch, too." She paused. "I should have made Molly work more in the house, though. She's always wanted to be outside and riding a horse, so she isn't the best housekeeper we know, and I don't think we ought to ask Dave about her cooking."

"She did a pretty good job with the roast and baked potatoes the other night when she asked us to eat with them. There's still hope for her."

Kate put on her gardening gloves. "Jake, would you do something for me?"

He proceeded cautiously. "It's taken me a long time to figure this one out, but I'm not saying yes 'til you tell me what you want."

"Well, this cabin needs . . ."

"Don't say it. Sagebrush," Jake said resignedly.

"Please tell me you'll get it from the same place. That tall sagebrush is exactly what we need. I don't want to take any of it away from the Bunkhouse so . . ."

Jake put a hand over Kate's mouth.

Laughing, she struggled to free herself.

"Tain't funny, Magee," he said.

"You told me that one time years ago. I wish I could remember why you said that."

"I don't remember either, but this isn't the first time since then you've bamboozled me."

"I just thought of something, Jake. You said you always liked hearing that old radio show, 'Fibber Magee and Molly'. Is that where you got the name for our Molly?"

"I never thought of that. I just liked the name. It seems to fit our Molly okay and I don't even remember much about Fibber's Molly now."

"Oh, well, back to the sagebrush. We planted the first one in the spring and it grew, so I guess this is a good time to plant some more."

"Yes, but you kept the first one in a tub in the house all winter before we put it out." He threw up his hands and added, "But, don't ask me. You're the sagebrush expert."

She gave him a gentle slap on the arm. "I'll help you dig some up and we can plant it together."

"Thanks a lot. I've got some work to do at the barn right now." He slipped out the door before she could say anything more.

———•———

"You are going with us to Matt's graduation, aren't you?" Kate asked Charlie the next morning. "I assumed you would."

"Oh, yeah, I want to see that boy get his diploma. And maybe I can get a little more mileage out of that suit."

Kate chuckled at his good-natured way of looking at things.

A steady rain dampened Matt's graduation day. He and Elaine had agonized over their carefully planned but spoiled picnic until a friend of Elaine's, who lived in Laramie, insisted they all come to her parents' house.

"It will be a bit crowded but it will be better than out in the rain," she told them that morning.

The graduation ceremony was all they had hoped it would be, and their indoor gathering turned out okay, too. Jake and Elaine's dad, Walt Howard, hit it off right away, both being ranchers and having the same interests. Jake knew Walt had served in the Wyoming Legislature for several terms so there were plenty of issues to talk about concerning ranchers. Kate and Elaine's mother Janice visited while trying to help with getting everyone fed.

Since Matt planned to take Elaine to her home in Douglas on his way home to the ranch, there were only Jake, Kate, and Charlie in the new Chevy pickup Jake had bought a few weeks earlier.

Kate sat between Jake and Charlie. Her mood was upbeat. "Our kids are all living their own lives, so I guess we're through raising kids," she said.

Jake gave a dry response, which evoked a snicker from Charlie. "Yeah, all we have to do is plant sagebrush these days."

———•———

That fall, Jake and Dave said they could do the feeding by themselves. Charlie was so miserable with his rheumatism that no one wanted him out in the cold.

October brought a happy announcement when Molly and Dave trekked up to the cabin.

"We have something to tell you," Molly said gleefully. "Come next summer, you are going to be grandparents."

"Oh, oh, oh, that is wonderful," Kate said, clasping her hands together.

"Congratulations, you two. But, let me give you some advice, Dave," Jake piped up.

Dave knew his father-in-law well enough to realize when Jake was serious and when he wasn't. "What kind of advice?" he asked in a lighthearted tone.

"You leave here before this baby is due and get to a hospital in time for the birth."

"Are you afraid he'll have to deliver our baby in the car, like you did me," Molly interrupted.

"Dave, you don't want to do that," Jake said seriously.

"Oh, don't listen to him," Kate said, slightly exasperated.

"Right," Jake corrected. "Don't let my experience with Molly spoil this moment of happiness."

"Oh, Dad," Molly said. "Don't be such an old codger. Think about what a great granddad you'll make."

# Chapter Thirty-Five

**Jake and Kate were called** to the nursing home the next spring on the afternoon of April 10, 1985. Solemnly, Kate told Molly before they left, "She's not expected to live through the night so we'll stay with her."

Molly wiped away tears and said, "I said my goodbye yesterday when I was in town for my checkup. I don't think I can stand to see her die."

"It's okay. She might not know we're there but we should be with her. And, we've been expecting this for the last week. I'll call you," she added before she hugged Molly.

Jake drove up to the Bunkhouse to pick up Kate. When she got into the car, Jake told her that the priest was on his way to give Maureen the last rites but he would wait for them to get there if he could.

Maureen passed away quietly about four the next morning with Jake and Kate each holding one of her hands and talking softly to her. After Maureen's body was taken out, Jake and Kate made the arrangements for the funeral and graveside service at their Mc-Clary cemetery.

On the day of the funeral, Jake and Kate stood arm in arm at the graves after everyone left. "I guess it's the way of things, but Mom outlived most of her friends and the very few of them left weren't able to go to a funeral." Jake's words were softly spoken but from his heart. Kate tightened her arm around his waist.

Charlie's words at supper that night were prophetic, although they all thought he was being lighthearted.

"I guess I'll be next. I'm about the only old codger left in these parts."

"I don't know" Jake offered. "I've been called an old codger myself."

"You can't hold a candle to me, Jake," Charlie said.

About five weeks after Maureen's funeral, Charlie picked up the basket to gather the eggs. On impulse, Molly said, "I'll go with you just like we used to do. You'll have to slow down, though. I can't move very fast anymore, you know." She patted her stomach and said, "Just think, the baby is due in three more weeks. I can hardly wait."

They were headed for the house with Charlie carrying the basket of eggs when he stumbled and fell face down on the ground near the gate.

Molly bent down to help him up. "Charlie, are you okay?" she asked. When he didn't answer, she ran as fast as she was able around the garage where she could see her mom working in the yard at the cabin. "Mom, Mom, come quick," she yelled, "Charlie fell and can't get up."

"Oh, dear God," Kate exclaimed, running toward the house, where she could see Charlie lying motionless on the ground. "Get your dad. I think he's in the barn."

Jake had heard Molly and was already coming.

As Jake turned him over, Charlie clutched his chest. "My chest hurts—bad," he said weakly.

Jake picked him up and carried him into the house and to his bed. They all gathered around while Kate took his pulse. Charlie's face had become ashen.

They settled him in bed. Kate stood on one side and Jake on the other. They each held one of Charlie's hands. "I need to go call a doctor," Jake said.

"No, no doctor." They knew he meant it, but Jake intended to do it anyway. With labored breathing, Charlie spoke, "I don't want to go anywhere." He squeezed Kate's hand. "No man ever had a sweeter daughter." He looked at Molly who was fighting tears next to her mother. "I love all of you."

"We love you, too," they said in unison. They stood, transfixed as Charlie closed his eyes and his breathing slowed until there was no more.

Jake came around and pulled Kate and Molly into his arms. There was no need for words. Finally Jake said he would go call the coroner.

Charlie's brother, Will, and Will's wife, Alice, arrived the next morning. Will had asked Jake if the funeral could be set at the end of the week so their two sons and a daughter would have time to come from where they all lived near Colorado Springs.

They all sat down at the dining room table in the Bunkhouse. "You know, Jake, when you and Charlie lived in Saratoga, and Martha was living, we were able to spend more time with them. I guess we've neglected Charlie some in the past years. He was content here and didn't travel much."

Jake handed Will a cup of coffee then put a hand on his shoulder. "I guess we don't think much about what time we have left or what we should have done with the time we have, but I can tell you this for sure, Charlie felt close to you. He told me several times he ought to go see you and I even encouraged him to take a few days off. He always found work to do here so he would put it off."

Jake took a sip of his own coffee and added with sadness in his voice, "I don't know how we'll manage without him. He's been like family to us."

Will turned to Kate. "Kate, I'm sure you know that you had a special place in Charlie's heart. He always longed for children and you were the daughter he needed in his life. We will always be grateful to you for giving him such joy."

Alice chimed in, "And being thought of as Grandpa by your children meant so much to him that if we didn't know better, we would have thought they were actually his grandchildren."

Tears welled in Kate's eyes and her throat was too tight to speak. She just blinked away tears and tried to smile.

"Charlie told us that when he died, he wanted to be buried here in your cemetery. Thank you for doing that for him."

"We're glad he wanted to be buried here. He gave a lot of years to this family."

Kate had just fed the dog on the porch of the cabin when she saw Matt driving into the yard. She met him at his pickup door and hugged him silently as they both dealt with the pain of their loss. Finally he said, "I guess I wasn't surprised when Grandma died, she had lived such a long time. But Charlie has always been here and I can't imagine him not being here when I come home."

"I know, sweetheart." She took his hand. "Come in and eat something. Everyone brought so much food."

Jake and Kate, along with Will and Alice, had arranged for the priest to say Charlie's funeral Mass in the meadow just below the cemetery. Don, Marie, Brad, and Emily came from town for the services. Will and Alice's family arrived the night before the funeral. Many of their neighbors joined Charlie's few relatives and the McClarys to pay their last respects and lay him to rest in the cemetery on the hill.

When everyone had gone, Molly said tearfully, "Things won't be the same here. I miss him so much."

Kate held her close and said, "We know, honey. All of us will miss our dear Charlie."

Late that evening, Jake told Kate, "My heart has a big hole in it."

"Mine does, too," whispered Kate. "Molly and Matt are so heartbroken that my heart aches for them as well."

———•———

Then, right on June seventh, her due date, Molly delivered Jason David Fitzpatrick in the Jackson hospital. Jake and Kate left the hospital exhilarated after meeting their first grandson and congratulating the happy parents.

"Well, that brings back memories," Jake said.

"So it does. Isn't he the cutest thing you ever saw?" Kate asked.

"You said that about Molly, then Matt, now little . . . what's his name . . . oh, I remember, Jason."

Kate giggled and put her arm through his as they walked to the car.

In the days to come that summer, Kate spent a lot of time at the Bunkhouse helping Molly. When they started to hay, Molly thought she could juggle a schedule of working in the field and nursing the baby too while Kate did the cooking. Finally, Molly had to give it up so she stayed in the house while Kate worked in the hayfield. Kate learned to run the baler and most of the time, everything went well. She also tried to help Molly out as much as she could.

One night, Kate told Jake, "I think we'll all be glad when haying is over. I'm about out of steam."

"No wonder," was his sleepy response.

 # Chapter Thirty-Six

**One morning** in April of 1986, Sam Peterson drove into the ranch yard and proceeded around to the front of the cabin. A knock on the door surprised Kate as she wasn't expecting anyone.

"Morning, Kate. Is Jake around?"

"He's out checking the ditches, but he ought to be in pretty soon. Come in, I just made the coffee. How's your family?"

"I wish I could say fine. It's quiet since all the kids have grown up and moved away. None of them want to stay on the ranch and they seem happy with their careers."

Kate handed Sam a cup of coffee.

Jake came through the door. "I saw your pickup out there—come to visit my wife, did you?" he said, jokingly.

"Hi, Jake. I like visiting with your wife. But I want to talk over something with both of you."

"Sure. What's up?"

"Well, I was just telling Kate that none of our kids want to stay on the ranch. And, we've had some bad news. Jackie went to the doctor last week and she has been diagnosed with breast cancer."

"Oh, no," was Kate's immediate reaction.

"Boy, we hate to hear that, Sam," Jake added with genuine concern.

"Jackie and I are getting too old to do all the work. We've been dreading another winter of snow and cold and we've been wishing we could go south, at least for the winter. Now, Jackie needs to be near doctors and hospitals so we have decided to put our ranch up for sale. I contracted Ward Kelly to put up our hay this summer. You know, he put ours up last year."

"Yes, I know," Jake responded.

Sam crossed his arms on the table top and looked squarely at Jake. "I am offering you first chance to buy me out."

Jake and Kate both sat up straight, surprised that Sam wanted to sell and that he was giving them first right of refusal.

Jake mulled it all over in his mind and looked at Kate. She didn't know what to say either. Finally, Jake said, "We don't know what to tell you except that we will think about your offer. And I'll get back to you right away."

"Good enough, my friends." Sam got up. "Thanks for the coffee, Kate. You make good coffee."

"I'm glad you like our cowboy coffee," Jake said. "I wanted to buy her an electric pot one time but she said no to that."

They watched Sam walk to the pickup, bowed and bent from years in the saddle and hard work.

The only thing Kate could think of at the moment was Jackie. She went right to the phone. "Oh, Jackie, we are so sorry that you're sick. What can we do for you?"

"I know you pray all the time, just include us in those prayers."

"I'll be praying for your complete recovery. You know that."

"It was scary finding a lump in my breast and devastating to learn that it's cancer. I have an appointment in Salt Lake next week so we'll know more then. The doctor seemed to think I'll be spending some time in Salt Lake for treatments. We'll just have to see."

"Let me know if we can help with anything."

"I will, thanks. By the way, were you surprised about what Sam told you about the ranch?"

"Of course, we had no idea."

"We can't think of anyone who should have this place more than you two."

"We'll be talking about what to do," Kate assured her.

"Great."

"Take care of yourself," Kate said.

Jake came into the cabin just as Kate was hanging up the phone.

"Jackie is so brave," she told him. "She's also hoping we'll take their place."

Over dinner, she and Jake talked over Sam's offer.

"I hate to go into debt at this late stage of our life," Jake said, "but if by some small chance Matt wants to be on the ranch, it could be possible."

"Did you ask Sam about his cattle?" Kate asked.

"No, but we'd need to take them, too, or buy more." He continued to ponder. "Matt and Elaine plan to be married after she graduates this spring. Matt told me the other day that she hadn't found a job teaching English and there isn't an opening in Lander for an English teacher. He likes his job in Lander but thought they should try for a school where they can both teach. He said that so far, they don't have any prospects for working in the same school."

"Sounds like we can't really decide anything until we see what the kids want."

Jake called Matt that night to tell him about Sam's visit and was quite surprised at Matt's response.

"Dad, there's nothing I want more than to be on the ranch. I would have come right out of college, but you already had Molly and Dave there and I didn't see how the ranch could support all of us."

"Well, we could have talked about it."

"I know, but I want to tell you something else. Elaine is graduating in June. We don't know what to do about getting married. I'd either have to go where she gets a job or she'd have to come here and work at something else."

"So there is a chance you'd come to the ranch?"

"I haven't signed my contract here for another year. I need to talk to Elaine and see what she says."

Kate, who had been watching Jake listen to Matt but not say much in return, surmised, "Matt and Elaine could live at the Peterson place. And maybe Matt and Dave could work together haying and taking care of the stock."

"I don't see why not. We could still help out with haying and moving cows. Of course, we wouldn't be able to go on any cruises or plant sagebrush or anything like that."

"You're incorrigible!"

"You've told me that so many times I can't count it on one hand."

Two days later, Matt called back and said that he and Elaine wanted to come to the ranch. Jake and Kate had already been discussing the possibility of that and knew in the event the kids wanted this opportunity, they had to talk about financing a sale.

Kate got out her recent investment papers and showed Jake what they had in stocks. Jake looked over the totals. "I hate to use your money. We might have a quarter of his price in the ranch accounts and we can borrow the rest."

Kate pursed her lips. "Jake McClary, how many times will it take to get it through your thick head that it is not *my* money, it is *our* money. However, if you insist that it's my money, I want to buy that ranch with it."

Jake sat quietly.

Kate prodded, "Well?"

"Okay, if that's the way you want it."

They went to see the Petersons the next day.

"How much do you want for your ranch?" Jake asked when they had all seated themselves at the dining room table.

Sam named a price. "To be honest, we'd like to spread payments out over several years. That would give us enough to live on and we wouldn't have to pay the whole tax at once." He looked to Jackie to concur and she nodded her head when he said, "We've talked it over and we would be willing to charge interest at two percent lower than today's rate."

Jake and Kate looked at each other. They had talked about how much they could afford to pay for the ranch and since it was higher than Sam's asking price, Jake felt comfortable saying, "If Kate agrees with me, I think we can accept your terms."

"I'm fine with it . . . especially since we don't have to come up with the full amount right now," Kate said in response.

When they agreed on the terms and Sam said he would have the papers drawn up, they shook hands on their deal. On the way home, Jake said, "I don't think many ranchers have that much ready money to buy another ranch."

"It's simple. You're not like other ranchers."

He tilted his head at her and said, "I know. Old cowboys don't go out just like that and buy a ranch. And they don't . . ."

"Plant sagebrush," she finished for him.

———•———

Things happened fast that summer. When Jackie and Sam learned the treatment schedule, they were anxious to close the sale and eliminate constant travel to and from Salt Lake. They were off the ranch before haying so Jake was glad that Ward Kelly would be putting up the hay. Matt moved in as soon as Petersons left and Elaine came to look over their new home.

"They make me dizzy with all their plans," Kate told Jake after a quick visit to see what was going on.

"Me, too. I guess Matt is up to all the work they want to do there. He'll learn soon enough what he's expected to do. I doubt that she cares about sagebrush, though."

"I'll tell her how nice it is to have sagebrush in the yard."

"Let me tell you something," Jake said, trying to sound serious. "A mother-in-law should not interfere in her kids' lives."

"A father-in-law ought to remember his own advice," she retorted.

All too soon, it was September and time for Matt's wedding. Elaine had spent the summer with her parents in Douglas, planning the wedding with a lot of help from her mother and two sisters. Elaine's brothers were married and had young children so Molly knew she and Dave wouldn't be the only ones with a child there. Molly and Kate shopped for a dress for Kate in Casper on the way to Douglas, and Jake had the western style suit he'd bought at the Cowboy Shop when Molly got married. Molly was set since she was to be one of the bridesmaids.

Brad and Emily arrived in time for the rehearsal. Kate immediately asked where their little Jacob was.

"At Grandma's house," Brad replied. "By the way, Mom and Dad wanted to thank you for inviting them, but neither of them are up to traveling much anymore."

They were walking into the restaurant at the time and Jake pull-ed Kate back so he couldn't be heard and whispered, "I hope Grand-ma Marie and Grandpa Don are up to babysitting. It might have been easier to travel."

Kate grinned up at him. She had been thinking the same thing. The last time they saw Marie and Don, she was glad to see they were doing okay but keeping up with a two-year-old takes a lot of energy.

This time around, Elaine's mother was the teary-eyed one. Kate and Jake were emotional at seeing their son married but it was not quite the same as for Molly's wedding day. This time it seemed more like gaining a daughter than giving one away.

Elaine was a beautiful bride in a brocade white dress with long train. Elaine's sister, Melanie, served as maid of honor. Her other sister and Molly were bridesmaids and all wore beautiful rose color-ed gowns. Brad was best man. Dave and one of Elaine's brothers served Matt as groomsmen. Her other brother had a little daughter to be a flower girl, and a boy just the right age to be a ring bearer. All in all, it was a perfect day and a joyous time for the families.

Telling everyone goodbye only took Matt and Elaine a short time. They were anxious to leave for their honeymoon to Yellow-stone Park. They expected to be back at the ranch in five days and do some more remodeling before time for roundup.

Jake and Kate started for home from Douglas. When they came to Red Canyon in South Pass country, Kate asked Jake to pull over.

They got out of the car to look over the great expanse below them. "I don't think I ever told you this," Kate said, "but the day I came to the ranch, I had come from spending the night in Riverton and stopped right here. My grandfather had shown me this great canyon and I was thinking of him."

Jake stood silent next to Kate.

"It made me even more determined to drive into their ranch," she said, lost in her own thoughts. "I wasn't capable of making good decisions at that time after losing David and Jeremy. It must have been divine guidance that made me so anxious to get back where Grandma and Granddad seemed so close."

Instinctively Jake put his arm around Kate and held her close. They continued to take in the majestic view before them.

She looked up at him. "If I'd gone on to Jackson that day, I wouldn't have gotten stuck in that ditch and you wouldn't have found me there."

They didn't speak again until they were back in the car. Then Kate said, "We've had a wonderful life."

Jake took her hand. "We were both blessed, and you've made me a happy man all these years." He turned the key in the ignition and put their new Buick in gear. "Hey, we didn't do anything for our twenty-fifth anniversary and we have an anniversary coming up in a few days. Would you like to do something special this year?"

"I thought you'd never ask," Kate said.

"Uh, oh. I see you've already thought about it and it's either going to cost me money or you have something for me to do."

"Our thirtieth anniversary is in two years and I suppose we ought to wait until then but since you asked, I'd like to go on an Alaskan cruise sometime soon." She poked him in the ribs and added, "You're not getting any younger."

He laughed and said, "I've heard guys call their wives, 'my old lady.' Be careful or I'll be doing that too."

After a while Jake said, "I suppose if we ever want to travel a bit, we ought to be getting at it."

# Chapter Thirty-Seven

**Jake drove over** to Matt's place one morning and met Matt as he was coming in from the barn.

"Want a cup of coffee? I think Elaine still has some in the percolator," Matt asked his dad.

"Sounds good." After Matt sat down to join him, Jake said, "Do you think you and Dave can take care of things for a couple of weeks?"

Matt looked alarmed.

"Oh, nothing's wrong," Jake said quickly. "But I've been thinking Mom and I might go south for the winter. Winters haven't been so tough the last few years, but we'd like to go where it's warmer."

"I think we can handle things without a boss for a while," Matt said with a grin. "You two deserve a break. Go and have a good time."

Back in their cabin Jake said, "Kate, what do you say about this? Let's go to Arizona or New Mexico or wherever you want for a few months and get out of the winter here."

Kate looked askew at him. "Do you honestly think either one of us can leave when it's time to feed the cattle this winter?"

"Matt tells me that he and Dave can take care of the ranch and we ought to take things easy. We've fed cattle for many years, and it'll be hard to give it up, but it's time. Besides, we need to let these kids run the outfit."

"You're right. But I can't imagine leaving home." Kate wrung her hands. "I hope they can all get along," she said.

"How many times have you told me, 'Don't borrow trouble'? It's time we just enjoy this place and look over new country when we want to."

"Then let's saddle the horses and go for a ride," she suggested.

"Yes, Ma'am." He saluted and added, "I always do what you tell me to."

"Uh-huh," she said with a pert expression.

Jake saddled the horses and brought them to the cabin yard and called Kate to tell her he was out there. She climbed into the saddle and said, "I'm ready." They headed eastward and passed the old Orland house where Kate had spent the summers of her youth. "I guess we ought to tear it down, it's about to fall apart," Jake said when they got close enough to see that it had lost a lot of shingles, and some of the bricks of the chimney were broken away. I thought about trying to fix it up for Matt at one time, but we'd have to bring electricity up here and do so much work on the house, it didn't seem reasonable."

"I have to agree. It was a pretty good house in its day but it seems to me that a house deteriorates when no one is living in it. My grandparents loved this old house, though."

"Look at the barn, the roof is caved in. I wonder what year that barn was built."

"Granddad bought this place from a man who homesteaded it about 1912 and that man built the barn himself. No wonder it's falling in."

They went on through a gate at the southeast corner of the property and out through a canyon following a stream that carried water down to the ranch when snow was melting but was dry the rest of the year.

"Have you ever been up here before?" Kate asked when they were up another draw and several miles from the ranch.

"I rode up here a few times. I came once with my dad to hunt elk and we found several in a clearing just beyond those pine trees. Neither of us enjoyed the trip out. Our pack horse wasn't very gentle and didn't appreciate what we wanted him to do. But we made it and he actually turned into a good pack horse."

They rode along in silence among golden leaves filtering down from the aspens. "We'd better head for home," Jake said. "We didn't tell the kids we were leaving and they might get worried."

"I suppose so but I hope we can do this more often. It seems like there has never been much time to explore these mountains."

"We'll do that next summer. Now we need to decide if we really want to go south this winter."

Kate thought about that. "I don't want to go until after Christmas. What do you want to do?"

"I was thinking we had better do the taxes before we go, so that suits me. Maybe one of these days we can turn over the bookkeeping to the kids, but I'm not ready to let go of that yet."

They rode back to the barn and unsaddled the horses. Molly, carrying the baby, came to the barn door just as Jake and Kate were putting oats into the horses' feed boxes. "Where have you two been? It's not like you to take off without telling us where you're going."

"I guess we didn't think. It's kinda nice to know you kids are looking after the place. We will probably do this more often so don't worry."

———•———

"Jake," Kate called over her shoulder while she was driving the teams to feed the cattle in early December, "Dave wants to pick out a Christmas tree before we go back to the house. Let's just enjoy their tree this year. We don't really need another one."

"That's fine," Jake said noncommittally.

A few days later, Molly asked Kate to go with her to Pinedale to do some shopping. Kate agreed, figuring she could keep Jason in the car while Molly shopped, and then pick up a few things she needed herself.

It was nearly dark when Molly dropped Kate off at the gate of the cabin.

"Thanks, Mom. I hope Dad fixed you some supper. If not, come up to the house and you can eat with us."

"I appreciate it but we have plenty to eat here, and I'm ready to stay in where it's warm. See you tomorrow."

Kate got the surprise of her life when she opened the door to the cabin. It was totally dark inside except for the fireplace that lit one corner and the Christmas tree lights that glittered in every nook and cranny of a huge shrub of sagebrush. It took Kate's eyes a moment to adjust until she could see Jake leaning back in his recliner watching for her reaction.

"Oh, Jake, what a wonderful surprise! I love it!" She walked over and sat in his lap, put her arms around his neck, and kissed him. "I love you, too," she said.

Jake had warmed up some stew. They sat in the glow of the fireplace as they ate their supper. Kate was so delighted with the beauty of her "tree" that she called Molly and Dave to come see it early the next morning. Matt and Elaine came after they finished feeding.

They all got together in the cabin to celebrate Christmas Eve and open presents. They kept the lights down low so everyone could enjoy the twinkling lights of the unusual Christmas tree. Watching little Jason play with the boxes and wrapping paper, Kate said to Jake, "Reminds me of our first Christmas with Molly."

Jake nodded. "Yeah, and a couple years later, Matt did the same thing. Like I said then, it's a waste of good money to buy babies presents."

On New Year's Eve, Kate and Jake offered to babysit so Molly and Dave could go out for the evening with Matt and Elaine. At the Bunkhouse, Molly came from Jason's room and said he was asleep in his crib and she would leave a bottle of milk for him in case he woke up before they got home.

After the kids left, Jake said, "New Year's Eve isn't the same without Charlie, is it?"

"No. We had wonderful times dancing and having peach cobbler with real cream. I guess those days are gone forever."

"Not entirely, Katie," Jake said, using Charlie's pet name for her. After Molly and Dave get home tonight, I intend to crank up the Victrola and dance a waltz or two with my partner."

She nodded, "I'd like that."

"I'd ask you to play the piano but I don't want to wake Jason," Jake whispered to Kate after he put a log in the fireplace and sat down with her on the couch to watch the leaping flames.

They were still awake when they heard Molly and Dave come in accompanied by Matt and Elaine a few minutes before midnight.

"We decided to come home, bring in the New Year with you, and not have to be tired when it's time to feed the cattle tomorrow," Matt said.

"That's nice," Kate exclaimed.

Just before the clock was nearing midnight, Dave and Matt brought out glasses of wine for everyone. They toasted each other with "Happy New Year" and kisses all around.

Jake and Kate went back to their cabin and as he promised, Jake turned on the phonograph and they enjoyed dancing for a while. They had brought the Victrola with them to the cabin amid the protests of their kids who thought they ought to buy a new record player. A few years ago, they were lucky enough to find new records to replace most of the old ones that had been in the Victrola for years.

The next morning they were up early enough to drive to Pinedale for Mass and then to a restaurant to eat.

By the middle of January when roads in the state were reported to be open, Jake and Kate left for Arizona. Mostly, they traveled, spending a few days then moving on. By the first of April, Jake was restless as a hungry bear and in about the same mood. "Let's go home," he said to Kate on a Monday morning.

"I'm ready. I'm surprised you stayed this long."

So they were back in Wyoming by Friday and greeted warmly by their kids but warily by Jason. It didn't take long for him to decide his grandparents were okay.

Molly's news later that spring that she was expecting a baby in February had Kate thinking they just couldn't go south again.

"Now, Kate, you know we did this pregnancy thing by ourselves. I don't think they need us here."

"So you want to go to Arizona again?"

"I didn't say that. But, surely Matt and Elaine can look after Jason while Molly has her baby and we can go somewhere."

"Maybe so, but I want to be here when the baby is born. Let's stay home during the winter and go on our cruise next summer."

"I didn't see that coming but I'm not surprised," he said, chucking her under the chin before he went out the door.

# Chapter Thirty-Eight

**After the births** of Molly's Amanda and Matt's Christian in 1988, there wasn't room in the cabin for everyone at Christmas time. Then it became a tradition for the families to gather in the Bunkhouse for Christmas Eve. Being there for special occasions, helping out during haying season, and new babies in the families made Kate and Jake think they were needed so they stayed around to do what they could. Two years later, Kate was on hand to babysit Jason and Amanda and Jake helped Matt feed the cattle while Molly and Dave were in Jackson awaiting the birth of their third child.

Alex was born in March, and in June Elaine had Caleb. There was so much to do Jake and Kate kept putting off the cruise. A couple of years later, Elaine and Matt became parents again, this time to Curtis who promptly became Curt to all of them.

Finally, in July of 1995, they were set to leave for their cruise to Alaska. Matt, Elaine, Molly, Dave, and all the grandchildren were on hand to say goodbye and to tell their folks to have fun. As they started down the road, Kate looked back and waved again and again.

"I hope you don't cry," Jake said, putting his hand on her thigh.

"I feel like it, you know."

"Let's concentrate on having a good time. How long is it since you flew in a plane?"

"I never have."

"Never? Come to think of it, you've never mentioned it. I haven't flown since I was in the service. I guess this will be a new experience since we fly from Salt Lake to Vancouver."

They spent the night in Salt Lake after trying to work out the logistics of putting the car in long-term parking and getting the baggage checked. Kate sat next to a window part of the way and told Jake he ought to trade for the last part of the flight. The take-off and landing were smooth and Kate hardly realized when they left the ground and was mildly surprised when they touched ground again.

"I liked that," Kate said after they retrieved their baggage and met the van that was to take them to the ship. Later, Jake held her hand as they boarded. Then he moved away and snapped a picture of her looking a little peaked at the sight of land slipping away.

Kate woke up the next morning in the ship's cabin. Jake was outside on the deck waiting for the sun to rise. When he decided he ought to wake her for breakfast, he slipped back in the cabin.

"Good morning, Mrs. McClary," he said. "I ordered room service this morning. It should be here any minute."

"Good morning to you too, Mr. McClary."

There was a knock on the door. Kate pulled the covers up and waited until breakfast was wheeled in before she got up. She exclaimed, "My goodness, look at all that food."

They spent a lot of time on the deck and investigating all the amenities on the ship. "I'm afraid we're going to get fat," she commented to Jake as they filled their plates with an assortment of unaccustomed fare.

"I know what you mean. We'll worry about that later," Jake said as he picked up a dill seasoned roll.

As the ship moved up the Inside Passage, Kate and Jake enjoyed the company of other sightseers but kept to themselves most of the time.

"Gosh, there are so many things to see," Kate declared one afternoon when they were able to see whales on either side of the ship.

Standing beside her on the deck, Jake pointed to a mountain in the distance. "I wonder how high above sea level that mountain is."

"Not as high as our mountains, I'm sure," Kate responded.

"I wonder how things are at home," Jake mused.

"Busy, I'm sure," she answered. "We had instructions not to fret over what is going on at home."

"I know."

"We'll be docking in Juneau just before lunch," came over the loud speaker one morning. "If you elected to have lunch on the ship, stay aboard, all others may choose a place to eat in town."

They left the ship and toured the town and found a place for a light lunch then hurried back to the ship.

Standing on the deck as the ship began moving again, Jake said, "It seems odd to me that Juneau would be the capital of Alaska since the only way to get here is by boat or airplane."

"I know," Kate added, "it's a beautiful city." She chuckled, "And we think we live in an isolated place."

Although they enjoyed everything about the cruise and seeing the sights, when the time came to head back to Vancouver, they were growing weary and wanting to go home.

As they were leaving the ship, Jake said, "It's been a trip of a lifetime."

"It took a lifetime to get you off the ranch," Kate kidded.

They both slept much of the way back to Salt Lake. "I hope we can find our car," Kate said rather anxiously as they left the terminal.

"It might be the only one with a Wyoming County 23 license plate," Jake said.

There were several Wyoming license plates in the lot but they found their car easily. As anxious as they were to start home, they spent the night so Kate could do some shopping in the morning. As it was, they got home late that night and were hardly awake when Molly and the kids came to see them early the next day.

———•———

Jake was anxious to see how things were going on the ranch. Kate walked to the Bunkhouse and spent part of the first day with the grandchildren, who wanted to know where she and Grandpa had been. When she said, "We went to Alaska," Caleb asked, "Did you see any polar bears?" She laughed and said, "No, I wish we could have but they were out on the ice, I guess."

The kids soon tired of visiting and went to play. Molly caught Kate up on all the news in the area that she knew about.

After finishing a cup of coffee, Kate got up to go back to the cabin. "I'd better go get everything unpacked and some laundry done. It sure was a great trip. Even your dad enjoyed seeing so much."

"We're glad you're home safe and sound," Molly said. "Do come for supper. We all want to hear about sailing on a ship."

Matt and his family came soon after Kate and Jake went to the Bunkhouse for supper.

They'd all greeted each other, then Matt said, "We've been slaving away here getting the hay put up and you're off having fun."

"We planned it that way," Jake replied.

They had lots of questions and Jake told them he especially enjoyed the stops they made along the way so they could see the coastal country. "Even the boat ride was interesting. We could see land a lot and believe me, they treat you well on one of those cruises."

"Lots of wonderful food all the time," Kate chimed in.

"Did you take a lot of pictures, Grandpa?" Caleb asked. "Grandma said you didn't see a polar bear."

"We did take some pictures. And we saw whales and sometimes we saw fish swimming near the boat."

"I have to send the film to be developed but we'll show you the pictures when we get 'em back," Kate told them.

No one wanted their help with the dishes so they sauntered back to the cabin, grateful that their families seemed glad that they were home.

— ◆ —

Jake and Kate had oftentimes looked after some of the kids when the parents had work to do. Occasionally, they offered to stay with the grandchildren so the young couples could go out. But, with Jake and Kate in their seventies and the kids going to school, Molly and Elaine seldom asked Kate or Jake to take care of any of them.

By that time, all of the children from the ranch rode the bus into Pinedale. It made long days for the younger ones but they adjusted and somehow even the high school students were allowed to participate in some sports. Molly or Elaine and sometimes the men car-pooled and managed to give their kids some of those advantages. Jake and Kate usually went to sports events when their grandchildren were playing but were most content to stay home unless they needed something from town.

When Kate suggested, with tongue in cheek, that some people buy motor homes and travel in the winter time, Jake looked at her askance.

She said, "Never mind, I don't want to go either," and laughed at him.

One thing Jake enjoyed, and Kate liked, too, was taking short trips around Wyoming. They often fished in streams they came to and sometimes camped in a tent. Jake had been to Yellowstone Park as a youngster but that had been so long ago, he only remembered seeing bears.

"I suppose that anyone who lives a couple hundred miles from Yellowstone ought to take time to visit the famous park once in a while. How about we spend a week or so exploring Yellowstone Park?" Jake asked Kate one evening.

"I'm all for it," she replied. "I think it would be fun to stay in that historic Old Faithful Inn and watch Old Faithful Geyser erupt a few times."

Actually, they were gone over two weeks because they decided to go into Montana and see some new country. They returned by way of Sheridan, Buffalo, and through the Big Horns to Ten Sleep and Thermopolis and back over South Pass.

They arrived one evening and learned that Matt's youngest, Curt, had broken his arm. He'd tried riding a colt in the Little Buckaroo Rodeo. Although they sympathized with him when they saw him, Jake was more philosophical. "We've had kids get hurt and these kids will likely have more mishaps. We just hope it's never anything serious."

# Chapter Thirty-Nine

**Since the boys** were doing most of the work on the places, Jake and Kate often went out riding. Jake usually mentioned in a casual way that they ought to check on the cattle. Then they'd spend most of the day looking over the McClary's cattle grazing on the forest permits. They rode up draws into the mountains adjoining the ranch.

One bright morning of sunshine, Jake and Kate were sitting on the porch of their cabin enjoying a cup of coffee when Matt drove by on his swather and Dave followed with the baler on their way to the hayfield. They all waved at each other. Jake watched as the boys drove their equipment through the gate into the meadow.

"Remember haying in the old days? I'm glad I lived during the times when we used horses for everything. All this machinery is so impersonal," Jake complained.

"I know," Kate agreed. "I miss the horses and the machinery we used. All this new technology is changing our way of life. I guess those computers the kids have are good for something but I'm too old-fashioned to try one."

"You're right. The kids don't even milk a cow anymore. Of course, after our last Mrs. Cowley died, we didn't even know where to find another milk cow."

Kate nodded. "I miss the cream. Can't even make sour cream raisin pie like I used to."

"I've noticed," Jake teased. He shook his head. "I'm worried that the grandkids won't have the same feel for the land that we've enjoyed. Even our kids go along with all this new stuff—they've been talking about how we need a four-wheeler on the place."

"On the other hand, dear," Kate said as she touched Jake's arm, "remember when we wanted the convenience of electricity and a telephone, even though we had managed without those things before? Then we had to have television. I guess we have to keep moving with the times," she said resignedly.

"I guess, but I hate to give up the way it used to be. I've talked to a couple of people who even have a phone in their *car*. What will they think of next?" Jake sighed. "Most of all, I miss our work horses."

"Well, at least we can still ride our Bonnie and Clyde," Kate offered.

"Good idea. I'll go saddle the horses while you put on your boots and a hat."

———•———

As the years wore on, they went riding less. Sometimes they went exploring in their four-wheel-drive pickup, driving over many of the two-track roads along the foothills of the Wind River Mountains and onto the hills around South Pass and took time to wander through the restored town of South Pass.

"How'd you like to spend a night in that jail?" Kate asked as they read the history of the jail sitting by itself along the road.

"Might make a fellow think twice about getting drunk and causing trouble."

They explored the Upper Green area, Hoback Basin, and the Wyoming Range, always awed by mountain and meadow scenery. They looked for new wild flowers, and loved the fresh scent of new mown hay.

When they passed through town, they picked up books at the library. Reading had always been a favorite pastime of Kate's and she continued to read avidly. Jake chose mostly westerns but he liked history, especially Wyoming history. Jake lost interest in watching much TV. "They don't have those good old westerns very often. And, I've usually seen 'em if I do find one. One day, Kate held the control and was clicking through channels looking for an old movie when she came across a soap opera. Jake watched the half-hour show with a bemused look on his face.

Finally Kate said, "What's so funny?"

"Is that how people live out in the world?" he asked.

"How would I know?" she said, laughing.

----•----

As they approached their fortieth anniversary in 1998, Kate dismissed Molly's suggestion that they have a big party for them. Matt was there and he thought they should do it at the Bunkhouse.

Kate firmly vetoed the offer and luckily, Jake backed her up. "We're such homebodies, who would even come?" she said, hoping she wouldn't disappoint Molly and Matt too much.

"Actually, we figured that's what you'd say, so we've asked Uncle Jesse, Aunt Mary Anne, and all their family to come out here. Brad and Emily would come, I know. We want to have a picnic where the big rock is among the aspen trees," Molly said triumphantly.

Jake panicked slightly, wondering what Kate's reaction would be to celebrating their anniversary at the very spot where he'd spanked her on her sixteenth birthday.

"That's the perfect place to celebrate our anniversary," she said, sending a knowing glance Jake's way.

Jake relaxed visibly and shook his head in amazement. He spoke in a low tone so only she would hear. "Wonders never cease with you."

----•----

On the day of their celebration Kate woke up early to find Jake propped up on one elbow beside her.

"Wanna go skinny dippin'?" he whispered.

"I can stand it if you can," she said, batting her eyelashes at him.

Jake fell back on the pillow. "Um, I've changed my mind. We have to get ready for that picnic."

"Let's ride Bonnie and Clyde over to the picnic," Kate said. Tongue in cheek, she added, "I'll help you get on your horse."

"You're not serious. How can you? I have to help you first," Jake teased back.

They led their horses to stand in a dry ditch near the cabin and mounted fairly easily although both of them could get on their horses on level ground if they had to.

"Look at that," Jake said, as they approached the aspen grove. "Looks like everyone is here, even Don and Marie." The old couple sat in camp chairs and both were beaming.

"You don't know how glad we are to be here in this beautiful wooded spot. Of course, most of the leaves have fallen but it's that time of the year," Marie said as Jake bent to kiss her on the cheek.

Jake held Don's hand between both of his and said, "It means a lot to us that you were able to come. Now, this is a party!"

A long table was laden with different dishes of beef, chicken, and pork. There were several kinds of salads, and a card table had been set up for the cake.

Everyone said the common Catholic grace together and Matt told Kate and Jake they were to go first. "Better get yours before we turn the kids loose," he joked. They were urged to sit at a card table with Don and Marie whose plates were filled for them by Molly and Elaine. Emily was pouring punch for everyone.

The afternoon was spent with the kids playing baseball with their dads. At one time or another everyone congratulated Jake and Kate. About three o'clock Brad told Don and Marie he would take them home whenever they were ready.

Matt stood up and got everyone's attention. He said, "We ordered this beautiful fall day to celebrate our parent's forty years of wedded bliss. Before we leave, the ladies have some champagne ready, and there's Kool-Aid for the kids. I'll propose a toast, but first I'd like to take a moment to remember the people who made it possible for us to live in this incredible valley. Mom's grandparents and her dad are buried over on the Orland Place, and Dad's parents and grandparents are on that little hill," he said, pointing to the McClary cemetery. "We can't forget our beloved Charlie, either. I'm sure they are all together, smiling down on this happy occasion."

After a few solemn moments of reflecting on what he said as several of them brushed away a tear or two, small plastic glasses of champagne were given to all the adults.

"To Mom and Dad. We wish you many more years together," Matt said.

"We'll be looking forward to your fiftieth anniversary," Brad said as he stood ready to help his parents get up from their chairs.

"I hope we're here to help you celebrate our fiftieth," Jake joked. "We're getting pretty old."

"We made it and you will, too," Don put in, shaking his cane at Jake. "You're in a lot better shape than I was when we'd been married forty years."

Marie said, "We just hope we get to fifty-eight. It's coming up." Everyone clapped when she said that.

Jake helped Marie to Brad's pickup while Brad held onto Don's arm. Kate and Jake watched them drive away, hearts full of gratitude for such dear friends.

When the festivities ended and everyone was loading up tables, chairs, and leftovers, Kate and Jake untied their horses and walked them to a ditch where they could climb on easily. Jake held the reins of Kate's horse and said quietly, "I hate to think how you were hurting the last time you got on your horse at this very spot."

Today, she hadn't thought about that day when he had spanked her, then shoved her off his lap and her arm broke when she hit a rock. Now, she looked at him with tenderness and said, "Let's not think about that day. Let's just remember what a lovely day we've had here with people we love."

Several grandchildren saw them leaving and gathered around them with obvious excitement. All talking at once, they informed their grandparents that they must come to the Bunkhouse for supper.

"Gosh, I don't think I can eat anymore today," Kate said.

"You have to come," Amanda pleaded.

Several of the other grandchildren chimed in, "You gotta come, Grandma and Grandpa."

"Okay, we'll come," Jake assured them.

Back at the barn, Jake and Kate unsaddled the horses and took off the bridles. They fed them some oats and then turned them into the pasture.

On the way to their cabin, Jake remarked, "Wasn't that a great way to celebrate our anniversary?"

"It sure was. I don't know how we can pack in anymore to such a wonderful day." She grinned at Jake and added, "You look as tired as I feel."

Jake said he was tired but, "We've got this bunch of kids so let's see what else they want us to do."

They were headed for the Bunkhouse when Jake seemed lost in thought and said, "Not long before Mom died she told me that after she'd given up any hope that either Jesse or I would become a priest . . ."

Kate stopped in her tracks and tried to picture *that* in her mind.

Jake said with a chuckle, "She said God told her it would take too much work to turn us into priests."

They laughed together and Kate stumbled. Jake put out a hand to catch her and made sure she was steady again then went on.

"Seriously, she prayed hard that we would find good wives. And her prayers were answered better than she could ever have imagined."

They were nearing the house when their two youngest grandchildren came running to meet them and pulled them into the dining room to see all the desserts set out on the table. Again, they were told to go first. Kate spooned a serving of peach cobbler onto a paper plate and glanced toward the living room. All the furniture had been moved to the edges of the room. She suspected that there might be a dance in the works.

Knowing how their parents and Charlie loved to dance to the old Victrola, the kids had put out waltz tapes to play in their tape player.

After dessert, Matt herded everyone into the living room. "We're going to have a dance." The grandkids squealed. He started the sweet sounds of the *Missouri Waltz*.

Matt and Molly and their spouses, along with Jesse and Mary Anne, joined them as Jake pulled Kate into his arms. By the looks of it, it was obvious that Jake and Kate had passed on their love of waltzing to their kids.

Near midnight, Jake and Kate had danced the waltz and two-step so many times they were growing weary.

Everyone, including the youngest of all, accompanied them back to the cabin. They were hugged and kissed and congratulated all over again. But, no one left as they stepped to the door. They soon realized why when they heard "surprise!" shouted from the small crowd.

When Jake pushed the door open, the cabin was lit with soft light and they saw what had been put there for them to see. In the middle of their little table were a couple dozen red roses—all arranged between tall branches of a sagebrush.

Neither of them could speak for a minute or two but both finally were able tell everyone thanks for such a special gift and for their celebration. They stood arm in arm on the porch watching as their wonderful family walked back to the Bunkhouse.

Jake turned on the tap for a glass of water. He drank one and took another to Kate, who sat mesmerized by the beautiful display of roses and sagebrush.

After a while, Jake put a record on the old Victrola in the corner, started the music, and walked over to Kate. "May I have this dance?"

She stepped into his arms and they danced to the *Missouri Waltz* again. When the last notes died away, Jake said, "We need to have one more dance before we go to bed."

He put on another record, turned the handle, and set the needle down. He pulled Kate close. "This is for Charlie," he whispered. She looked into his blue eyes, ran her fingers into his thick, graying hair, and nodded with tears forming in her eyes as a knot caught in her throat. His arm tightened around her and they stepped into the familiar one, two, three rhythm of the *Tennessee Waltz*.

—∗—

THE END

# ACKNOWLEDGMENTS

Once again, Gail Kearns of To Press and Beyond edited my manuscript and guided me through the publishing process. And once again, Sue Sommers of Sommers Studio did the book design, illustrations, and prepared the book for production. Together with Kathy Brown of Sheridan Books, they brought the book to its conclusion and I thank them for their hard work.

For proofreading the manuscript, I thank Susan Lehr and Deanne Bradley.

My brother, Donny Marincic, provided the cover artwork and continues the website for my books. Thanks, Donny.

I learned some factual information from Albert Sommers, Jonita Sommers, Jep Richie, Mardell Fear, Kay Malkowski, and Jane Wardell. I am grateful to all of you.

Having the support of my family and friends is gratifying and encouraging. I thank them and also Eric Marincic for the use of the Marincic family brand in the publishing house logo.

*Helena Linn*

# ORDER FORM

Name  _______________________________________________

Mailing Address  _______________________________________

_______________________________________________

_______________________________________________

Telephone  ___________________________________________
E-mail  ______________________________________________

**Summer and Sagebrush**
    No. of copies x $24.95                         _________
           Subtotal                               _________
    Shipping and handling (no. of copies x $5)    _________
                       **Total**      $ _______

**Winter in the Bunkhouse**
    No. of copies x $22.95                         _________
           Subtotal                               _________
    Shipping and handling (no. of copies x $5)    _________
                       **Total**      $ _______

---

## BUY THE SET AND SAVE

Order both *Winter in the Bunkhouse* and
*Summer and Sagebrush* for $52.90 per set,
including shipping (regularly $57.90).

Please send me ______ sets of both novels at $52.90 per set.

**Total**      $ _______

---

Mail with your check or money order to:

**Seven Cross Lazy L Productions**
**P.O. Box 308, Big Piney, WY 83113, USA**

For more information, email helenal@tribcsp.com
or visit www.7crossproductions.com.